# Swindler's Revenge

## *Karina Cardinal Mystery Book 5*

## Ellen Butler

*To Sam~ Enjoy!*

*Ellen Butler*

A
*Karina Cardinal*
Novel
K.C.

*Power to the Pen*

*P.S. I hope it keeps
you awake!*

Power to the Pen
PO Box 1474
Woodbridge, VA 22195

Digital ISBN 13: 978-1-7343650-1-6
Print ISBN: 978-1-7343650-2-3

Categories: Fiction, Thriller & Suspense, Mystery, Female Sleuth, Amateur Sleuth

# Chapter One

The knock, or I should say pounding, on my door startled me out of the rainy Saturday morning HGTV home renovation coma I'd slipped into. The clock read half past ten, and I realized I'd been watching back-to-back shows for over three hours. I picked up my coffee to finish it, but the half inch at the bottom of the mug had gone cold and skimmed over.

*Bang! Bang! Bang!*

I clicked off the show. "I'm coming! Keep your pants on!"

The knocking likely came from one of my fellow condo neighbors. Winding my auburn hair into a bun and tightening the knot on my chenille robe, I shuffled to the foyer.

"Who is it?" I asked, peeking through the peephole.

The man on the other side wore a long overcoat opened to reveal a barrel chest in a dark suit, white shirt, and striped tie. He had gray-brown hair and a bulbous nose. Not a neighbor.

"If you're peddling your religion, you can move along. I'm quite happy with my own beliefs. Thank you!" I hollered.

"FBI. Open the door, Ms. Cardinal. I have a warrant to search the premises." He held his badge in front of the peephole. It read "Gerald Newcomb".

*Warrant?* I turned off the security system, unlocked the deadbolt and the floor bolt, and pulled it open. "May I see the warrant, please?"

The agent, a little shorter than my five-foot-nine height, invaded my personal space as he laid the piece of paper onto my open palm. "We're looking for Michael Finnegan."

"Mike?" I glanced over the sheet. "Your information is out-of-date. We broke up a few months ago, but feel free to search away." I pulled the door wide, and two other agents wearing Men's Warehouse suits followed Newcomb into my tiny foyer. The first guy was in his late twenties, with freckles and reddish blond hair. I held out a hand to stop him. "Your ID, please."

"He's with me," Newcomb snapped.

My mouth flattened and I delivered him a side-eye. "It wasn't a request. *Identification, please.*"

"Brandon Keller, IRS, fraud division." The freckled fellow held out his card.

The olive-skinned, black-haired man following Agent Keller held up his badge as he entered, but he needn't have. I recognized Amir from the last time he'd been in my home more than a year ago. "What?" I mouthed. Ever so slightly, Amir shook his head. Something slammed in my kitchen. Newcomb and Keller had already begun their search of my two bedroom, two bath condo. Abandoning Amir, my fluffy pink slippers and I shambled over to investigate.

My kitchen was U-shaped with an island in the center. Newcomb opened and closed each cabinet, needlessly slamming them shut with a bang. However, he had no such luck with the soft-close drawers that were put in when I updated my fifty-year-old condo a few years ago.

"Wow, it's ten thirty on a Saturday. Judge—let's see . . ." I scanned the paper in my hand. "Here it is—Judge Robinson must really love you."

The agent didn't respond and started with the lower cabinets along the back wall.

I leaned against the island and drawled, "Mike is six foot tall and a solid 185 pounds. Do you really think he's going to fit in the cabinetry?"

"Please stand back, Ms. Cardinal, and let us do our job," Newcomb stated.

Crossing my arms, I moved aside to allow him to check out the island cabinet behind me. "I'm telling you—you're barking up the wrong tree. We broke up over two months ago." My volley didn't receive a response. "Agent Newcomb, what division of the FBI did you say you worked in?"

"White Collar," Newcomb replied in a clipped tone as he pulled open the cabinets beneath the sink.

*White Collar? Hm, did I just fall down a rabbit hole with Alice?* Mike worked in the Cybercrime division.

Newcomb opened the tiny microwave above my stove, and I rolled my eyes.

"You know, Mike once told me that they found an entire safe inside the dishwasher. Maybe I've stuffed him in there." I pulled it open and whipped out the racks. Dirty dishes rattled and clanked. Newcomb jerked upright, putting a hand to his hip in an action I'd seen from Mike. Amir hustled in from the other room.

"Nope, not in there. Don't forget to check the fridge. Oh, and there's a washer and dryer in the pantry." I pointed. "Maybe he's hiding in there."

Newcomb was not amused. "Ms. Cardinal, I can arrest you for interfering in an investigation, or you can go sit down and wait until we're finished," he said in a menacing voice.

"Interfering? Why, darlin', I'm just tryin' to help," I explained in my sweetest southern debutant accent.

Amir cleared his throat and caught my eye. His silent message was clear: "Don't."

"Okay, fine." I threw up my hands. "I'll leave you to it. Let's see what the tax man is up to."

I discovered that Keller had moved from the living room on to my bedroom, and he was searching my dresser drawers.

"Is fingering my lingerie part of the warrant, Mr. Keller?"

His freckled face bloomed like the red tide.

"Then I suggest you get your mitts out of my panty drawers and check places where an adult male might hide. Under the bed, closet, bathroom. You get the picture," I snapped.

He slammed the drawer shut.

"Leave my shoeboxes alone, too. He's not hiding in them, either!" I delivered the parting shot and strolled across the living room and down the hall to my guest room, where I found Amir searching the walk-in closet.

"Amir," I whispered, "what the hell is going on? Is Mike in trouble? What are you doing with White Collar? I thought you worked in Cybercrime."

Amir put a finger to his lips to shush me. "Ms. Cardinal, I believe Agent Newcomb asked you to take a seat while we finish the search," he said in a normal tone. Then he took my hand and placed a tiny, folded piece of paper in my palm.

Shoving the paper deep into my robe pocket, I harrumphed, "Fine. I'll go wait in the living room." I stomped to the living room, plopped down onto the sofa, and flicked the TV back on to the home renovation show.

A few minutes later, Newcomb came into the living room. I turned up the volume.

Keller also joined us in the living room. "The bedroom is clean."

"Did you check under the dining table?" I snarked, then caught Newcomb staring at the sofa. "Oh, for the love of Pete!" I muted my show, stood, and picked up the cushions one at a time. "He is *not* in my velvet couch. And if he did dare to try and crawl in there, *you* would be the least of his worries!"

Newcomb didn't seem convinced and continued to stare.

"What? Do you need to check behind the couch?" I yanked the armrest and it moved about six inches.

Keller trotted over to give the backside a gander. He pulled it out farther and shook his head. "Nothing back here."

Shoving my favorite piece of furniture back in place, I collapsed down and put my fluffy feet on the coffee table.

Newcomb pulled up the safety bar and unlocked the slider.

I sighed as he spotted the door on the far-right side of the deck. "You'll need the key for the utility closet."

"Please open the closet, Ms. Cardinal," Newcomb requested in a very nice way.

Amir joined us in the living room. "All clear in the guest bedroom and bath."

"Agent Amir, would you please retrieve my car keys from the glass bowl by the front door?" I asked sweetly, copying Newcomb's tone.

When Amir returned, Newcomb indicated I should open the door for them. Instead, I plucked out the key to the closet and held it between two fingers. "I prefer to keep my distance from the creepy closet. Last fall, a copperhead slithered in there while I was replacing the furnace filter. I locked that sucker tight and haven't been in since." I wiggled the key. "It's all you."

With interest, Newcomb took the key. All three men piled onto my tiny deck, standing tense and at the ready, as if waiting for Mike to jump out of the closet like a jack-in-the-box.

"Be careful. That deck gets slippery when wet!" I hollered from the comfort of my couch. I considered shouting "boo!" when they opened the door, but I decided I might get shot.

The agents were doomed to disappointment. The door swung open, revealing my furnace and rusted water heater. Newcomb said something to Keller. The poor guy pulled a small flashlight out and dove into the depths of the three-by-five-foot snake- and spider-infested room. I hated that closet and shivered in disgust just watching him. He returned dusty and holding a dried-up snake carcass.

Jumping to my feet, I cried, "See! I told you there was a

copperhead."

"Ma'am, it's just a rat snake. They're good snakes. They eat rodents and vermin."

"There is no such thing as a good snake if it's in my home," I replied to Keller's misconceptions. "There's a dumpster out back where you can dispose of it, please." I added the *please* in a particularly wheedling tone, because there was no way I wanted that snake to be dropped in my kitchen trash.

I guess the show was over, because after closing and locking the closet, Keller and Amir filed through my apartment and out the front door.

Newcomb returned my keys. "Your boyfriend—"

"*Ex-boyfriend,*" I clarified.

"—is in big trouble. He's wanted for questioning. If he contacts you, please give me a call." He passed me his business card.

Following Newcomb to the door, I said, "Pardon me, but I'm having a difficult time believing my Boy Scout ex did anything illegal. What exactly is he accused of?"

No one responded.

"Hello?"

Newcomb paused, with his hand on the halfway closed door. "It seems he's scarpered off with one point two million dollars. We need to find out why." The agent shut the door in my mouth-bobbing shocked face.

# Chapter Two

I must have stared at the door for a full five minutes before coming back to earth. *Mike stole over a million dollars?*

*No.*

*No and no and no.*

There was simply no way that could be correct.

Mike and I had been good friends in college and reconnected here in D.C. We danced around a relationship for a while, finally sealing the deal after I played a role in finding the killer of a sitting senator. Our relationship ended in neither acrimony nor on the best of terms. We simply didn't see eye-to-eye on some of my past escapades, and I'd become tired of his censorship of my life choices. Mike accused me of seeking chaos and questioned my judgement. I accused him of being a boring prig and never there for me. And on that note, we both decided it was time to end our romantic interlude. While I didn't speak with him on a daily basis, we'd forgiven each other for the unkind words, and stayed in touch through social media. Mike was a good man, and I still considered him a friend. Newcomb's accusation seemed unfathomable; however, it caused my gut to clench in fear, and I reached for my cell.

The call went directly to voice mail. "Mike, it's Karina. I've had a rather unnerving visit from an FBI agent Newcomb in the White Collar division. Can you please give me a ring when you get this? Thanks."

I spent the next twenty minutes on my laptop searching Mike's social media accounts for any indication of where he might be. Not that he ever "checked in" anywhere, but still, he'd occasionally post a picture from an identifiable D.C. location. Per usual, his Twitter account hadn't been used in over a month. Facebook's most recent post was a funny meme on Monday about coffee, and he posted an Instagram photo last weekend of the Lincoln Memorial lit up by a gorgeous orange-and-pink sunset, probably taken during one of his runs.

On the off chance he hadn't changed his Netflix password, I tried logging into his account. Success. Thursday night he'd rented an action flick, and it looked as though every night before that he'd been working his way through the second season of *Breaking Bad*. However, there must have been a mistake, or another person had used his account, because on Tuesday, the account showed a seven-hour marathon of *Breaking Bad* at a time when Mike would've been at work. The rest of his Netflix account revealed nothing of value, except for the fact that he'd watched a number of *The Baby-Sitters Club* episodes. Must have been a new guilty pleasure—one I'd enjoy ribbing him about the next time we spoke.

Having run out of social media ways to stalk my ex, I contemplated the next move. His sister's and parents' phone numbers were still in my contact list, but I didn't think it wise to phone and possibly alarm them. Perhaps one of my contacts at the FBI—

"Karina, you dope!" My voice echoed in the empty dining room. I gave myself a mental head smack and dug out the wadded piece of paper Amir had given me. In sharp, slanted handwriting was a phone number with a Maryland exchange and the words,

**Call after 5. Don't use your phone.**

The mantel clock revealed the hour closing in upon noon. I needed a shower and a visit to the grocery store—two things that would help while away the time until the appointed hour, when I hoped my overwhelming curiosity would be satisfied by Amir.

At 5:05, I trotted across the hall and let myself into my neighbor's apartment. The aroma of vanilla and jasmine enveloped me from the Glade PlugIn by the door. A new flavor. Tim was branching out; he usually stocked the fresh linen scent. Tim Spencer was a traveling salesman for a tech company. Three years ago, he'd given me a key, asked me to water his plants once a week, and keep an eye on the place. A move which turned out to be a lucky one for him after a pipe burst last winter while he was in Oregon. Normally, Tim traveled during the week. However, he'd garnered so much comp time and airline miles, he'd recently started taking more holidays and three-day weekends to fantastical places such as Bali and Iceland. Since I refused to accept any sort of monetary payment from him, Tim invariably brought back little gifts from his excursions, including a silk scarf, keychain, gorgeous postcards, and my favorite—local wines.

Tim's condo could best be described as stark minimalist. The few items of furniture were either white, black, or gray, with sharp lines, and the tables made of glass and chrome. The only color came from the half dozen plants sitting in front of the sliding glass door. Tim and I were probably two of the few people left in the D.C. metro area who still had landlines in our apartments. A few years ago, I'd listened to some of Tim's messages and understood why he'd kept a landline. The voice mails were all from women. All of them asking when he was coming back to town. Tim was an average-looking guy—about my height with bronze hair and physically fit—but what he might have lacked in the looks department he made up for with natural charisma and melt-your-boots brown eyes. Clearly, Tim charmed lady loves across the nation and gave them his home phone number so they couldn't bother him while he was working . . . or possibly visiting other women. Whatever the case, Tim's need for a landline came in handy for me today.

He picked up on the third ring. "Amir speaking."

"Well, Amir, would you like to tell me what the hell is going on?"

"Karina, I assume."

"Excellent guess." I pulled out one of the polished metal stools at the counter and sat. "I'm assuming the FBI has tapped my phones, which is why you asked me to call from another location."

"I'm not quite sure what Newcomb is planning, but I haven't put it out of the realm of possibility," Amir replied.

"Are they expecting Mike to contact me?"

"They're covering their bases."

"And as the ex-girlfriend, they think he might call me."

"So goes the thinking."

Playing with my necklace pendant, I swiveled to face the living room. "Read me in on the situation?"

"Just tell Mike to contact me if you see or hear from him," Amir said.

"Oh, no. We are *not* playing that game. If you want my help with Mike, you need to tell me what's going on. Otherwise, you'll get no help from me. You know I have friends who can make the FBI's investigation very difficult if I ask." My threat hung like a water balloon about to be released from four stories up.

Amir took a beat before responding, "Two weeks ago, an account at Mike's bank, in Mike's name, was opened. On Monday, one point two million was transferred from a numbered account in the Cayman Islands to the new account."

"Well . . . that doesn't sound right. Maybe it's a different Mike Finnegan. There must be other Mike Finnegans in this area."

Amir continued as if I hadn't spoken. "On Tuesday afternoon, a man matching Mike's description walked in with a briefcase and walked out with the entire one point two million in that briefcase."

I gulped. "Well, lots of men fit Mike's description."

"You're correct. The height, weight, and hair color match Mike."

"What about his face? There are monitors all over banks these days."

"He was wearing a ballcap and avoiding the cameras. We didn't get a facial recognition match."

I let out a relieved sigh. "Then it must be someone else. Besides, if it *was* in the middle of the day, Mike would've been at work."

Amir dropped the anvil. "He called in sick that day. His prints were left on the withdrawal documents and a computer monitor."

"Geez." I scrunched my eyes shut and pinched the bridge of my nose. "Did anyone in his apartment complex see him that day? What about traffic cams? Did he drive to the bank?"

"Street cams tracked him to the metro. Then he disappeared."

My head popped up with a thought. "Wait a minute, did you say Tuesday?"

"Yes."

"Well, I did some of my own digging, and according to his Netflix account, he was watching a *Breaking Bad* marathon all day. Surely that shows he was in his apartment all day."

Amir paused, and I waited with bated breath. "It won't hold water. Once you tune into a Netflix series the episodes simply continue to run until you turn them off. Makes for a weak alibi."

My sigh blew audibly across the handset. "Yeah, you're right. So, you're telling me no one has seen Mike since Tuesday?"

"He returned to work on Wednesday. However, he left for lunch on Friday and never came back. No one has seen him since. His disappearance verified Newcomb's theory and kicked the investigation into high gear. Newcomb pulled strings to get search warrants on a Saturday."

"You realize I'm having trouble swallowing this."

"If it makes you feel any better, I am too," he said solemnly.

"Is that why you're on the team looking into it?"

"I've been tasked with figuring out who owned the account in the Caymans."

"Good." I nodded even though he couldn't see me. "Amir, one thing I don't understand. How did the FBI get onto this account transfer and subsequent withdrawal?"

"The government works with the banking industry to track all transactions over ten thousand dollars. A raw data report is delivered once a week to the IRS and various divisions at the Bureau. The IRS tracks it for fraud and tax purposes," Amir explained.

"That would explain why that Keller guy was with you. Is he the bean counter that found the transaction?"

"The data drops into their laps on Wednesday. On Thursday, Keller was having lunch with another FBI agent in counterterrorism and mentioned his finding. He asked the counterterrorism agent if he knew Mike. He didn't, but it was Mike's bad luck, because Newcomb was having lunch at a table nearby and overheard their conversation."

"And what or who is Newcomb to Mike? A friendly like you? Or just an agent doing his job who's been assigned to this case?" Realizing I was pulling hard on my pendant, I let it drop before I accidentally broke it.

Amir whistled a sigh. "That's the problem. Mike started his FBI career in White Collar. I don't know the entire story, but there's bad blood between Mike and Newcomb. This isn't just an assigned case. Newcomb started the investigation against Mike, and he's gnawing on it like a dog with a new chew toy. It's like he's getting some sort of sick pleasure out of it."

I digested all the information Amir revealed. It still didn't add up in my head. "So, is the FBI's working theory is that Mike took a bribe from a bad guy?"

"That's one of the theories."

"Newcomb's theory?"

"Yes."

"And you're in charge of investigating the Cayman account, where the money originated."

"Correct."

I hopped off my stool and began pacing the living room. "So, what's the problem? Can't you get the Cayman bank to give you the name on the original account?"

"It doesn't work like that. The lenient tax laws make the Caymans the fifth largest financial banking center in the world. Banks, such as Deutsche Bank, where the transfer originated, provide complete anonymity and security to their clients. Making it nearly impossible for U.S. agencies to track the money," Amir explained.

"In other words, the money came from an unnamed, numbered account, and this Deutsche Bank doesn't want to play ball with the FBI."

"That is correct."

"Hm, have you considered a different angle?" I pivoted and paced back to the kitchen. "Maybe Mike was forced into moving this money for someone. Maybe it's blackmail. Have you checked on all of his family members? Is everyone safe?"

"We've considered it." He paused, and I stopped pacing in anticipation. "Field agents searched his family members' homes this morning. Everyone seems to be in perfect health."

"Are you sure? None of them seemed twitchy or reluctant to help you?"

"I wasn't there, but I spoke with two of the agents who conducted the search warrants. Neither felt the family had any idea what was going on."

I rubbed a hand down my face and groaned. "I simply don't

get it. He's not the type to go on the run with a bunch of money. He's got family and ties to the community. Can you give me one good reason for Mike to do such a thing?"

"No, I can't. Newcomb is working along the theory that an opportunity presented itself to Mike, and he's taken advantage of it."

"Amir, have you ever seen Mike do something sloppy in his work? In the field?"

Without hesitation he answered, "No."

"No. Mike is methodical. He's smart. He knows about these transaction laws. What you've described is sloppy. Fingerprints. Taking a briefcase. Getting caught on camera." I ticked off each piece of damning evidence. "Hell, having the money transferred to his own bank. Isn't there a Deutsche Bank downtown?"

"Yes."

"Then why on earth wouldn't he just go there? Couldn't he access an account at the local branch?"

"All excellent questions, which I can't answer. I've got another call ringing in and must go. If you hear from Mike, have him contact me. I can bring him in safely." Amir hung up before I could ask another of the million questions reeling through my noggin.

The plants looked a little thirsty, and I gave them a drink while I stewed over my next steps. It took about ten minutes for me to realize the next steps belonged to either Mike or the FBI. I'd left a message for Mike, and there was no other way for me to contact him. If he was as smart as I thought he was, he wouldn't come near me or his family.

# Chapter Three

Saturday night brought little sleep, which is why I didn't get out for a morning run until after eleven thirty. A number of my friends assumed I had a high metabolism and that keeping a relatively curvy, yet decent weight, came naturally to me. They would be mistaken. My mother passed on her Irish peasant ancestry, which made it easy to pack on the pounds by just looking at a donut, and, I'll admit, I wasn't fanatical about eating healthy. Things such as jogging and yoga helped to keep me from ballooning into a plump Irish partridge on her way to the county fair. Running didn't come naturally to me, but after the upsetting events from yesterday, I figured I needed to get out of the house.

Luckily, the rain had ended sometime in the night and left behind a crisp breeze with the scent of spring upon its wings. February was coming to a close, and March was around the corner—one of my favorite times in the D.C. area. The Tidal Basin would soon be surrounded by cherry blossom trees in full bloom, and brightly colored tulips would greet me as I jogged past, their heads nodding in the gentle wind. Though the breeze was cold, the sun warmed me. Quite a few folks were out enjoying the fine weather, which was why it took me so long to notice I'd gained a tail. At least, I thought it was a tail.

The woman seemed to be pacing herself about twenty feet behind me no matter how fast or slow I ran. Reaching Jefferson Memorial, I trotted over to the steps to rest and tighten my laces. Surreptitiously, I watched the lady in the pink and black spandex jog past without giving me a second glance. She was of

Asian descent, and her beautiful black ponytail bobbed innocently with each step. Eventually, the crowds hid her from my sight.

I didn't see her again, but the incident, or should I say non-incident, preyed on my mind, and in conjunction with my recent FBI visit, I had that creepy feeling that I was being watched. Maybe it was plain and simple paranoia. The rest of my run I kept checking my six, turning what should've been a stress-relieving run into the exact opposite. When I got back to my car, I opened the rear passenger door to toss in my sweatshirt and happened to glance down the line of vehicles parked along the curb. I caught a glimpse of those bright pink-and-black leggings as their owner climbed into a black, extra-long panel van that seemed familiar to me. I slammed the door and strode down the sidewalk to rap sharply on the side door.

It remained shut, and I banged again. "Who's in there? Hernandez? Josh?" The door slid open, and a fearsome face stared back. "Jin! Good to see you. It's been a while. Have you been out of the country on assignment?"

Jin grinned back at me, making the long, jagged scar across the left side of his face pucker. He was former military special operations, and I'd once heard he'd gained that scar in Afghanistan. He had black hair and eyes and was almost as tall as me, but his build was wiry and whip strong. "Hello, Karina," he greeted in his well-modulated voice. Not that Jin spoke in a monotone, but I'd never seen him get excited or angry. He always seemed to roll along on an even keel. As a person whose emotions could fluctuate vehemently—which I blamed on my Irish ancestry—I often envied Jin for his Zen-like-style.

"I must say, I'm surprised to see you here." I glanced over his shoulder at the high-tech computer and surveillance equipment lining the inside of the van. I'd once accused the Silverthorne crew of stealing the van from the FBI. They'd denied my accusations, and after seeing some of the proprietary equipment in action, I realized it was far beyond something the FBI could afford—more on par with military intelligence or CIA. "I thought this van was the property of Hernandez."

"Though he doesn't like it, sometimes he has to share," Jin replied. "Besides, he's out of town on assignment."

"Would you like to explain why Silverthorne is tailing me today? Is there something I can help you with?"

"Damnit!" cursed a disembodied voice.

I leaned my head into the van and spotted the pink-and-black clad jogger sitting on one of the squat stools in the back. "Hi there." I gave a finger wave, then returned my attention to Jin. "New recruit?"

He simply shook his head and chuckled.

"Is money exchanging hands right now?" I asked. It was widely known among the Silverthorne Security team that Jin never laughed . . . except when I was around. Many a man had lost good money taking bets against me.

"No—"

A firm hand came down on my shoulder, and I jumped sky high. "Eeyow! Don't sneak up on me like that!" I put a hand to my heart.

"Sorry, didn't mean to startle you." Rick's silvery gaze met my startled green. "I was just going to say that I've banned the team from placing bets when it comes to you and Jin."

"Why? Did you keep losing?" I taunted.

"No. I've learned never to bet against you." He gave my ponytail a gentle tug.

Like Jin, Rick was former. . . something. Could've been military intelligence, CIA, NSA—I wasn't very clear on where Rick's training came from. I guessed his age to be around forty, and like all the Silverthorne employees, Rick was in excellent shape, with broad shoulders and a trim waist. His tree-bark brown hair was cropped military-style, shot through gray at the temples.

He rarely smiled, but when he did . . . whoa, Nelly! He was the head of Silverthorne Security—a private company based in D.C. They provided protection for foreign diplomats visiting D.C., worked private security in warzones and sketchy countries, and Mike once hinted that they did wet work for the CIA—though I'd never received confirmation on that score. I'd met Rick well over a year ago, when he'd saved me from a gruesome fate at the hands of a knife-wielding mafia thug who didn't like my investigation into a stolen painting. I'd once given Rick the moniker of Batman because of the way he swooped in and out of my life. However, I'd come to rely on him, and other Silverthorne operatives, to help me get out of some sticky situations.

"When did you pick up on our surveillance?" he asked.

"Maybe a mile into the run. I recommend less identifiable clothing next time. Also, I thought it might be . . ." I trailed off, unsure if I should reveal that I'd originally believed she was an FBI tail.

"You thought it might be . . . ?" Rick prompted.

"Uh, nothing." I returned my gaze to Jin. "So, want to introduce me to the new recruit?"

"Karina Cardinal, this is Sonia Lee." Jin indicated the woman.

She was petite, maybe five foot three, with slashes of black brows, almond eyes, and a wide, flat nose.

"Hey, Sonia." I reached a hand back and she reluctantly leaned forward to give it a short shake.

"Hi." Her tone was clipped.

"What's your background? Military? Police? FBI? CIA?" I probed.

"Military," she stated with reluctance.

I decided not to push her. I wasn't sure if she'd taken a dislike to me, or if her reticence was due to embarrassment from having been spotted by a civilian such as myself. Instead, I returned my attention to Rick. "Is this just a training op, or is there a reason you're tailing me?"

"Training op," Rick responded. "Jin, why don't you and Sonia head back to the office for a debrief? I'll meet you there. I'm going to walk Karina to her car."

"Sure thing, boss." Jin slid the door closed.

"I'm glad to see you're branching out and hiring women for field work," I said. The only woman I'd seen at the Silverthorne offices was the receptionist, Regina, a black woman in her fifties with a high-pitched, sing-song voice and lovely smile.

"I have four women in the field right now."

Taken aback, I paused a step. "I've never seen them. Are they here?"

"Out of country." He quickly changed the subject. "Want to tell me why you're so jumpy and on the alert for a tail?"

I sighed and stared down at the sidewalk. "I had a visit from the FBI yesterday. They arrived with a search warrant. Mike's in trouble."

"Boy Scout?" he asked incredulously.

"I know. They believe he's taken a one point two million dollar bribe."

Rick frowned. "From whom?"

"That's the rub. They don't know. However, it's likely they've tapped my phone."

"And bugged your apartment?"

"Oh, Lord." My head popped up. "I hadn't even thought of that. It's certainly possible."

"I'll send someone over later today to sweep the apartment and your car."

"Probably a good idea." I scowled.

"Have you heard from him?"

"Mike? No." I shook my head.

Rick's sculpted features scrutinized me. His six-foot frame had me tilting my head only slightly to meet his scrutiny.

"What?" I asked.

"I'm trying to decide if you'd lie to me even if you *had* heard from him."

Removing my sunglasses, I opened my eyes really wide and gave him a hard stare without blinking. "No, I have not heard from Mike," I repeated in a monotone.

We gazed at each other for a few beats before Rick broke away. Thank goodness, because my eyes were starting to dry out, and I had to blink a few times to restore moisture.

"You can always come to me if you need help," he reassured me.

I lowered my lids and dropped my head forward. "I know. I'm just hoping I don't have to."

He lifted my chin with a finger, and we gazed at each other, only inches apart, so close I could feel his minty breath on my face. A bolt of electricity zipped down my spine. It wasn't the first time the attraction had come on hard and fast like that. I'd been ignoring it for months. However, I was fairly certain I was the only one feeling it, so, per usual, I disregarded the sensation and waited for Rick to say his piece. He didn't. I stepped back, squinting at the Silverthorne van as it cruised past. Rick glanced over his shoulder and raised a hand in farewell. The van drove off, but Rick continued to survey the scene across the street. Tourists walked the pathway to visit the Martin Luther King, Jr. Memorial. An octogenarian sat on a bench drinking coffee. A woman with a stroller waited to cross the street.

"Have you got a ride back to the office? I can give you a lift if you need one." I replaced my sunglasses.

"No thanks. I've got my truck." His eyes were narrowed as his attention returned to me. "You might be right about an FBI tail."

I sucked wind, but he raised a finger to his lips to shush me.

Softly, he murmured, "I want you to get in your car and drive straight home. Don't drive like you normally do." I opened my mouth to protest, but he continued, "You drive like a maniac."

My jaw snapped shut.

"Obey the speed limits and other rules of the road. I'm going to follow and see if you're being tailed. Okay?"

"Fine. But I resent the aspersions you're casting on my driving skills." I shook a finger at him.

"I never said you weren't a skilled driver. You just drive like you're on the Daytona Motor Speedway every time you get behind the wheel," Rick observed as he opened my door.

I harrumphed as I folded myself into my car.

"I'll contact you later and let you know what time someone will be coming over to sweep the apartment." And with that, he shut my door and sent me on my way.

# Chapter Four

The text I received from Rick was nothing if not succinct.
**Mission inconclusive. Joshua. 4 p.m.**

Roughly translated, we were back to square one and unsure if the FBI had put a tail on me. Meaning, my old lady driving through Old Town Alexandria, which garnered more than a few angry horn honks, had turned out to be a waste of time. Also, Josh was due at my house around four to sweep for bugs. Fabulous. Josh was one of the first Silverthorne Security guys I'd met and had become a favorite of mine. In his former life, he'd been a Navy SEAL and a medic. To my irritation and embarrassment, Josh had to put his medical skills to work by patching me up . . . on more than one occasion. He treated me like an annoying but loveable little sister. I always felt safe when Josh was around.

At ten past four, I opened my door to the bulky, blond man. He wore jeans, a navy-blue polo with a Silverthorne logo on it that fit tight across his muscular chest, and a Washington Capitals ballcap. He carried a duffle on his shoulder.

"Hey, Josh, good to see you."

"You, too." He leaned in for a side hug and whispered directly in my ear, "Paper and pen."

I nodded—"Come on in." —and guided him into the kitchen, where I'd left a legal pad and marker on the island for just this occasion.

He set the duffle on the counter and wrote *talk normal.*

"What can I get you to drink?" I asked. "I've got iced tea,

lemonade, water, and diet soda."

"I'll take an iced tea." Quietly, Josh unzipped the duffle and removed a little black box similar to one I'd seen Rick use on my apartment in the past.

"I made some cookies this afternoon. Would you like some?" Josh methodically moved about the dining room with his bug detector. "What kind?"

"Chocolate chip."

"Absolutely."

While I prepared our drinks and set a handful of cookies on a plate, Josh moved into the living room.

"A slice of lemon with your tea?"

"If you've got it," he said, distracted. Something behind my television had garnered his attention.

I carefully cut two perfect lemon wedges and dropped them into our glasses. Carrying the whole kit on a serving tray, I placed it on the coffee table. Meanwhile, I wracked my brain trying to think of a new topic for discussion.

Josh turned, and I spotted his ballcap. "Did you catch the Caps game yesterday against the Penguins?" I asked.

"I was at the game," he replied. "Helluva thing."

"I saw on the news the score was one to one up through the third period. Then, *wham!* Ovechkin scored twice within minutes." I wrote on the pad *Did you find one?* and held it up for Josh.

He nodded. "The Penguins scored twice, but then Carlson and Panik each scored for the Caps, and that was the game."

"Do you think we have a chance at the Stanley Cup this year?"

"Possibly." He shrugged and abruptly changed the subject. "I need to use your bathroom. I'll be back." He trotted down the hall to my guest bathroom.

I sat back, sipping tea and speculating if the FBI's bugs were strong enough to pick up the sound of me nibbling on my cookie. Josh left me cooling my heels for a solid fifteen minutes before flushing the toilet for our listening audience.

*Anything?* I wrote.

He nodded and pointed to the glasses. "Which one is mine?"

I handed him one. "How about a cookie?"

"Thanks." He swallowed half the glass in a gulp and the cookie went down in two bites. "Mm, these are really good. I didn't know you were a baker."

"I enjoy doing a bit of light baking now and then." I wondered if the FBI was enjoying our scintillating conversation.

"Could I get the recipe?" he asked as he scribbled *Bedroom next* on the notepad.

"Sure, let me copy it down for you before I forget." I nodded, pointing to the closed door off the living room. A memory of Keller rifling through my lingerie came to mind, and flipping to the next page, I penned *Check the dresser drawers.*

Josh acknowledged and entered my private domain.

Closing my eyes, I pinched the bridge of my nose. *Great, my panty drawer was getting more action than I was.* While Josh fingered my lingerie, I moseyed to the kitchen with the notepad and proceeded to copy the cookie recipe from the back of the Nestle Toll House chocolate chip bag.

Finally, he finished and waved me out to the back deck.

"Here is the recipe you wanted."

Josh stuffed it in his back pocket and closed the door behind me.

Before he spoke, I put a shushing finger to my lips and held up the note. *They were out here, too.*

Josh rolled his eyes and used his little mechanism to search the small deck. The furnace moaned and wheezed like an old man as it turned on, and I pointed to the door, mouthing the word "inside".

But he shook his head. "They wouldn't have put one in the utility room. Too much ambient noise between the furnace and water heater."

"What did you find?"

"A GSM is plugged in behind your television where all your electronics are. There's also an RF bug in a lamp on your dresser."

*Great.* "So, you're telling me there's a van parked somewhere in the vicinity listening to my conversations."

"Not necessarily. The GSM, global system for mobile communication, bug is being transmitted to a computer somewhere. However, the radio frequency in your bedroom would need something closer. Maybe a few miles radius. I suspect they're listening to your phones and the GSM. If they hear something, it's more likely they'd plant additional RF bugs and set up a nearby listening post," he explained. "I doubt they've put the manpower into a twenty-four-seven surveillance team. Right now, they're shaking the trees to see what falls out."

"Have you removed the bugs?"

"No." He shook his head. "That's what we need to discuss."

My lips flattened unhappily. "If you remove them, a team might return to replace them?"

"Or they'll become suspicious and amp up their surveillance on you."

I crossed my arms and chewed on his theory. "In other words, I have to leave them."

He lifted his muscular shoulders and delivered a sympathetic face. "It's up to you."

Shifting to the edge of the balcony, I drummed my fingers on the rail and squinted down at the parking lot below, debating my options. I wasn't thrilled having my life invaded by the FBI. However, if I went along on my innocent way, maybe they would get bored and focus their efforts elsewhere. "How long can they leave the bugs active?"

Josh shrugged. "Depends on what they hear. Frankly, I'm surprised they got permission to plant them to begin with. They'll probably stop listening if Mike turns up."

My brows drew together in thought. "I'm not happy about the one in my bedroom. Are you sure that's the only one? You checked the closet and bathroom?"

"As best I could with this equipment. I can have Jin return with the van if you want. We have higher end gear . . ."

I tapped my chin in thought. "Let's remove the one in my bedroom. I'll leave the one behind the TV. Who knows, maybe it'll come in handy."

Josh nodded in agreement. "One other thing—Rick gave me a prepaid phone for you. It's in my duffle bag."

I crossed my arms. "I don't suppose he likes the FBI listening in on our communications?"

"He'd prefer not. Let me take care of the bug in your room." Josh pulled open the slider, but I suddenly had an idea and placed a hand on his arm to stop him.

"Wait."

The door slid shut. "You want to leave it?"

"No, but I also don't want them to know I found it. You said it was on the lamp on my dresser?"

He nodded.

I flicked my hand and tsked. "Well, I never really liked that lamp anyway. Follow my lead."

Josh's face gave way to confusion, but he trooped behind me into the bedroom.

I shut the bedroom door with force and cried out, "Oh, Josh, you naughty boy. Yes, oh, baby." I commenced with heavy breathing and little moans.

Josh looked at me like I'd gone bonkers.

I took the dresser and slammed it against the wall. Josh's eyes bulged. I grimaced and waved him forward. "Oh, Joshie, oh, yeah. Give it to me." More panting.

Finally, the big guy clued in to the game. He came over and we knocked the dresser against the wall a few more times. When the offending lamp didn't fall on its own, I gave it a swipe and it crashed to the floor. The shade crumpled and the green ceramic base broke apart in large pieces.

"Sorry," Josh mouthed and then said breathlessly, "Oh, yeah, do it like that some more." He reached down, plucked off the offending bug, and crushed it with the toe of his boot.

"Can they hear us from the one in the living room?" I whispered.

His lip curled up. "It's unlikely with the door closed, and if you're speaking in normal tones."

"Loud voices they'd be able to hear?"

"Possibly."

I sighed. "I suppose we better finish."

His eyes darted back and forth. "Uh . . ."

"Oh, Josh, yes, give it to me, big boy!" I cried, jumping on the bed. "Yes! Yes! Yes! Give it to me." I slammed the headboard against the wall and bounced up and down. "More! Just like that! Don't stop! Don't stop!" Josh stood frozen in place as I continued our little one-act play. Finally, I ended it with, "Yes! That's it!" and flopped back onto my pillows with a moan of ecstasy.

The silence that followed was so quiet, I could hear the ticking of Josh's watch.

Finally, he cleared his throat and drawled, "Would you like a cigarette?"

I slapped a hand to my mouth to smother the laughter while Josh grinned at me. "An Oscar-worthy performance, if I do say so myself."

"Most definitely," he agreed.

"Are you going to tell the boys back at the office about your conquest?" I snickered.

He paled and his face dropped. "I don't think that would be a good idea. Someone might get the wrong impression."

I thought about his reaction for a moment and decided I didn't want anyone to hear about it, either. "Yeah, you're probably right. We'll never speak of it again. I suppose we should wait a few minutes before we go back out."

"I guess so." He shrugged, looking uncomfortable.

I patted the bed next to me, but he shook his head with a quick, jerky movement.

Eight long minutes later, we exited my bedroom. Josh finished the cookies and gulped down his tea before gathering the electronics. We spoke about the weather and the new SARS virus spreading through China again. He left the phone on the coffee table and wrote down the number. By the time I showed Josh to the door, he'd recovered his equilibrium, but I couldn't help messing with him one more time.

"Thanks for the afternoon delight, lo-ver. It was ... exhilarating," I cooed breathlessly, à la Marilyn Monroe. My fingers trailed across his forearm, making his hair stand on end.

Poor Josh's face flamed, and his eyes bugged.

"Call me." I winked and made kissy noises as the door closed behind him. My body shook with silent laughter.

****

Later that night, the burn phone Josh left with me rang. I slipped into a pair of flip-flops and headed outside. "Hello."

"Are you in your apartment?" Rick asked.

"I just stepped onto the back deck. Josh said there weren't any bugs out here."

"Good. Joshua debriefed me on your situation. If you don't want to remove the bugs, I can provide you with a jammer so they don't transmit."

I considered his proposal for a moment. "No. I think Josh is right. If I remove or mess with the bugs in any way, the FBI will be up in my business in no time flat. For the moment, I'm going to let this play out. I simply can't believe Mike did what they say he did." I picked at a piece of flaking paint on the railing. "As a matter of fact, the more I think about it, the more I'm getting worried. I have a bad feeling that Mike is being forced to do something against his will."

"You might be right."

The paint came off in a long strip, and I flicked it over the edge. "Amir told me this Newcomb guy hunting Mike has a beef with him and probably isn't following any other avenues except the assumption that Mike is guilty."

Rick paused before answering, "That doesn't bode well for your friend."

"No, it doesn't." The dead air hung between the two of us. I desperately wanted to ask Rick for help, but I had no idea how he could help, and I didn't want to waste his resources on a wild goose chase.

"Is there something I can do to help?" he asked.

Of course, Rick would make the offer. I rubbed my temple. "I'm not sure what I should be asking you to do. I've got no leads on Mike. No direction for you to follow." I gave an ironic bark of laughter. "Right now, Mike would be telling me to 'let the FBI handle it,' and keep my nose out of it."

Rick didn't respond.

"You think he's right, don't you?"

"I think . . . this entire situation smells like a dumpster at a seafood restaurant. I no more believe Mike took a bribe than you do. And I'm bothered that you're caught up in it, even if it's peripherally." He said the words in neutral tones, but I thought I heard an undercurrent of anger belying that neutrality.

"Yeah. Me, too," I harrumphed.

"Do you miss him?" His question came out of the blue and threw me off.

"I beg your pardon?"

"Mike. Do you miss him?"

"You mean, being a couple?" I frowned. "Sometimes, when I get lonely. I don't miss his censure, that's for sure. However, I still consider him a friend, and he's a good agent. I don't like seeing his name smeared like this. It's unfair."

"What do you want me to do?" Rick sounded frustrated. As a man used to fixing things, he probably didn't appreciate my waffling.

"Nothing for the moment," I stated firmly. "Let's see where the coming week takes us. If the pressure of having the bugs in my apartment becomes too intense, I'll contact Newcomb and tell him he can take his bugs and shove them up his patootie. Speaking of the FBI—you couldn't discern if I had a tail?"

"No. I don't think you did, but I'm not counting out the possibility. Joshua searched your car for bugs and a GPS tracker. Nothing. But if they've bugged your cell, they're probably also using its GPS," he warned.

"No problem," I said with assurance, "I always turn my locater off, except when I'm using GPS to find an address."

"They can still be tracking you using data such as the phone's time zone, and information from other apps like social media, a weather app, and anytime you make a call, or send a text."

My mouth turned down, and I got an icky feeling in my stomach. Mike had warned me about things like that. I simply didn't take into account that one day the FBI might be using those techniques on me. "Ugh. You've just ruined my evening."

"Put it in the back of your mind and go about your daily business. I imagine this entire thing is simply a mix-up and will sort itself." Rick tried to reassure me.

"Okay. I'll try."

"Are you coming in this week for a lesson?" he asked.

I'd been taking self-defense lessons from the guys at Silverthorne off and on for a while. After my sister's kidnapping, Rick added some time at the shooting range. "I've got time tomorrow evening. Will someone be around to work with me?"

"I'll make sure of it. Come by at seven thirty."

# Chapter Five

Monday started with a whimper. I couldn't stop thinking about the damn bugs in my apartment, and it took forever for my brain to stop spinning and get to sleep. When the alarm buzzed me awake, instead of snoozing, I hit the button to turn it off and proceeded to oversleep, which made for a hellish morning of rushing around. I burned myself with the curling iron, bruised my knee running into the corner post on my bed, and had to change my entire outfit after spilling coffee down the front of my blouse and pencil skirt. The most frustrating part was I had a morning meeting in D.C., but I had forgotten some materials at work. I would have to stop by the office first rather than drive directly into the city.

My office was in the heart of charming Old Town Alexandria, while my condo lay on the outskirts. Old Town is a historic district built along the Potomac River with cobblestone streets and eighteenth-century townhomes. Laid out in a grid pattern, the narrow neighborhood roads were marked with speed limit signs of twenty-five mile per hour, and lights or four-way stops at each corner. There were a few major thoroughfares running north and south through the city that D.C. commuters used. Without traffic, I could be at my office in five to ten minutes. That was usually anytime between ten at night and four in the morning. The rest of the time, traffic varied and my commute ranged from ten minutes to half an hour. Lucky for me, my coworker Rodrigo was known for his morning punctuality. I phoned him on the way to the office.

"Rodrigo. How may I help you?" he chirruped.

"Hey, it's Karina."

"Are you on your way to the meeting in D.C.?"

"Not yet. That's why I'm calling. I'm running late—"

"Oo, why? Did a new man in your life keep you up late?" For some reason, Rodrigo was fascinated with my dating life.

"What? No!" I brushed away the memory of me and Josh disposing of the bug in my bedroom. "Rodrigo! Focus! I left the research numbers for the urban health care initiative on my desk. Can you please, please, get them and put them in one of the binders for me so I can take it? I've got the cover and everything else in my bag, but I've got to have those numbers. I should be at the office in five minutes." Traffic came to a halt, and I slammed on my brakes, stopping mere inches from the car in front of me. "Crap! Make that ten minutes."

"Hm. I don't know. What's it worth to you?" he said thoughtfully.

I rolled my eyes because I knew he'd do it for me anyway. "What do you want?"

"The coffee shop came out with a new Frappuccino flavor . . ."

"Seriously? You're blackmailing me for a Frappuccino?"

"Well—"

"Done." Frankly, I was so desperate, he could've bargained an entire week's worth of Frappuccinos out of me. "Meet me at the elevator. I'll call you when I'm on the way up."

"Tah, dahling. See you in a jiff."

Twelve minutes later, my impeccably dressed coworker stood outside the elevator wearing a light gray suit, hot pink shirt, and purple paisley tie. The colors set off his black hair and Puerto Rican skin tone perfectly. He held the materials out to me, and I didn't even exit the elevator. "You're a lifesaver. I'll be back in the office around two. Frappuccinos on me."

"You've got lipstick on your teeth, and your blouse is buttoned crooked!" he bellowed as the doors slid closed.

There was something to be said for having a gay work-husband. Most men either wouldn't notice, or if they did, simply wouldn't say anything. I rubbed away the lipstick, rebuttoned the blouse, and fast-walked back to my car. For once, reliable Old Bessie let me down. I cranked her twice and heard nothing but a *click, click*. She'd been having a slow start on these cold mornings, and I'd been planning to get her a new battery this weekend. With the FBI and everything else, I'd completely forgotten to take care of it. I did what any sane woman in my position would do. I jumped out, kicked the tire, and yelled, "Crap!"

A passerby gave me a frightened stare and picked up her pace.

The King Street metro station was a few blocks away, and I was unexpectedly glad I'd spilled my coffee and changed into a pants suit. Hustling my way down the uneven brick sidewalks, I kept my eye out for a tail, because if either the FBI or Silverthorne happened to be following, I would've approached and begged for a ride into the city. Unfortunately, I couldn't identify anyone.

My phone rang, and I pressed the button on my Bluetooth headset. "Karina Cardinal."

"Karina, it's Jonathan Sumner with the Urban Health League." His voice boomed at me, and I winced. "I'm stuck in a traffic jam on the beltway. I'm going to be late."

I slowed to a walk, and mumbled, "Oh, thank God."

"I didn't catch that?"

"Sorry, it's no problem. I'm running late also. Car trouble." *And a mess of other reasons, too.* "Are you good to meet at nine thirty?"

"That should work fine. See you at nine thirty."

By the time I arrived on the metro platform, my breath had slowed to normal, and the timeclock indicated I had four minutes before the next train. Placing my stuff on a bench, I checked to make sure Rodrigo had gotten everything I needed. Sure enough, it was all there. Maybe my day was turning around; I had two minutes to sit down. The train rolled in with about half the number of cars it normally carried. Being that it was the tail end of rush hour there were no seats, so I took a position mid-aisle and grabbed onto the pole for support. Other passengers packed in, the doors closed, and off we went.

At L'Enfant Plaza a fair amount of people got off, but just as many, if not more, got on. I began inching my way toward the doors since my station was coming up in two stops. The train squealed to a halt at the Archives, and I felt a distinct pinch on my butt. Whipping around to give the creep a piece of my mind, I found myself staring into a pair of dark eyes, fringed with thick lashes, that I knew well. They were the only identifying feature I recognized. Immediately, I questioned my judgement. He wore an odiferous, dark fleece jacket, baggy, ripped jeans, and a multi-colored knit cap with dreadlocks hanging out. His beard had moved past five o'clock shadow, but wasn't fully formed yet, and he'd done something to darken and thicken his eyebrows. He looked like a stoner. Was I seeing what I wanted to see, or was it a case of mistaken identity?

His lip quirked up, as only Mike could do, and he departed out of the closing doors while I gaped at him like a prize goldfish from a carnival fair. The crowd shifted, the train pulled away, and I lost sight of him. My stop came up next, and I considered crossing the platform to catch the incoming southbound train. A ridiculous thought. I knew Mike would be long gone by the time I got back to the previous station. Besides, my meeting started in fifteen minutes; I didn't have time to chase a ghost.

The long escalator chugged the mass of people out of the darkened Gallery Place metro station into bright sunshine. The high-pitched trill of someone's cellphone rang near me on the escalator. They didn't answer, and it finally silenced as the moving staircase spit me out onto the sidewalk. However, heading down Seventh Street, the phone started up again, and I glanced around, trying to figure out who wasn't picking up. It had an annoying ringtone, and I wasn't the only one trying to identify the location of the piercing sound. Finally, it stopped. Squinting against the sun, I dug into my pockets for my sunglasses. My hand met a square object—not my sunglasses—and I removed it. I found the glasses atop my head and pulled them down to assess the item from my pocket. The unfamiliar, black phone was cheap—something you'd pick up at a convenience store—not dissimilar from the one Rick had given me.

It began its shrill ringtone, and this time I answered. "Hello?"

"K.C.?"

"I was wondering what that cheeky incident on the metro was all about. Did you enjoy yourself?"

"I'm in trouble," Mike stated.

"I know." I continued striding down Seventh Street and lowered my voice. "They searched my apartment."

"They may be monitoring your phones. That's why I dropped a burner in your pocket," he explained.

"Hold on a sec, don't hang up." I jaywalked across Seventh Street, dodging a pair of cars that honked at me, and jogged onto a grassy area in front of the National Portrait Gallery away from busy commuters. There was some sort of monument with a globe atop; I wandered over to it and pretended to read the plaque. "Okay, I'm back. They left behind two ugly little bugs in my apartment."

"They bugged your apartment?" he said incredulously. "That seems overly invasive."

"Indeed. There's a possibility the FBI has put a tail on me as well, but I can't confirm it."

"Jesus. It's worse than I thought," Mike groaned. I heard the sound of traffic in the background and figured he also walked the

D.C. streets.

"What the hell have you gotten yourself into?"

"I'm not sure, but I have my suspicions."

I had to ask. "Did you do it? Are you being blackmailed or threatened?"

"No," he denied, "I've been set up."

Needing answers, I continued to press. "Where were you last Tuesday when you didn't go to work?"

"I spent the majority of my time in the bathroom tossing my cookies. I think I was poisoned."

"Poisoned!" I got a strange look from a passerby. I turned away and lowered my voice. "Who poisoned you? Where? How? Why?"

He took a beat before responding. "I ate at that Chinese restaurant a block away from the office. You know the one—I've gotten takeout from there."

"Yeah, I know, the Red Dragon. The one with the good dumplings."

"Not an hour after I got home, I was praying to the porcelain god. It went on all night long and into the morning. I was so dehydrated I could barely pick myself up off the floor."

It sounded bad, but I wasn't ready to let him off the hook. "Why did you run? Amir said you left on Friday for lunch and disappeared."

He sighed. "Hold on." I heard his breathing increase, then the traffic noise behind him diminished. He must have entered a building. "A friend contacted me through a specific channel. Said Newcomb was coming after me and it was bad. Real bad. I did some digging before I left and found the bank account in my name. A man matching my description removed over a million dollars from the account."

"One-point-two, to be exact."

"What do you know?" His voice was urgent.

Briefly, I outlined what Amir told me. Mike wasn't happy when I mentioned the fingerprints.

"My fingerprints? They've got my fingerprints!" he exclaimed. "Are you sure?"

"That's what Amir said."

"This is bad."

"Mike, I don't understand. How could they have gotten your fingerprints?" I asked him the one question that had been weighing on my mind from the beginning. Fingerprints were fairly damning evidence. Initially, I thought someone might have forced Mike into removing the money. Now, he was claiming it wasn't him at all.

"Believe it or not, there are ways of creating another person's fingerprints. There isn't time to explain right now, but one day, I'll tell you."

"Okay," I agreed, checking my watch; it read nine twenty-five. "Who's doing this to you? Why?"

"That's the million-dollar question. If I figure out the who, I'll know the why."

We were talking in circles, and I was running out of time, so I cut to the chase. "My meeting starts in five minutes. Why did you put this phone in my pocket?"

"I need a favor."

*And there it was.* "What kind of favor?"

"Do you still have the key to my apartment?"

"Ye-es . . ." I replied hesitantly.

"You remember that cardboard box in the laundry room where I throw all my junk mail?"

"Yeah, you fill it up, and then take it into the office to shred on your super-duper, military-grade shredding machines."

"I need you to search through and find anything that has to do with baseball. It had the Nationals logo on it . . . a calendar . . . maybe an invitation to buy tickets . . ." He hesitated as if searching his mind. "Something like that. Promotional material. That's all I can remember."

"You want me to dig through your junk mail and find anything to do with baseball?" I frowned with confusion. "I don't know, Mike. They're definitely watching your place. They might be tailing me, or at least tracking my cellphone. If I go in, I'm not sure I'll get far before they pick me up. I don't have a hankering to spend the night in an FBI interrogation room."

"You won't have to. I've got a plan," he assured me. "You left behind some makeup and that Outer Banks sweatshirt."

"Is *that* where it is?" I snapped my fingers. "I've been looking for that sweatshirt for months."

He spoke in a quick urgent tone. "It's on the shelf in my closet, and the makeup is under the sink in your little purple travel bag. Go in. Get your stuff. Hide the junk mail. If you're stopped, show them the items you've picked up. Tell them you were worried with all that's going on, you might not have another chance to get it, or something along that vein."

"Michael Finnegan, are you asking me to lie to the FBI?"

"It's not a lie."

"But it's not the whole truth either," I pointed out.

He sighed. "You're right. I'm sorry. I never should've asked you—"

I cut him off. "Oh, Michael, I'm yanking your chain. I'll do it. Now, I'll plan to head over there tonight. Where should we meet up for the exchange? Or do you want to do a dead drop?" I'll admit, I was getting a little excited about this covert mission.

"Exchange. Dead drop. You're talking like a spy. This is exactly the sort of thing I've warned you against getting involved in with Silverthorne."

I rolled my eyes. "Yet, here you are, dragging me into your own shenanigans."

"I know. I can't believe it myself. Rick was right—you're a

magnet for trouble."

"That's not it at all. My friends know they can count on me when they're in a bind. I'll do this for you because I believe you. I know in my heart you didn't do this, and I'm going to help you prove it. But, Mr. Boy Scout"—my tone turned sharpish— "you're certainly dancing across the lines into the gray area, and I don't *ever* want to hear you question my moral compass again. You got me?"

"I get you," he replied begrudgingly.

"Now, how are we going to do this?"

"I'll call you later with the details. Keep this phone on, and when it rings, find a place that isn't bugged."

"Roger that." I delivered a small salute even though he couldn't see me.

"Oh, and you'll need to reconnect your car battery if you want to drive home tonight."

"Why, you . . ."

He hung up.

I fast walked down the next block to my meeting, to which I was now running late.

# Chapter Six

After work, I reconnected my battery, and even though Bessie gave a sluggish *rrww-rrww*, she did start up. I made a mental note to hit the auto parts store. Mike's apartment was in Arlington, Virginia. I decided to run home and change into comfortable clothes before heading over—just in case I ended up spending time as a guest of the FBI. I also wanted to leave my two burner phones in the safe in my apartment. Ironically, Mike helped me install the safe not long before we broke up. If the FBI did detain me, I didn't want to have to explain why I was carrying around three different phones.

Mike lived in an airy one-bedroom apartment in the Ballston neighborhood of Arlington. His decorating style was a mishmash of Ikea furniture, hand-me-downs from his parents, and good quality consignment finds. He had a dreadful, brown leather couch that I'd originally disdained, but after sitting in the reclining seat that hugged you, I eventually forgave the couch for its ugliness.

I let myself in and was surprised to find the alarm disengaged.

"Yoo-hoo. Anyone home? Mike? FBI people?" Nothing. The apartment had the scent of stale air.

I locked the door behind me and went directly to his box of junk mail, flipping on lights as I walked through the apartment. He'd been correct, there wasn't much inside. It didn't take long to sift through the small stack. The only piece of junk that had to do with baseball was an oversized postcard with a Washington Nationals' season calendar on the back. I folded the postcard in half and stuffed it beneath my newsboy cap. Then I rescued my sweatshirt, cosmetic bag, and a half bottle of conditioner I'd left behind, and put all of it in the tote bag I'd brought with me. Reversing my steps, I flipped off the lights and exited as quickly as possible. My heart pounded in my chest as I slid the key into the deadbolt and heard the snick of the lock. It wasn't until the elevator doors closed that I drew in a deep breath of relief. *Success.*

I made it all the way to my car before being accosted.

"Excuse me."

Turning, I found a man in a dark overcoat with matching black hair. We stood beneath one of the streetlamps. His stiff bearing screamed "fed".

My brows rose. "Can I help you?"

"FBI." He flashed a badge identifying him as John Daniels. "What's in the bag?"

"Do you have a warrant?" I pulled the tote to my chest.

Realizing I wouldn't cower at his badge, he changed tactics and delivered a disarming smile. "I noticed you just paid a visit to Michael Finnegan's apartment."

I could've denied it, but I'm positive I was speaking to this fellow because the apartment was under surveillance. "Yup, I sure did. I wondered if the feds would be watching."

"Can you tell me why?" He tilted his head and put his hands in his pockets. "Were you expecting to meet him there?"

"No, I was not," I said imperiously. "If you must know, I was picking up my stuff. *My stuff.* We didn't end on the best of terms when we broke up, and some things were left behind. Here"—I opened the tote bag and began pulling out items—"I left behind a full bottle of my favorite conditioner. Which is half empty now because the twit has been using it. This is a twenty-five-dollar bottle of conditioner, you know." I handed it to the FBI agent. "And here is a little bag of cosmetics I left behind. It had my favorite Lancôme lipstick. Also rather expensive. You may look inside if you wish."

I pushed the purple bag onto him, and he unzipped it.

"*And* I left behind one of my favorite sweatshirts from the Outer Banks." I shook the sweatshirt in his face, before dropping it back into the tote. "Do you need to check my pockets, too?" I proceeded to pull out both the pockets of my parka. "I'm wearing yoga pants, so no pockets there."

After poking around the cosmetic bag, he rezipped it and handed the items back to me. "May I ask how you got in?"

I held up my key ring and jangled them. "Mike and I never got around to returning our keys to each other. Now that he's on the lam and the FBI is hunting for him . . ." I shrugged. "I got worried I might never see my stuff again. I knew he wasn't there, and I've really been wanting that lipstick back. As you can see, I came over to claim my stuff before his apartment becomes a—a crime scene or something." I hiked the tote up to my shoulder. "By the way, y'all forgot to reset the alarm. Don't worry, I did it for you."

Daniels didn't acknowledge my dig, instead deflected with his own question. "Has Finnegan been in contact with you?"

I lobbed my own questions back at him. "Why? Is there a reward for finding him?"

"No, ma'am. Has he been in contact with you?"

Lying to an FBI agent was a federal offense; I had to be very careful with my words. My eyes went wide. "With me? Are you *expecting* him to contact me? Should I be on the lookout?"

"Not necessarily. We're simply following all leads. Now, if you don't mind, I'll take that key off your hands."

I jammed the key ring into my pocket. "I'm sorry, Mike hasn't given me permission to turn the key over to you. So, unless you have a warrant or plans to physically wrest it from me . . ." I allowed the comment to dangle and glanced pointedly around the rather busy parking lot. It was half past six, and commuters were arriving home. The front door of the complex repeatedly opened and closed as tenants went about their evening activities. "I think I'll just hang on to it for the time being." I clicked my tongue and winked.

Daniels didn't push. "Please be sure to reach out to the FBI if you hear from Agent Finnegan." He passed me his card.

I promptly dropped it into the tote bag. "If you don't mind, I'd like to leave."

The agent stepped back. I tossed my stuff onto the passenger seat and got the hell out of there.

My hands shook driving back to my apartment. I didn't remove the hat until I'd gotten safe inside my own place with the alarm turned on and the door properly bolted.

After some deep breathing exercises and a commune with Enya's "Orinoco Flow" to calm my frayed nerves, I ambled across the hall to Tim's apartment with Mike's burner phone and gave him a call. He didn't answer, and he hadn't set up a voice mail account. I hung up and texted instead.

**_Found a baseball postcard. Call me._**

Not known for my patience, I waited only five minutes before giving up and returning to my condo to retrieve my workout bag for my lesson at Silverthorne.

****

The last bullet in the seven-round clip of the Ruger 9mm went wide of the target. I laid it down on the platform in front of me and removed my hearing protection. Rick pressed the button and the circular target zoomed up range to where we stood. Early on, the Silverthorne guys would hang the black targets shaped like a human being. The kinds we've all seen cops in movies and television shows use. When I'd balked at taking aim at the paper man, Jin suggested using ones with circles instead to increase my comfort level. Ever since, I'd made sure to request those colorful circles.

In addition to a full gym, a SCIF room, and elevators secured with card readers and access codes, the Silverthorne building had a few subbasement levels. On one of them was a two-lane gun range. I shuddered to think what was on the others. Possibly more offices, but it's conceivable there was some sort of detention center. I'd once asked Rick if the waterboarding happened down in the subbasements. I'd never gotten an answer. Though, I'd admit it could all be in my head. The Silverthorne crowd was known for being mysterious and short on words. That was why they got all those fancy security clearances—I suppose loose lips and all that.

The target came to a halt, and I grinned. "Hey, check that out. All the rounds made it onto the target today." Granted, only one hit the center ring, but still, it was a far cry from where I'd started. My shots were no longer quite so erratic.

Rick simply replaced the target with a clean one and sent it back down range. "You can do better. Try again." He handed me a fresh clip. "Only this time, I need you to slow down and focus."

"I am focused," I complained as I removed the spent clip.

"No, you're not."

"Yes, I am!" My fist tightened around the grip.

Rick's brows rose and he tilted his head.

Gently, I laid down the gun. "You're right. I'm distracted by all this stuff with Mike. Maybe target practice was a bad idea. Why don't we go upstairs to the gym and try some self-defense? I could use some punching and kicking."

He shook his head and laid his hand on top of mine. "If I take you upstairs while you're this distracted, you're more likely to get hurt, and I don't want to hurt you. Now, what's eating at you?"

Those gray eyes softened, and my emotions warred with my head. Rick had been a shoulder for me to cry on in the past. He'd given me a safe place to turn when I'd been struggling with the guilt, pain, and stress of a previous misadventure. I wanted to tell him about Mike and my visit to his apartment, but it felt as though I'd be betraying Mike. I also wanted Rick to have plausible deniability, although I wasn't sure why. Silverthorne didn't have any connections to Mike, so it was doubtful the FBI would be knocking on Rick's door.

I chose a half-truth. "It's the feds. The bugs . . . tracking my phone. And it's possible I spotted a tail on the way over here." I pressed my fingers against my eyes.

"There's something else." He gripped my wrists and pulled them away from my face.

He knew me too well. It was as though his assessing gaze could see right into my mind, and I found it disconcerting. I glanced away and made an effort to arrange my features into blankness. I *did not* want to outright lie to Rick.

Sighing, he released me and ran a frustrated hand through his cropped hair. I noticed the silver at his temples had expanded in the past months. I'd probably been the reason for some of those extra grays.

"Do you know where Mike is?" he asked.

My head rotated back and forth.

"What aren't you telling me?"

I didn't respond.

Rick paced away, spun on his heel, then paced back.

"Nerve wracking, isn't it?" I asked sweetly.

"What do you mean?"

"Asking questions that don't get answered. You could say I learned from the best." I'll admit, I reveled just a tiny bit in giving the gander some of his own sauce.

His face turned grim. "I don't like seeing you dragged into his mess."

I shifted tactics. "Do you think you could teach me how to properly ditch a tail?"

He stroked the five o'clock shadow along his jawline. "Drive like you normally do. Nobody will be able to keep up."

I crossed my arms and delivered a withering stare. "Can you help, or should I ask someone else?"

He chuckled. "I have time tomorrow during lunch."

"Lunch is good."

"I'll swing by your office at noon."

"Okey doke. So, are we finished with target practice today?" I asked in a hopeful tone. It wouldn't hurt my feelings if Rick wrapped things up early tonight.

However, he shook his head. "I'm not letting you off that easy. You'll need to work through your distractions and do better if you want to leave tonight."

"It could be a long night," I grumbled, replacing my ear protection. Out of the corner of my eye, I saw Rick flash one of his rare smiles.

At quarter to nine, Rick threw in the towel. The practice had been helpful. Eventually, I'd been able to push aside my worries and focus. On the last clip, my aim was solidly within the inner circles.

As Rick escorted me up the elevator to the main level, his phone rang. "Donovan," he answered. The elevator doors opened, and I exited. Rick followed, still on his mobile. "Yes. Yes. Okay."

The exit lay at the far end of the tiled hallway. I turned, gave Rick a finger wave, and mouthed, "See you tomorrow."

"Wait up, Karina." He held out his hand. "Yes, we just finished. I'm with her. Okay. Thank you." He shoved his phone in the back pocket of his blue jeans. "That was Jin. I asked him to do a perimeter check. He said there's a fed staked out half a block away."

The news didn't surprise me. My little visit to Mike's apartment tonight probably amped up the FBI's surveillance of me. I wondered if they'd replace the bug in my bedroom. "Does that mean I'm getting my lesson on ditching a tail tonight?"

"Why? Are you going somewhere else that I should know about?" His voice held genuine concern, not just curiosity.

"No, I'm going home," I said truthfully.

"Then we'll leave it for tomorrow. I suspect the FBI team will have a boring night."

"Okey doke. Any other sage words of advice?"

Rick gave me one of his searching looks and rubbed his jaw. "Do you think the feds still believe you and Mike are an item?"

I shrugged and sighed with the realization that my visit to Mike's apartment could've been misconstrued. "I hope not, but I can't be sure. If they've put a full-time surveillance team on me, maybe they don't believe we broke up."

"Do you want to help them believe it?" He swung open the glass entry door.

"Sure, but how?" I trotted to the car and tossed my duffle into the trunk.

"We'll give them something else to think about," he said cryptically.

Turning, I found Rick inches from me. The lights in the parking lot illuminated half of his unreadable features, leaving the rest deep in shadow. He was so close I could feel his body heat radiating against mine.

I swallowed. "You want to expand on that?"

He placed his hands on my shoulders. "Relax, *pequeña ave*," he murmured, referring to a Spanish code name Silverthorne once used for me. It meant little bird.

His lips came down on mine, soft and gentle. Stunned by his action, I didn't move. His hands slid off my shoulders and ran along my back, pulling me against his warm, hard body. Electricity flowed down my spine and shot straight to my lady bits, and I was no longer an inert statue. I was *into* it. My hands ran up his neck and burrowed into the soft bristles of his shorn hair. I plastered myself against him. He deepened the kiss, a hand slid down to grip my behind, and he shifted me against the car. I was unclear how long the kiss lasted. The space-time continuum kind of warped around us. When we finally broke apart, my breaths came out in little pants, and it sounded like Rick's breathing was heavier than normal. His face hovered above me, but now it was completely eclipsed. Meanwhile, the harsh lights lit up my own wide-eyed expression.

Rick tilted his head back and whispered, "You're not going to smack me, are you?"

Lowering my lids to shutter my emotions from him, I opened my mouth to answer but could only get out a pitiful squeak. I cleared my throat and tried again. "No. You're safe."

He loosened his grip and our bodies separated. "That should give the feds something to think about. If they believe you've moved on, maybe they'll back off."

"Uh, yeah." A thought occurred to me, and I bit my lip to keep the giggle that bubbled in my throat from leaking out. Considering yesterday's show with Josh, and now tonight's smokin' hot kiss with Rick, we'd probably confused the hell out the feds. I knew I sure was.

Rick opened the car door and held my hand as I slid into the driver's seat, giving it a quick squeeze before releasing me. My hands were shaking again, only this time it wasn't from fear. It took a moment to start the car as I fumbled to get the key into the ignition.

When I glanced up to wish Rick a good night, he leaned in and whispered, "One more for the road."

This time it was hard and quick. It still set my hoo-ha on fire.

He shut the door and I whipped out of the parking space, oblivious to anything around me. I must have driven home on autopilot, because suddenly, I realized my car was parked in a space, and my building rose in front of me. The ringing of one of my new phones drew me out of my brain-spinning stupor.

Groping in my purse, I grabbed the first one I touched. "Hello."

"Are you home yet?" a masculine voice asked.

"Yup. Just got home." I didn't know which mobile I'd picked up in the dark, and from the short sentence, I couldn't determine who was on the other end.

"Good. We watched the feds follow you down the street."

*Aha! Rick!* "Anything of interest to report?"

"No. Just checking in."

A topic for conversation eluded me, and an awkward hush lay between us.

Rick cleared his throat. "Well then, I'll see you tomorrow."

"Great! Tomorrow! Lunch!" I chirped. "Bye!"

My forehead banged against the steering wheel. Rick was a professional. As such, he wouldn't be one to dally with a client.

*He used the kiss as subterfuge to throw off the FBI.*

*It meant nothing to him.*

*It means nothing to me.*

*Liar.*

When I reached my apartment, I discovered a folded piece of paper taped to my door.

**Come over when you get home. I've got something for you.  — Tim**

Great. My neighbor returned early. That would mean my options for taking elusive phone calls were now reduced to the back deck or my condo's hallway.

I tapped on Tim's door.

"Hey, you're back." He leaned against the doorjamb, giving me his signature boot-melting smile.

Not that I had succumbed in the past, but tonight, I was

completely and utterly immune. "Hi, Tim. From whence have you returned, my favorite world traveler?"

"Amsterdam. For you, O Lady of the Plants, giver of green life, I brought"—he leaned out of the doorway and returned with a pretty lavender box in his hand—"Puccini Chocolate Bonbons."

"Tim, you're a doll." I gave him a quick hug. "Normally, I would say, 'you shouldn't have', but I've had a hell of a day, and I'm in desperate need of chocolate. So, I'll simply say thank you."

"Anything I can do to help?"

"You've already done it." I wiggled the box.

"Want to come in for a beer?"

"Not tonight. I'm worn out." I edged toward my own door. "Thanks again. Text me the next time you leave."

Giving up, Tim shrugged, said, "Goodnight," and shut the door.

Ten minutes later, I sat on my couch with the box of chocolates and a bottle of red wine, contemplating that kiss. It had certainly set my loins afire. I snickered. Loins. What a funny word. It reminded me of a medieval Scottish laird. Another bonbon slid sumptuously down my throat, and I chased it with a gulp of wine. Did the kiss set Rick's loins on fire?

I gave myself a mental head slap and flicked on the TV to divert my musings, only to be interrupted by one of my many cellphones. Mike's, this time. Pulling on a sweatshirt, I headed to the deck.

"Talk to me," I answered.

"Where are you?"

"On the balcony."

"Is it safe?"

"Josh swept it on Sunday. It's clean," I assured him. "However, after my little visit to your place, the FBI saw fit to definitively put a tail on me."

"Damn it to hell!" he cursed. "I'm sorry, K.C. I can't believe Newcomb has gotten so intrusive into your life. It seems . . ."

I shrugged. "It was a calculated risk."

He paused, as if hesitating to ask the obvious. "Did you find anything?"

"A postcard for the Nats season. It has a calendar on one side. Opening day info and an invitation to purchase season tickets on the other."

Silence.

"Mike? Want to tell me what's going on?" I probed.

"Is there writing on it? A note? Anything?"

I squinted at the cardstock in the gloom of my darkened deck. "Nothing that I can see." I flipped the card over and leaned closer to the illumination coming from the sliding door. "But you know the lighting out here isn't great. I can get a better look at it in the morning light. What am I looking for? A clue?"

"I think the card *is* the clue. I'm simply wondering if he left a message."

My curiosity piqued. "He, who?"

"A money launderer. I was closing in on him four years ago, but he bolted before we could arrest him. We tracked him to the Caymans and then South America, but then the trail went cold."

One of my neighbors' sliding doors opened and closed. I moved into the back corner away from the edge and lowered my voice. "Was he a bad dude?"

"He wasn't a killer, if that's what you're asking. He liked to collect baseball paraphernalia—signed balls, bats, and rare baseball cards."

"Because of a postcard, you think it's this guy? Mike, this postcard was probably mailed to thousands of people. Hell, I might have tossed one into the recycling."

"I can't explain it. It's a gut feeling. I need to get that postcard from you. There's something important on it." His tone held frustration.

"If you're right, what's the likelihood this guy is still in the U.S.? If it *is* this money launderer, don't you think he would've skipped town with the $1.2 million by now?"

"Maybe," he snapped.

I paused a beat before replying, "Mike, I think you should come in."

"And what? Turn myself over to Newcomb? I'll never get a fair shot. I'd rather chew broken glass!" Mike bellowed so loudly I had to pull the phone away from my ear.

Instead of belting back at him, I took a few deep breaths and answered in the calmest voice I could muster, "I was thinking we reach out to Amir. However, since we're on the subject—tell me, why does Newcomb hate you? What's his beef? Amir said there was bad blood between you two."

"I'm sorry for barking at you," he said in a chastised manner and continued in a cooler tone. "Back when I worked White Collar, I was on a case with Newcomb. He wasn't thrilled to be stuck with a young agent, and as the case unfolded, I figured out why. I could never prove it, but I believe he stole money from an embezzlement case. A witness told me that our perp had told him there was four hundred thousand in the walls of his garage. Newcomb got to the garage before any other agents and found the money. But there was only three hundred and fifty thousand behind the wall. After Newcomb 'interviewed' our perp, he clammed up and agreed there was only three hundred and fifty behind the wall."

To stay warm, I paced from one end of the balcony to the other. It took only six steps. "You think Newcomb took the money?"

"Yes. I confronted him. It didn't go well. I was practically a rookie, and I didn't think it would look good on the resume to accuse a more senior agent without any evidence. So, I never reported him to the Office of Professional Responsibility—"

"The office of whose-whatsit?" Turn, six more steps.

"Office of Professional Responsibility. It's like Internal Affairs for the FBI," he explained. "Anyway, word got around that I had my doubts. I was transferred out of White Collar two weeks later."

I paused midstride. "Nothing ever happened to Newcomb?"

"No, Newcomb had been in the department for a dozen years. I was still green. Most of the agents came down on Newcomb's side."

"Do you still think he did it?"

There was a pause. "His daughter was born with a congenital heart condition. She'd had five surgeries by the time she was two. His wife had to quit her job to take care of her."

"That's sad." The pacing resumed. "So, you think he took it to pay off his medical debt?"

Mike gave a grunt. "Probably."

"How did he hide the money?"

"Pay for a lot of things in cash. Groceries. Gas. Restaurants. Coffee. Shovel those savings into the medical debt. Do that over a couple of years and eventually everything gets paid. No one's any the wiser."

"You were wiser," I stated.

"Like I said, I had no proof, and I made a dangerous enemy in the process. Newcomb has never forgiven me," Mike explained.

"So, when this juicy case fell into his lap, he decided to come after you with all the might of the FBI?"

"Precisely."

"Okay, so Newcomb is out." I tried a different tack. "I'm sure Amir could be of help. Maybe if we saw the security footage from the bank, you could positively ID this money launderer."

"*No*," he snapped, then softened his tone to explain, "I don't want to drag Amir further into it. He's already put his neck out talking to you. If I make contact, I'll put him in a very tricky situation that could easily ruin his career. No need to flush two careers down the toilet."

My feet came to a halt. Mike was right, we didn't need Amir. "I have another idea, but you're not going to like it."

"What's that?"

"Silverthorne." The silence stretched. I shivered and pulled the sweatshirt hood over my head. "Too risky?" I finally asked.

"Nooo . . . actually, they might be the only people I *can* go to for help. Do you think I can trust them?"

"Do you trust me?"

Mike distinctly paused before responding, "Yes."

"I trust them. Let me talk to Rick tomorrow. I'm meeting him for lunch. He's going to teach me how to ditch my tail."

"You're sure you're being tailed?"

"Rick saw them follow me away from the Silverthorne building." I shivered from both cold and a touch of fear.

"I can't say I'm thrilled he's teaching you how to elude the FBI." His voice held the old censure that always put my back up when we were together.

"Well, Michael, if it weren't for you, I wouldn't be having to do this," I said rather testily. "You can't have it both ways. Either you want my help, or you don't. If you don't, then I'm chucking this phone and you're on your own. If you do, then you can't poo-poo the tactics I'm using to keep us all from being thrown in jail."

A long, windy sigh blew at me across the phone lines. "You're right. I apologize. I'm a terrible person for dragging you into this."

I took my tone down a few notches. "You're not a terrible person. If you were, I would've turned you in myself. You're simply stressed, and worried, and in a bad situation. Speaking of a bad situation, where are you staying? Homeless shelters?"

He hesitated before replying, "At a townhouse the FBI seized last month."

"You're squatting?" I said incredulously.

"That's one way to put it."

I frowned. "That seems a little risky."

"It's actually not. The house has already been processed and stripped. It won't go to auction for a few more months. It's just sitting idle until then."

Well, at least he was relatively safe. "Do you have money?"

"Enough for the moment. I emptied the cash out of my home safe before bolting."

As I stood shivering on my back deck, a thought occurred to me—tonight's temperatures were supposed to plummet down into the twenties. "Does your townhouse have running water? Heat?"

"All the utilities have been shut off," he replied.

"Really, Mike, you can't continue to live like that. I'm reaching out to Silverthorne and I don't want to hear any more arguments," I stated in a no-nonsense manner. "Now, I'm freezing my ninnies off out here, and I want to go back inside to finish my glass of wine. I'll contact you tomorrow. Stay warm." I hung up before he could respond and returned to my cozy, warm living room, with chocolates and wine, and gave nary a thought to Mike, huddling in a cold townhouse with no heat, water, or electricity.

# Chapter Seven

"What's going on?" Rodrigo stood in my office doorway in a slim fit, indigo-blue suit with a printed white shirt and red tie, looking as though he'd just stepped off the cover of a *GQ Magazine*.

"Nothing much." I dropped my pen and rolled my neck from side-to-side. "I'm reading over the statistics on the white paper from the Urban Health League. The numbers are making me cross-eyed. That's a nice-looking suit. Is it new?"

"Birthday present from Alphonse," Rodrigo said rather abruptly and made a brushing motion with his hand.

"Trouble with your signification other?"

"No. We're fine. That's not what I'm here to talk about."

I tilted back in my chair. "What are you here to talk about?"

"I invited you to a free lunch at McGarrity's fundraiser this morning and all you did was grunt at me."

"First of all, I don't grunt. Second, I apologize, I was in a rush to get on a conference call with Hasina and the Diversity Committee. Third, normally, I would come with you, but I have plans for lunch today." I held up a finger for each point.

"With who?"

"Whom," I corrected. "What does it matter?"

His eyes narrowed, and he moved from the doorway and laid his palms on my desk. "Something. Is. Going. On."

I crossed my arms. "Why would you say that?"

"I know you, Karina. I've been through a few escapades with you. You've got that harried look, and you're being awfully evasive with me right now."

It's true. Rodrigo and I had been on a few adventures, including being chased up I-95 by a rogue Mossad agent turned mercenary intent on killing us, and last summer our vacation to Mexico went to hell when a fake Egyptian funerary mask turned out to be a magnet for conmen and killers. While Rodrigo had jumped into the mercenary thing on his own, he'd been an innocent bystander in Mexico. I still felt terrible that his vacation was ruined by the death mask debacle. There was no way I'd drag him into Mike's mess, so I took the easy way out.

Uncrossing my arms, I opened them up in wide innocence and answered, "Fine. I'm having lunch with Rick."

His face changed from interrogation to interest and he plopped into my guest chair. "You mean *Rick*? As in the rock-hard, intense, silver-eyed, badass man of mystery who's the boss of your favorite security company? The one who's dragged your bacon out of the fire on more than one occasion? That Rick?"

Retaining a look I called interested neutrality, I answered, "Yes. That Rick."

"Hmm." He rubbed his jaw. "A very fascinating development. I want details. Is this a first date?"

"It's not a date at all." My snappish answer had been a simple knee-jerk reaction, and I realized I'd made an error denying it, because it would only lead to more questions. I decided to tell Rodrigo a version of the truth to get him off my back. "If you must know, I've told you that I take self-defense lessons from Silverthorne, and today Rick is taking me out to teach me how to lose a tail."

"Lose a tail?"

"Yes," I replied calmly. "Just in case I need to do it one day."

Rodrigo held up a finger and opened his mouth. My lips pursed, my chin went up, and one of my brows rose in anticipation of his coming words. However, his finger deflated, his mouth closed, and his expression drew down as he pondered my comment. "Considering all the crazy exploits you've been involved in, I can see where losing a tail might one day come in handy."

"I'm glad it meets with your approval," I replied drily.

"So . . ." He scrutinized me. "There's really nothing going on between you and Mr. Mysterious?"

Visions of the kiss came back to me, and I dropped my gaze to the pile of papers on my desk.

"Aha!" Rodrigo pointed at me. "Your face is as red as a radish."

I scowled and said through gritted teeth, "There is *nothing* going on."

"I don't see why not. You're free from your entanglement with Mr. FBI. He's single, right? And he's got to feel *something* for you. I mean, he's been putting up with all your exploits for a while now—"

"Just drop it, Rodrigo," I snapped.

"Geez, sorry. I didn't mean anything by it," he said in a hurt voice.

I got a grip on my irritation. "I know. It's just . . ." I exhaled. "There's nothing there, okay?"

"Oh, I get it. You want something to be there." His brows wiggled.

I wasn't up for going down this road with him. "Look, it's eleven thirty. Don't you need to get going to your luncheon?"

He glanced at his watch and jumped out of the chair. "You're right. Have fun with your little lesson." He paused in the doorway. "Just remember, if you do need to talk, I'm here. Like you were for me when Alphonse and I went through that rough patch."

I softened and allowed a small smile to emerge. "Thanks, pal."

When we'd gone on our trip to Mexico, I had noticed Rodrigo wasn't acting quite like himself. I'd chalked it up to the mad shenanigans that transpired during our trip. What I didn't know until after our return was, he and his partner had been on the skids and almost split up. I'd lent Rodrigo my ear and a few bottles of wine, and eventually they worked things out.

At noon, Rick texted.

**Out front. We'll take my car.**

Honestly, sometimes it was like communicating with a caveman. *Come. We go.*

Five minutes later, I climbed into an SUV, one of the Silverthorne company cars.

Rick was in the driver's seat, wearing black jeans, an azure polo with the Silverthorne logo on it, and a black leather jacket. "Buckle up," he said, pulling away from the curb.

"Why aren't we taking my car?" I asked.

Rick glanced in his rearview mirror. "I'm having Jin check it for bugs and tracking devices while we keep your friends busy."

"Doesn't he need my key?"

Rick leveled an arch glance my way. "It's not as though you're driving a high-end vehicle."

It was true. Old Bessie, a four-door Camry, had seen better days. She was a dozen years old, with a fist-sized dent in the bumper, multiple door dings, and a trunk that didn't always close the first time. I had a feeling, if it ever came to it, *even I'd* be able to jimmy the lock. Still, I was sentimentally defensive about her. "Hey, don't insult Bessie. She's reliable."

Rick didn't comment because his phone rang. He pressed the Bluetooth button on his earpiece and said, "Donovan . . . yes, uh-huh. Okay, notify me when it's done." He pressed some buttons on the dash, the radio came on, then his gaze flicked at me as he came to a halt at a stop sign. "Your tail is following us now."

"Really? Where?" I glanced over my shoulder.

"Dark blue sedan. Three cars back. Don't stare. Use your mirrors."

I pulled down the visor and slid the makeup mirror open. After fiddling with the adjustment, I zeroed in on our quarry. "Oh, yeah. I see it."

"First lesson—we're going to learn to identify a tail. If you aren't positive you're being tailed, you'll want to confirm your suspicions. The easiest way to do that is to keep your eyes peeled, identify the vehicles around you, and head into a residential area."

Old Town Alexandria was laid out in a grid pattern interspersed with lots of commercial and residential areas. Rick turned off the busy, three-laned Route 1 onto Queen Street, and we slowly worked our way through the residential streets. Stop signs and lights were at the end of practically every block. He turned left. Then right. Then right again. Traveling at twenty-five miles per hour and stopping at all the stop signs, it was soon apparent we had a tail. At one point, all of the cars behind us turned off onto other streets and the FBI no longer had a buffer. Instead, they held back by doing a slow creep.

"Once you've identified you have a tail that isn't being aggressive, but rather surveilling you, both you and the tail are going to want to keep a few cars in between. It makes them less likely to be spotted and gives you the chance you're hoping for."

"What chance is that?" I asked.

"Hold on. I need a few buffer cars." Rick turned onto North Washington Street, a busy six-lane thoroughfare. The FBI vehicle fell back three cars. "The easiest way to lose a government or other law enforcement tail is to run a stale yellow and hope the cars behind will stop for the red." The light fifty feet ahead of us turned yellow. Rick floored it and drove through just as the light turned red. Sure enough, the cars behind us halted at the red, along with the FBI. "Another way to pull that move is called shooting the gap. When you're at a red light in the left turn lane, if there isn't a green arrow, as soon as the light turns green, gun it and turn left before the other cars cross into the intersection. You'll leave the tail behind to wait his turn."

"Impressive," I murmured.

"Keep in mind, it doesn't always work if you're being followed by someone who doesn't care about breaking the law. There are other rules to ditch an aggressive follower," Rick said.

"Mm-hm, like our old Mossad friend. How else can I lose a tail?"

"Drive through a busy parking lot. Pedestrians can hold up a tail. Try to use a different exit. If you can get to a highway, it's best to keep speed with the rest of traffic. Try to get in front of a truck or large van to create a visual barrier between you and the tail. If the large vehicle is exiting or turning, go with the larger vehicle in hopes that you won't be seen exiting." He demonstrated by pulling in front of a box truck that had its signal on. Both vehicles turned right onto a side street. "The most important thing to do is remain calm. If you panic and begin speeding all over the place, taking risky actions, you might end up in a very bad accident."

"I already speed all over the place."

His jaw flexed. "I know. Don't take unnecessary risks. Also, don't head down deserted roads. Stick to main streets or highways."

"You mean like the dead end you had me go down with Rivkin following?" I snarked. Naftali Rivkin was a mercenary hired to kill Senator Harper—one of my earlier misadventures. The mercenary ended up chasing Rodrigo and me up I-95, and Silverthorne helped capture him by using us as bait to block him into a dead end. Silverthorne was paid the million-dollar bounty for him. Rick tried to give me my cut, but since I wasn't sure the bounty was on the up-and-up, I refused the check. Rick opened a line of credit, and any time I called upon Silverthorne to help, their fees were paid out of my portion of the bounty.

Rick delivered me an arch glare. "That was different. But, yes, don't do that if you haven't got a plan."

"I feel as though I should be taking notes."

"I'll send you some guidelines you can review on your own." He pulled into the parking lot of an Italian restaurant. "You ready for lunch now?"

"Yes. This is one of my favorite restaurants."

"I know," he replied.

*How does he know?* I didn't remember mentioning it to him. I gave him the side-eye. I thought about Rodrigo's probing questions. "Is this a date?"

Rick's head rotated to me. "I'm hungry. It's lunch time. A date is dinner and wine. Maybe dancing."

"You dance?"

"On occasion."

"Good to know." I buried that bit of treasure away for another time. "Before we get out, I need to tell you something."

His lids lowered to half-mast but otherwise his stoic expression didn't change. "I'm all ears."

"I've been in contact with Mike," I confessed.

The lids lowered all the way, and he pressed his pointer finger and thumb into the sockets. "Why am I not surprised?"

"He said he's being set up," I rushed to explain. "He thinks he knows who did it, but he needs access to a computer and some . . . other things I thought you might be able . . ." I suddenly realized I didn't know exactly what Mike needed, and involving Rick and Silverthorne was a much bigger ask than I initially thought it would be.

"You should tell him to turn himself in to the FBI," Rick advised.

"That will be hard. The guy who set him up did a good job.

Impersonated him. Left his fingerprints. Used false identification. And the FBI fellow in charge of the investigation is an enemy of Mike's. He won't give him the benefit of the doubt." I sought to keep the desperation out of my voice. "Mike might not get a chance to explain his own theory or have the chance to get the access to the tools he needs to prove that theory."

Rick's face turned blank and unreadable. "Sounds as though this guy did a number on your fed."

"He's not *my* fed. But he's still a friend and a genuinely good guy."

"How can you be sure he didn't do it?" he probed.

"If he took the money, why is he still here? Why would he take the chance of contacting me? Why didn't he hop a flight to Argentina? Or hire a boat to take him to Bermuda?" I punched my finger to the dash with each question. "Can you help him? Or not?"

Rick watched me with hard eyes. "On one condition."

"Name it."

"Go out on a date with me. A real one."

My breath caught. "Done."

"Fine." He opened the door. "I'm hungry. Let's eat."

As soon as we sat down, he declared a moratorium on phones. He removed his earpiece and tucked it in a coat pocket and instructed me to bury my phone in my purse. The lunch special was a penne pasta with meat sauce and salad, which we both ordered.

Once the necessities of getting settled and ordering were out of the way, I expected one of two things to happen—either it would get awkward with long silences, or we'd discuss our date deal. Neither happened.

To my surprise, Rick and I kept up a steady flow of dialog. Nothing meaningful or deep, but still a pleasant conversation to pass the time. We talked sports, and the weather—in regard to global climate change. Our discussion on sports was short due to my own limited knowledge. Once we turned to politics, the discussion shifted.

"Typical. A white male is against the Equal Rights Amendment." I sniffed.

"Hey now, plenty of white females are against it as well," Rick defended.

"None that I know." I went on to list the reasons why women needed ERA. Going so far as to quote former Supreme Court Justice Ruth Bader Ginsburg. "Each person will be judged based on individual merit and not on the basis of an unalterable trait of birth that bears no necessary relationship to need or ability."

He grinned at my arguments and threw out the old standby, "What about the fourteenth amendment? The fourteenth already gives you equal rights."

"As I'm sure you know, the fourteenth does not explicitly mention women. And while the nineteenth gives us voting rights, it remains narrowly scoped to voting rights only. Furthermore, if ERA does pass, it means that selective service is no longer limited to men. I would think you'd want that, to broaden the pool should we ever have another draft. Unless, of course, you believe women are not suited for combat," I drawled, leaning forward, practically daring him to contradict me.

His grin grew broader. "You know you're cute when you get wound around the axle about politics."

Then it hit me, something about his teasing demeanor had me pulling back. "You're not against the ERA, are you?"

He chuckled and shook his head. "Nope."

"But ... then, why?" I stuttered.

"Because it's fun to wind you up."

I crossed my arms and frowned. "So, my ideas are a big joke to you?"

The grin disappeared. He leaned forward and replied in a soft, earnest voice, "That's not what I meant. You're very impassioned and well spoken about the issues you believe in. The topic of politics is off limits at the office. Much like those who work for the Secret Service, we all have our own opinions, but we don't share them. We've got a job to do and can't allow politics to cloud our judgement or get in the way of protecting a client. You're smart, and I enjoy sparring with you. Even when we are in agreement."

His comments blew me away. I hadn't been looking for or expecting the compliment.

"And, by the way, I have no problem with women in combat." He folded his napkin and placed it on the table. "You were on your high school debate team, weren't you?"

"Yes. Did I mention it before?"

"I think, I read it in your dossier."

My gaze narrowed. "I have a dossier?"

He made a wry face. "All of our clients have one."

"Of course. Silly me." I sipped the last of my iced tea and stared into the middle distance.

"Karina, it's standard operating procedure," he explained.

"I get it." I waved his comments away, then thought better of it, and my gaze returned to his. "What does it say?"

Rick didn't answer immediately. Because he'd been so well trained, it was difficult to read his features, but I felt that he struggled internally.

Finally, he said, "Would you like to read it?"

I almost fell out of my chair. "You'd let me?"

"It's not something I offer lightly."

"Why are you offering it now?"

A brow went up. "Would you like me to rescind the offer?"

"No." I fiddled with the napkin in my lap. "I'd like to see it sometime."

The waiter effectively ended our conversation when he

arrived with the check.

On the way back to the office, I identified our FBI tail, which must have caught up to us via tracking my phone. Rick didn't bother to lose them.

"There's no point," he said. "You're going back to the office. They'd wait to reacquire you there." The SUV rolled to a stop and Rick shifted into park. "Jin texted while we were at lunch. Your car is clean."

"He cleaned it, or there was nothing to find?"

"There was nothing to find. Which may mean they're using your phone as a listening device as well as a tracker. Be sure to keep it buried in your purse when you need to talk."

"Fabulous." *The FBI has turned my phone against me.*

"I'll get you the details on how we can bring in Mike."

"Wait a minute." I threw up my hands. "Aren't you worried the FBI has been listening to our conversation the entire time?"

"No."

My arms fell. "Why not?"

"I have a jammer in the car. This button turns it on and off." He pointed to the black button next to the radio that I'd seen him fiddle with earlier.

I digested that tidbit. "Well, I suppose that's convenient."

"This isn't my first rodeo."

"I know," I said defensively. "Well . . . I guess we'll talk later." I opened the door.

"Karina?" He placed a hand on my arm.

I turned with brows raised, and he swooped in, planting a slow, burning kiss. At least, it left *my* lips burning.

"For the FBI," he whispered.

I gulped and nodded. "Huh."

Gaining the street, I came face-to-face with a gaping Rodrigo, who watched Rick's SUV roar down the street. I marched past him to the lobby and stepped onto an empty elevator. He followed, punched the button to our floor, and the doors closed.

"I don't want to talk about it," I stated clearly in the deafening silence.

Rodrigo snorted. Then the snort turned into a chortle. The chortle metamorphosed into full-on laughter. The laughter followed me as I stalked down the hall to my office. I could still hear it through the wooden door.

# Chapter Eight

Wednesday, I awoke to find a text from my neighbor Tim.

**Leaving on an early flight for Seattle. Plan to return late Friday. Please keep an eye on things.**

I texted in return,

**Have a safe trip. Thanks again for the chocolates. They were delish.**

It was nice to know I had another place to make my clandestine phone calls to the various people involved in Mike's case. Surprisingly, I'd managed to get a decent night's sleep and didn't have to fully rely on the caffeine in my morning cup of Joe to motivate me. I checked both the burn phones for messages. Mike's had a text.

**Anything?**

I sent back,

**Stand by.**

Rick had also sent me a text.

**Arrangements being made to pick up package. Will send instructions soon.**

I sent no response to Rick's message, instead tossed the phone, along with the rest of them, into my purse, gathered my computer bag, and headed off to a daylong seminar at the World Health Organization in D.C. At noon, we broke for lunch and I checked my phones while waiting in line for the bathroom. There was a new text from Rick.

**Will pick up package in Arlington. 17<sup>th</sup> and Kent**

*Street. North corner. 7 p.m. tonight.*

I responded,

**Roger that.**

I switched phones and typed the instructions into Mike's burner.

"How many phones do you carry?" The woman's voice from behind startled me.

Dropping the phone in my handbag, I turned to find a middle-aged brunette with curly hair wearing a long, boho-style skirt and sweater.

"I have multiple business ventures and need a phone for each one." The person in front of me entered one of the stalls and we moved up.

The brunette smiled at me in a friendly manner; she had a gap between her front teeth. "What kind of businesses?"

A toilet flushed and a door at the far end of the bank of stalls opened. "Oops, my turn." I shuffled down the row, locked myself in, and released the breath I'd been holding.

She may have just been a friendly attendee, or she may have been an undercover agent sent to spy on me. Either way, it had been foolish of me to conduct this business in public. I didn't think she'd seen my text to Mike but I didn't want to take that chance.

I texted Rick.

**Location may be compromised. Please send new package pick-up point.**

An hour later, I locked myself into a toilet stall again and found Rick's response.

**23rd Street and S. Ives. In front of Our Lady of Lourdes Church. Same time. Send confirmation.**

After checking above my head to make sure there were no friendly eavesdroppers leaning over the stall wall, I relayed the message to Mike. He hadn't responded to my earlier text. I hoped his phone hadn't run out of battery and he'd receive the instructions before tonight. By four, he hadn't responded, and I was getting nervous. If he didn't get back to me by six thirty, I'd have to tell Rick to call off the mission. The seminar ended at five, and I still hadn't gotten a confirmation from Mike. My mind began spinning with all sorts of worst-case scenarios—the FBI had caught up to Mike. He'd been attacked at the house he was staying in. He'd become ill and needed medical attention. I was in a panic by the time I returned home and fast-walked into my building. The elevator seemed to take forever, and I considered climbing the stairs. However, living on the fifth floor, I knew it would be no faster. Instead, I hopped from foot-to-foot while mentally urging the elevator to *hurry up!* Finally, it arrived. When it stopped on my floor, I bolted out, practically plowing into my neighbor, Mrs. Thundermuffin, who was waiting with her leashed cat, Mr. Tibbs. *Crap!* I did a funny little leap to sidestep the cat.

"Hello, dearie! So good to see you," she greeted me.

"Hi, Mrs. T., Mr. Tibbs. Would love to chat, but I've . . . uh . . . got to have a wee. Been sitting in traffic. You understand." Washington traffic was a universal language to those who lived here.

"I do indeed. One quick thing—I'm leaving for Florida tomorrow morning to visit my sister," she called as I trucked down the hall toward my apartment. "Keep an eye on things for me while I'm gone."

"Sure thing!" I hollered, turning the corner.

It took but a moment to drop off my belongings in the foyer and grab Tim's key and the two burn phones. My heart raced with anxiety as I fumbled with Mike's cell. One glance, and I realized he'd responded to my text sometime during the commute home.

**Confirmed. 7 p.m.**

My legs turned to jelly, and I collapsed on Tim's uncomfortable couch with a wheezing exhale. At ten after six, I sent a text to Rick.

**Package pick-up confirmed.**

Now all I had to do was wait patiently for Rick to contact me. I returned to my condo, changed into jeans and a sweatshirt, and made myself a grilled cheese sandwich for dinner. By six thirty, I was pacing loops around the apartment. At 6:35, I grabbed my keys, coat, and purse, and headed to my car.

Thirty minutes later, I waited as the iron gates at Silverthorne Security rolled open to allow me to enter. Rick came striding out as I parked in front of the large, red brick, warehouse-style building. He did not look happy.

"You're jeopardizing the mission," he said. "Joshua will be returning with the package soon, and you've brought the—"

"I ditched my tail," I interrupted his rant. "I used your shoot-the-gap move."

"Your phone—"

"*And* I left my phone at home."

The answers seemed to mollify him, but only slightly. His gaze swept the parking lot and surrounding area. "You'll have to move your car around back. It's too exposed if they decide to look for you here. There are six garage bays. I'll open number three for you." He strode away without waiting for a response.

A few minutes later, the industrial-sized garage door rattled closed behind Old Bessie. A fleet of SUVs ranging from black to silver to forest green spread to my left and right, two deep. In front of me, Rick stood on an elevated loading dock and motioned me to move all the way forward to the edge of the dock. Once I shut off the car, he hopped down to get my door.

"Was the pick-up successful?" I asked.

Rick nodded. "Joshua is on his way right now."

I got out, slinging my purse over my shoulder. "Any ideas where we should keep him? Have you got space for a sleeping bag in one of your sub-basement interrogation rooms?"

Rick didn't blink an eye at my supposition. "We've got bunk rooms we use when we're on twenty-four-hour shifts."

"Is it safe for your other men to know Mike is here?"

"Those who need to know will be read in. The others won't. And yes, I trust my team to keep their mouths shut."

"Why? Because if your men don't follow orders, people die," I said in my best Jack Nicholas voice from the movie *A Few Good Men.*

Rick stood with his feet shoulder width apart, hands on hips, and didn't crack a smile. "Essentially, that can be the case. Yes." This was when he reminded me most of Batman, with that brooding intensity.

The smart-ass grin dropped from my face. "Well, thanks for helping him."

"We'll see, Karina. I may have a soft spot for you, but I warn you, if I don't like what we find, and your fed did indeed steal the money—"

"He's not *my* fed. And *if* he did steal the money, I'll be dragging his ass and dumping him on the front steps of the Hoover building myself," I retorted.

Rick's jaw flexed and that uncanny gaze bore into me.

"Alright, he's kind of heavy, so I might need you or Josh to physically carry him to those steps."

The jaw relaxed and the curve of a smile crept across his face.

"Now, tell me about this soft spot you have for me." I sent out the probe.

His lids lowered and he whispered in my ear, "Now is not the time. Joshua will be here soon."

I shivered and my brow rose. "But there will be a time . . . to . . . uh . . . talk about . . . it?"

"One day," he said, giving nothing away.

A penetrating silence enveloped us as we stared at each other.

The clacking of the garage door had me nearly jumping out of my skin. "Cripes!" I spun around to find a black SUV rolling in behind my car. Josh shifted into park and turned off the ignition. The garage door began its chattering descent.

"Any problems?" Rick asked.

"None," Josh replied, opening the back door. "It's safe to come out now."

Mike unfolded himself from the floorboards and kind of fell out of the vehicle.

Josh caught his arm, so he didn't faceplant onto the hard concrete. "You okay, man?"

"My foot fell asleep." Mike hobbled a few steps away, shaking his left foot as he went. The beard had thickened since we met on the metro. His dark eyes were hollowed and tense from stress and lack of sleep. His cheekbones were more defined and the dirty jeans he wore hung loose at his hips. I'd never seen the brown parka or black knit hat he wore. The pungent smell of body odor and something sour wafted from him.

I cringed. "What happened? You look like hell and you don't smell much better. I thought you were staying in a townhouse."

He continued limping around with a wince every time his left foot hit the ground. The pins and needles must have set in. "I had to move and get new clothes. One of the neighbors may have spotted me. I know it stinks. I found it in the trash."

The smell came at me again, and I pulled up my shirt to cover my nose. "Geez, Mike. Where did you stay last night?"

"On the streets," he grunted.

"Tough break," Josh murmured.

I grimaced and glanced at Rick, wondering if he was regretting his decision to help.

Instead of finding his usual implacable expression, he looked at my filthy, tottering, ex-boyfriend with compassion. "Come inside. You can get cleaned up and something to eat. Tonight, you sleep in a bed."

Mike nodded and said humbly, "Thanks, Donovan. I know you're sticking your neck out for me. I don't know why, but I appreciate it."

Rick gave a sharp nod and led the way to the loading dock. He nimbly climbed up the four-foot-high concrete slab and turned to give Mike a hand. Then it was my turn. I wish I could say, I ascended as elegantly as Rick or even Mike. There was some scrambling, and eventually Josh put his hand on my ass and gave a shove, which deposited me ignobly at the feet of my ex-boyfriend, and the man who was currently threading his way into my erotic dreams. Rick reached down to help me to my feet. By the time I stood, Josh had already gained the platform. Looking past him, I noticed a set of stairs at the far end, and I mentally cursed myself. Josh punched in the code to a large, gray metal door.

We entered a part of the building I'd never been in. One side of the thirty-by-thirty room was lined with industrial shelving filled with duffle bags and black cases, and on the other side was a locked armory of rifles, shotguns, and semi-automatic weapons. A large, counter-height metal table stood in the center of the room. Josh didn't stop, quickly leading us through to a short, industrial white hallway, another secure door, and into a more public hallway with tile floors and light gray paint. This was a part of the building I knew. At the end of the hall was the elevator. Rick swiped his card, punched in a code, and the elevator opened for us.

Mike and I climbed aboard, but Rick stopped Josh from entering. "I need you to check in with tech ops. The embassy issued new security parameters."

Josh nodded, smiled good-naturedly at us, and gave a little

two-fingered salute. "Catch you later."

We got off on the third floor. I'd never been on this level. To the right was a set of restrooms. Rick took us to the left. Halfway down the hall, he stopped, opened a wooden door with the number four on it, and revealed a twelve-by-twelve room.

Twin beds lined the wall on the left and right, and two squat Ikea chests of drawers lay between the beds. A mirror was mounted above each one, and petite lamps sat on top. Desks with chairs sat at the foot of each bed, and there was a television mounted above a set of bi-fold closet doors. The setup reminded me of my college dorm days.

"You'll have the room to yourself. Down the hall on your right is the kitchen. You'll find sandwich makings, pasta and sauce, microwave meals in the freezer, fresh fruit and vegetables in the fridge," Rick explained. "If it's not in a bag or marked plastic container and doesn't have someone's name on it, feel free to eat it. Grocery delivery comes once a week on Fridays. There's a pad on the refrigerator. If you want something specific, add it to the list."

Mike stood in the center of the room, his hands jammed in the parka pockets, rotating his head around, taking in the space. "This is nice. Thanks."

"The bathroom is here, behind the door." Rick pulled the entry door closed halfway to show Mike. "Towels are on the rack. You'll find soap and toiletries underneath the sink. There should be a razor. Let me know if you don't find one."

Mike rubbed his scruff. "For the time being, I think I'll keep the beard."

"That's not a bad idea. It certainly makes it more difficult to recognize you," I put in. "But what to do about clothes? I can't go back to your apartment again. I'll have to go and buy you some new street clothes."

"Check the dresser drawers," Rick said. "There should be a

T-shirt, sweatpants, and socks. You can change into them for now."

"And, for all that is holy, throw that stinking coat out." I made an icky face.

"You can clean them. There's a basket in the closet and washer and dryer off the kitchen. We'll arrange to get you more clothes tomorrow," Rick said.

"I have money tucked in my sock that I can give to you for clothes, Karina. And for what I owe you." He aimed the latter at Rick.

"Karina's being watched. Shopping for you would be unwise. We're about the same size. You can borrow my clothes, or I'll have one of my men get some for you." I'd never really noticed, but Rick was right—he and Mike were of similar height and build. Mike was a bit thinner and Rick's shoulders were broader.

"You're right. I'm sorry, Karina, I wasn't thinking." Mike sheepishly glanced down at his dirty sneakers. "I'm aware of the risks you're taking on my behalf. Be sure to know how deeply appreciative I am."

"Settle in. Take a shower. Meet us in the kitchen when you're ready." Rick held the door, indicating I should take the lead.

I'd never seen Mike looking so sad and miserable, and he rarely ever called me by my name; I was usually K.C. to him. I went over to him and took his hand. "We'll figure this out. You'll feel better after you shower and rest." I gave his hand a squeeze.

His lip creased up in acknowledgement, and we left him to it.

The sleek, modern kitchen was a chef's dream—dark gray cabinetry, side-by-side subzero refrigerators, a six-burner gas stove, two dishwashers, a farmhouse sink, a prep sink on the commodious white-quartz-topped island, and a long table that would accommodate a dozen comfortably.

"You've been holding out on me." I dropped my purse on the counter.

"Clients generally don't see the bunk room level. It's for the guys when they're on twenty-four-hour shifts, or standby for a mission," Rick responded. "I'm going to make some coffee. Would you like a cup?"

"Only if it's decaf. I need a decent night's sleep. So does Mike, for that matter. Is that a cappuccino maker?" I pointed to a large, copper machine with buttons and levers. "Pretty fancy, boss."

"I don't know how to use it. Jin, Regina, and a few guys in tech ops make their coffee in it. The rest of us stick with the old-fashioned Mr. Coffee machine." Rick pulled a plain, black coffeemaker forward.

While he went about measuring the coffee and water, I prowled the kitchen and began pulling out pots and pans. "I'm going to make Mike some spaghetti. He looks as though he could use a decent meal." I poured a jar of tomato sauce into a small pot, filled a larger pot with water, and began chopping onions. "What type of mission would require the guys to be on for twenty-four hours?"

"More often than not, it's the tech ops guys who are on for twenty-four hours. When I have a team in the field, either local or international, we might require tech support at odd hours of the day. Usually, we try to rotate shifts. However, some of our guys are specialists, and we require their expertise." The coffeemaker's wheezing came to a stop. "Cream, sugar, both?"

"Both, please." I dumped the onions into the sauce and stirred. "Is this the first time you've hidden someone here?"

He didn't answer, and I glanced up from the stove to find a pained look cross his face.

"What is it? Wait . . . don't tell me . . . you can't talk about it." I rolled my eyes in frustration.

A moment later, he spoke. "There was a woman. She was being abused by her husband."

My mouth turned down and a queasy ball formed in my gut.

"How did it end?"

"She was a foreign national, her husband was an ambassador. We were providing local security for trips outside of the embassy. She wanted asylum, but our governments were in the middle of trade negotiations." He shook his head. "The State Department forced us to return her."

My stirring stopped. "Do you know what happened after she left?"

"Three days later, she fell down the stairs and broke her neck," he said, using air quotes. "Her body was shipped home for the funeral."

"That's horrible." The water came to a boil, and I dumped in the pasta. "You don't believe it was an accident?"

"No." He sat on one of the island stools.

"What country?"

"I can't say." He took a deep swallow of coffee. "However, I can tell you, it was the last time we worked for that particular embassy. The ambassador escorted his wife's body home, and State revoked his diplomatic visa so he couldn't return."

I wiped my hands on a towel and began searching the cupboards.

"What are you looking for?" he asked.

"Seasonings, maybe garlic powder for the sauce."

"Upper cabinet, to the left of the stove."

I located what I needed and returned to the topic at hand. "What else do you house here, Rick?"

"I believe you've seen most of the building."

"There are two subterranean floors I haven't seen." I stirred the spices into the sauce.

"Sometimes a little mystery is good for the soul," he replied.

I scooped out a piece of pasta and tested it. "In other words, it's none of my business."

"Your words, not mine." A slight smile hovered around his

lips as he took another sip.

By the time Mike ambled into the kitchen, clad in sweatpants and a gray T-shirt, the spaghetti was ready, and I was putting the finishing touches on his salad.

He paused, his wet hair gleaming beneath the canned lights. "This is quite the domesticated scene," he commented, shifting the laundry basket he carried on his hip. "What are you making? It smells divine."

"Spaghetti with salad. We're having coffee. Would you like some?" I dumped diced carrot pieces into a small bowl filled with lettuce and tomatoes.

"A big glass of water, if you don't mind. I'll have the coffee after I eat," Mike replied.

"Why don't you put those clothes in the wash while I get your plate ready?" I suggested.

When he finally sat down at the counter, Mike ravenously dove into the pile of food. He went through the salad, two helpings of spaghetti, and two glasses of water. I found a tub of cookie dough in the fridge and baked a dozen cookies while he gorged himself. We all had a fresh cup of coffee with dessert.

By the time he finished the last cookie, he looked more like the Mike I knew. Granted, he hadn't shaved the beard, but he did clean it up, and while the deep circles beneath his eyes were still prominent, his demeanor had improved for the better.

"So, what's our next step?" I asked, brushing cookie crumb remnants off my sweatshirt.

"I have men working on getting footage from the bank," Rick said.

I watched Mike to see if he showed fear, or any other emotion, for that matter.

He merely nodded. "Good, good. I was thinking, I'd like to see if there's any security footage from the Chinese restaurant where I ate on Tuesday night. I think I was purposely poisoned to be kept out the way."

"I'll see what I can do," Rick replied.

"K.C., did you bring the postcard?" Mike asked.

"It's in my handbag." I gestured to the purse on the counter, and Rick passed it over. I dug the postcard out of the bottom. "Here you go. See, an ad for the Nationals. Look on this side. It says opening day is April fourth, and on the back is the schedule for the home and away games."

Mike squinted at the postcard, flipped it over, then flipped it back. "Sonuvabitch," he mumbled.

"What? Do you see something?" I peered over his shoulder.

"You're blocking the light. Sit back," Mike said. "Does anyone have a magnifying glass?"

Rick shook his head.

I dug into my purse. "My mom gave me one for Christmas last year. Here it is." I handed the small, round leatherette pouch to Mike. "Push it right there."

He held the little magnifying glass above the postcard. "Just as I thought. There's a number underlined in May. Done in pencil, very, very faintly." He pointed.

Rick and I both moved in to see.

"The tenth," I said. "I didn't see that before because I never looked at it under bright light. So? What does that mean? Is that the day you tried to bust this guy?"

"Bust who?" Rick asked.

"Mike thinks the guy setting him up is a money launderer he was after a few years ago," I supplied. "You never told me—what's his name?"

"Terrance Matheson. We'll get back to him in a moment. Look here"—he flipped the postcard to the front—"see how the date April fourth is circled in red?"

"They wanted the date to stand out," I said.

"If you look closer, under the magnifying glass, you'll see it's not printed. I think he used a sharpie." Mike passed the magnifying glass to me.

"Well, I'll be damned. And look—the red line under the *W* is printed, but the one under the *N* is sharpie again." I passed the glass over to Rick. "So, we have April fourth, the number ten and letter *N*. But what does it mean?"

"I don't know," Mike replied, tapping a finger against the counter.

Rick got up, walked around the island, opened a drawer, and pulled out a pad of paper and a pencil. In his sharp, angular handwriting, he wrote 404, *N*, 10, and, and tossed the pad across the island toward the pair of us. "It's a location at Nats Park. Section four-oh-four, row *N*, seat number ten."

"Holy shit. Rick is right!" I got excited and shook Mike's arm. "Did this Terrance guy have season tickets? Was that his seat?"

"Yes, he had season tickets. No, that wasn't his seat. He had seats in section 128, behind the dugout." Mike's gaze narrowed as he continued staring at the postcard.

"I know what you're thinking. It's too dangerous, mate." Rick crossed his arms and studied Mike.

"Too dangerous for what?" Normally, I'm quicker on the uptake, but tonight, I simply wasn't making the connection.

Mike didn't answer, so Rick filled me in. "I imagine someone has left something at Nats Park for Mike."

*Ting!* The lightbulb went on. "Oh." I nodded.

"I could put my homeless clothes back on. Sneak in during the wee hours of the morning." Mike sounded as though he was trying to convince himself as much as the pair of us.

"You know better than anyone. Security around D.C. is tight, and that park has eyes everywhere. Ever since the attack on our embassy last month in Ethiopia, Homeland Security has maintained a Level Orange, or high, threat level," Rick explained. "If they don't catch you on the way in, they'll nail you on the way out. You *will* get arrested if you try."

"What do you expect me to do?" Mike snapped, flicking the card in frustration; it spun across the long counter. "Wait until opening day?" He rubbed a hand across his eyes.

Rick surveyed my beleaguered ex-boyfriend. "You're tired and need rest. I'll work on getting the footage you've requested. Tomorrow, we'll review what we know with fresh eyes and determine a course of action."

Mike looked as if he was about to argue, but I cut in. "Rick is right. I'm tired, too. Ever since the FBI came knocking on my door, I haven't been sleeping well. Let's reconvene tomorrow, say six thirty, and you can tell us all about the Terrance Matheson case. I'll bring takeout."

"*Not Chinese!*" Mike barked.

I jerked back. "Whoa! Relax. I was thinking barbeque."

A loud buzzing that went on for a solid fifteen seconds interrupted whatever Mike was about to say.

I put a hand to my pounding heart. "What the hell was that?"

"Washing machine," Rick answered.

"Cripes. You think you could turn it down from heart attack level?"

"We keep it up high so you can hear it down the hall," he explained.

"Well, at least you've got some clean clothes, Mike. Let's hope the stench of trash came off that coat," I said.

Mike slid off the stool. "You and me both. I guess I'll see you tomorrow."

"Yup." I hopped off the stool and held up my hand to give a finger wave. Mike misinterpreted my movements and leaned in for a hug. I pulled back, he pulled back, and we ended up with an awkward shoulder pat sort of thing. "See you tomorrow." My face burned with embarrassment, knowing Rick had watched the entire bizarre exchange.

Mike meandered to the laundry room; his shoulders hunched dejectedly.

"I'll escort you out," Rick said.

I slung my purse over my shoulder. "What about the SUV behind my car?"

"Joshua already moved it."

"Well, that's efficient." I covered a yawn.

"Joshua is very efficient."

"Is this the part of the evening when we exchange witty repartee?"

"If you'd like." Rick put his hand on the small of my back and led me out of the kitchen.

I yawned again. "Actually, I think I'm having a sugar crash—"

"I'm not surprised, considering how much you put in your coffee."

I gave him the side-eye. "I meant from the cookies."

"Sure. That's what I meant, too."

"This is exhausting. We can try witty repartee tomorrow." I said the last in the midst of another yawn.

"Would you like me to drive you home?"

"No, I need my car. I'll be fine when I get outside in the cold, fresh air." The elevator arrived. Once the doors closed, I asked the question that had been topmost in my mind, and one that needed asking out of earshot of Mike. "So, do you think he's lying?"

Rick didn't hesitate. "No. He's trying to unravel the mystery. If he did do it, he wouldn't want us to get the bank footage."

"Do you really think you can get ahold of it?"

He tilted his head. "Of course."

I rolled my eyes. *Silly me.*

Josh waited for us on the main level. "You're needed in tech ops, ASAP."

"Escort her to the car and make sure she gets out okay. See you tomorrow," Rick threw over his shoulder as he strode down the hall.

"Tomorrow," I replied. There would be no goodnight kiss. I was kind of bummed about that.

It was past eleven when I returned to the condo, and for my listening fans at the FBI, I announced, "I'm home!" I almost added, "Did you miss me?" But I figured that was a step too far.

# Chapter Nine

To my surprise, Rick called on my regular cellphone—the one the FBI was likely monitoring—around midday.

"Hello?"

"I'm confirming your self-defense lesson tonight at six thirty," he said.

I was confused. "Uh . . . yeah. I'm going to bring some dinner over . . . for afterward. Would you . . . uh, like me to bring some for you?"

"That would be nice. See you tonight." He hung up.

Immediately, I pulled out the burn phone and texted,

**What the hell was that about?**

His reply was instantaneous.

**Giving you an excuse to be here tonight. Don't bother to lose your tail.**

For a moment, I thought about making the argument to lose the tail, but my work phone rang, distracting me, and I tossed the phones back in my purse.

At quarter to seven, I rolled in to the Silverthorne parking lot with a takeout bag that filled my car with the droolworthy scent of brisket, ribs, pulled pork, collard greens, slaw, and baked beans. My stomach grumbling, I entered through the front door and had the unexpected pleasure of seeing the Silverthorne receptionist at her desk. "Hi, Regina, you're working late tonight."

"Well, hello, Karina. It's been a while since I've seen you. How have you been?" Her sweet voice serenaded me.

"Can't complain. What about you?"

Regina pulled on her coat. "I'm good. My daughter is coming up from South Carolina to visit this weekend."

"Wonderful."

"What have you got in the bag? It smells good."

"Barbeque from Sweet Fire Donna's. I . . . uh . . ." I wasn't sure if Regina had been read into the third-floor visitor. "Rick said he'd never tried it, so I . . . brought some . . . for the boys." I'm sure my cheeks bloomed like cherries.

"Aren't you a doll." She slung a large cheetah-print tote bag over her shoulder. Luckily, she didn't seem to notice my consternation. "Don't let the boys work you too hard."

"No, I won't." My gaze slid past her. Someone walked down the hall toward us.

"You're late," Josh said to me.

"I know. Traffic. Sorry." When running late, traffic was always a solid excuse. In reality, I'd lost track of time and left the office later than expected.

Josh nodded. "You leaving, Regina?"

"Yes, I am," she replied. "Do you need anything before I go?"

He shook his head. "Drive safe. Please lock the door on your way out. Karina is the only person we're expecting tonight. Follow me." The latter he aimed at me.

"Good night, Regina." I waved.

Josh took the takeout bag from me and led the way to the elevator. We ended up in the kitchen. Mike and Rick sat at one end of the long table with a laptop between them. Mike wore a pair of clean jeans and a gray sweatshirt. He looked better than yesterday, but the burgeoning beard didn't hide the gaunt cheeks.

"What did I miss?" I plopped my purse on the counter. "Did you get the bank footage?"

"We did," Rick replied. He wore a pair of jeans and a black polo.

Josh placed the takeout on the counter. "I'm going to bolt.

I've got plans for tonight."

We all said goodbye to Josh, then I sidled up between the two men's chairs and peered at the computer. "What are we waiting for? Let's roll it."

The footage was blurry, but I identified the man who was impersonating Mike when he entered the front door. He didn't look around but walked directly toward a set of desks rather than a teller. He wore khaki slacks, a white button-down, and a navy blazer, and carried a silver-colored metal briefcase. The body type seemed on target; however, he wore a ballcap pulled low, and seemed to know where the cameras were because he averted his face to keep from getting a direct shot.

"If it is Matheson, he's lost a solid fifty pounds," Mike commented.

"The gait is wrong," I said.

Rick paused and backed up the recording. "What do you mean?"

"He's got a hiccup in his step."

"A hiccup?" Rick frowned.

"There." I pointed. "And there. And there. Like he's got arthritis in his knee or hip, or it's been injured. Mike, go out of the room and walk back in. Like you have a purpose."

Mike pushed away from the table and followed my directions, while Rick and I scrutinized his gait.

"You also take longer strides than the guy at the bank. Maybe he's trying to hide the hitch by taking shorter steps," I suggested.

"Whatever the case"—Mike plopped back down on the chair with a sigh—"my gait isn't enough to get me out of this mess."

The guy walked out of frame, and a new camera angle picked him up as he spoke with a bank employee at one of the desks.

"He's got a pointy-er chin than you do. Your jawline is a little more oval." I glanced back and forth at Mike and the guy on the screen. "Well, I think it was, before the beard . . . and weight loss," I amended.

The employee is seen waving him into a glass-enclosed office, and we moved to another camera angle. Our impersonator took a seat. A few minutes later, a man in a nice suit walked into the glass room, closed the door, and sat at the computer. Both men were in profile, but we could see more of the employee than our subject.

"Who's the guy in the thousand-dollar suit?" I asked.

"One of the bank managers," Mike said.

They talked for a while. The impersonator shook his head a few times. Eventually, he pulled out his wallet and handed a driver's license to the bank manager, who held it at such an angle that it was useless to us.

"I'm assuming we don't have audio," I said.

"No audio," Rick confirmed.

The bank manager left with the ID, and the impersonator turned his back to the camera. He hunched over and was clearly doing something, but we couldn't see what. Then he rose and, with his left hand, turned the computer monitor and took a photo with his cellphone. I remembered Amir said they found Mike's prints on a computer monitor.

I turned to Mike. "Have you ever been in that office?"

"Me? No. Why?" he asked with surprise.

Rick paused the recording and both men looked at me.

"It's one of the places they retrieved your fingerprints." I thoughtfully tapped my chin. The computer monitor had information on it, but the film quality was too poor to make it out. I squinted, but it made no difference. There was something else wrong with the scene, but I couldn't figure out what it was. Giving up, I sighed, "Keep rolling."

The perpetrator returned the monitor to its place and sat down. A minute later the bank manager came back, again closing the door.

Then it came to me. "Wait! Pause it," I declared.

Rick tapped the space bar.

"Back it up to when he moves the monitor around." I squinted at the footage as it ran at normal speed. "Back it up one more time. Can you put it on slo-mo or something?"

"I can make it go frame by frame," Rick replied. He backed it up again and slowly tapped the arrow key.

"Stop!" I called. "Right there. What's that on his left hand right above the cuff? A birthmark?"

Mike put his nose practically on the screen. "Or a tattoo. Can you blow it up at all?"

Rick moved the mouse, right-clicked, and tapped the little magnifying glass icon. Unfortunately, the larger he blew it up, the blurrier the picture got. "It could simply be a shadow."

"Can't you clean it up?" I asked.

"Not on this computer," Rick responded. "I'll see if tech ops can do something with it. Let's finish the footage."

The man signed some paperwork. I could clearly see where his left hand held down the withdrawal slip. Probably the piece of paper that Amir referred to, the one on which they found Mike's fingerprints. I kept waiting for the imposter to switch the papers while the bank manager wasn't looking. However, I could detect no sleight of hand, even after I had Rick run it frame by frame. The impersonator gave the briefcase to the manager and waited patiently for his return. When the manager came back, the case was clearly heavier. He handed the imposter an envelope and the case. Mike's doppelganger barely lifted the top high enough to check the contents and toss the envelope inside. Clamping the locks closed, he rose, shook hands with the manager, and headed out of the building at normal speed. Nothing in his movements indicated apprehension or agitation. Just a normal guy, on a Tuesday stroll, with $1.2 million in hand. A guy who looked remarkably like Michael Finnegan.

I scrunched my nose. "What denomination would he have asked for in order to fit all that money in a briefcase? I thought money took up a lot of space. Wouldn't you need a duffle bag for a million dollars?" I whipped out my Silverthorne burner phone to Google "*how big is a million dollars in one-hundred-dollar bills*" but Rick interrupted my search before it finished.

"He only took two hundred thousand in cash," Rick explained. "The rest was probably in the envelope as a cashier's check."

"Hm. Interesting." I tapped my chin. "That isn't what Newcomb indicated. Can't the FBI track the cashier's check?"

Mike shoved his chair away from the table and ran a frustrated hand through his hair. "They probably are. Either he'll sit on the money or deposit it into a numbered Swiss bank account."

"And the FBI can't track that?" I asked.

"Depends," Mike replied unhelpfully. "There are a lot of banks that do their utmost to remain discreet. Don't forget we're dealing with a money launderer. He's going to know how to hide it."

"What I can't figure out is how he left behind your fingerprints. We see clearly on the footage where he touched the monitor and the withdrawal slip. I didn't see him use sticky tape or another tool to lay down your prints. How did he do it?" I mused aloud.

"There are ways it can be done." Mike stood and paced over to the fridge to get a bottle of water. "You said you got footage from the Chinese restaurant?"

"I did. And I think you'll find it very interesting." Rick closed out of the bank footage, moused through a couple of folders, and clicked on a numbered file. I sat down in Mike's seat. Rick placed the laptop in between the two of us, and our silent movie began.

The Red Dragon restaurant was long and narrow with an aisle

down the middle and tightly packed tables on either side. The walls were papered in gold and decorated with framed Chinese symbols. A large, parade-style dragon was strung up on the ceiling from one end of the eatery to the other. Mike said it had been a Tuesday, so the restaurant was only at about 50 percent capacity. The footage wasn't much clearer than the bank footage, and it must have been cued up to a specific time after Mike had been seated and ordered. The waiter brought out a cup, saucer, and teapot. Mike moved the water glass to his left and made space for the cup and saucer on the right. The waiter returned a few minutes later with Mike's meal.

"Let me guess—Oolong tea, dumplings, and Kung Pao Beef," I commented.

"It's my favorite." Mike peered between our shoulders.

The phone on the table at Mike's elbow lit up. He checked the caller ID, rose from his chair, tossed the napkin on the table, and walked out of frame, heading toward the front of the restaurant.

Rick tapped the spacebar and the film paused. "Where did you go?"

"Out front. It was a call from the office."

"About what?" I asked.

Mike's brows drew down in thought. "I . . . don't exactly recall. I believe it was something . . . another division needed us to track down some information for them. I passed it along to an analyst."

"Which division? Was it White Collar?" I asked.

I had Mike's attention now. "May-be . . ." Mike sighed and pinched the bridge of his nose. "But I'm not sure. If I had my phone, I could check."

"Keep watching." Rick resumed the tape.

A man wearing a dark shirt and black ballcap sitting with his back to Mike's table turned and squirted a liquid onto his meal.

He had a dark beard covering the lower half of his face, darkened aviator glasses, and the ballcap was pulled down so low we couldn't see the top of his face, only the nose and beard. However, it looked disturbingly like Mike's current beard.

I gasped, placing a hand to my mouth, and Rick glanced to his right to watch Mike's reaction. Mike's gaze narrowed, but otherwise he showed no other emotion.

Rick paused the video. "Do you recognize him?"

"It . . . could . . . be Matheson. He never had a beard when I investigated him. Like I said, if it is him, he's lost fifty pounds since he fled the country. He also used to wear little round glasses." Mike made a circling motion around his eyes. "The beard and aviators cover up a lot of his face."

"It's probably exactly why he's wearing them," I observed.

A few moments later, Mike returned to the table and began eating his meal. The man remained with his back to Mike and the camera. Rick sped up the recording. I couldn't help the snicker that escaped me as we watched Mike shovel Kung Pao into his piehole at four times the normal speed, not to mention the other diners, and the waiters speeding around the restaurant. Near the end of the meal Rick slowed the video back to normal.

Finally, Mike's plate was empty; the waiter came to remove it and leave the check. Mike gulped the last of his water, paid the bill in cash, and left without further interaction with the waitstaff. We watched as the fellow in the dark hat turned around again and furtively checked to his left and right. The coast must have been clear, because he shook out his napkin and used it to pick up Mike's water glass. He dropped it in a plastic bag and shoved it in his coat pocket. He tossed a handful of bills on his own table and, with a distinct hitch in his gait, walked out of frame toward the front of the restaurant.

"I'll be damned," Mike murmured.

Rick and I both craned our necks to watch Mike who seemed

intent on his bottle of water.

"I'm assuming that's where he got your fingerprints," I said.

"That would be my guess."

"But"—I held up a finger—"how did he get them on the monitor and paperwork at the bank?"

Rick and Mike exchanged a look—a look that said they both knew how, leaving me in the realm of the cold unknown.

I sucked my teeth and crossed my arms. "Clearly, you two know exactly how it was done. Someone want to enlighten me?"

"He created a silicone overlay," Rick supplied. "If we go back to the bank footage"—he moused around and brought up the bank footage—"you'll notice his fingers touch the monitor in a very specific manner. He leaves a thumb in front and all four fingers in back. Most people doing something this surreptitious would use only their thumb and forefinger to turn the flat screen. Again, if you watch the way he places his hand on the withdrawal slip, making sure all his fingers touch, even his thumb gets on there, which is odd. I'm willing to bet all the prints are left-handed." Rick looked at Mike. "You moved the water to your left and used that hand to drink from it throughout the meal."

"So, he wore these silicone fingerprints into the bank and had them on the whole time?" I asked.

"No." Mike shook his head. "That's what he was doing when he bent away from the camera. Immediately afterward, he touches the computer monitor."

"Oh. Wow, this guy is pretty sophisticated." I pushed back from the table. "I had no idea you could wear other people's fingerprints. I thought that was only in the movies."

"It's real enough," Mike said with disgust.

"We need to get that footage to Amir," I said.

Mike squinted and rubbed his beard. "Let me think about it."

"What's there to think about?" I put my palms up in the air. "Mike, it's clear this is exactly how you've been set up."

"I'm not arguing with you. However, Newcomb can poke all sorts of holes in this theory." He spoke slowly and clearly. "I need to figure out the best way to approach Amir or lead him to the original footage."

*Okay, he has a point.* "Fine. So, the next question, which you've skirted, is why this guy would do this to you to begin with?" I got up and began pulling takeout boxes from the Sweet Fire Donna's bag. "We'd better eat, before it gets cold. Rick, where are the plates?" I took the lid off the coleslaw and shoved one of the plastic spoons into it. "What did you do to this guy that he hates you so much, Mike? How did you become his nemesis?"

While Rick and I sorted the takeout, Mike began his tale. "Terrance Matheson was a money launderer for a few people. Some were wealthy businessmen trying to hide money from an ex-wife or the government. But he also catered to a small clientele of organized crime—Serbian. That's how we got onto him in the first place. The Organized Crime unit and White Collar division paired up. Organized Crime wanted him to flip on the Serbians. White Collar wanted him to flip on Fred Tate."

"Wait, Fred Tate?" The brisket I held between a set of tongs hovered over the plate, midair. "As in Senator Fred Tate?"

Mike nodded. "The very one."

"What kind of money was he laundering for the senator?" Rick laid a pile of silverware on the table and began sorting it at each place.

"Fred was silent partner at a sketchy international adoption agency. He used his influence to acquire visas for the adoptive families and received a hefty fee for his 'help'."

"So hefty he needed a money launderer to hide his ill-gotten gains." I handed Mike a plate full of barbeque.

"That's the line we were pursuing." Mike put the plate on the table and returned for the next. "Matheson slipped through our fingers before we could make the case. We needed information from him, but he got wise to our investigation. I think the senator had a mole at the Bureau, because Tate retired that year, the adoption agency closed up shop, everyone affiliated with it disappeared, and Matheson fled the country."

"Tate was still popular in his home state." I finished piling a scoop of greens on the plate and handed it to Mike. "A group of us at work always wondered why he didn't run again. But then, a few months after he left Congress, he died in that car accident."

"What was Matheson's story?" Rick asked.

We all sat down and tucked in while Mike continued, "Matheson was both brilliant and stupid. For instance, at one of Matheson's legitimate businesses, a dry cleaner, he paid himself 60k a year. However, he put his two kids on the payroll at 250k, his deceased grandmother was making three hundred, and his wife one hundred."

"Um, I didn't know you could do that." I bit into a tender piece of brisket.

"You can't." Mike picked up a saucy baby back rib.

"So, what about to the wife and kids?" Rick popped the top on a can of diet soda. "Did they know what he was doing?"

"No." Mike wiped his hands on a napkin. "The wife and kids were in the dark. When the FBI moved in, we seized everything we could. He'd put the house in the wife's name, so we couldn't confiscate it, but it was mortgaged to the hilt and she couldn't afford the payments. Eventually, the bank foreclosed. She and the kids were allowed to keep their clothes, personal effects, and jewelry. She sold her furs and auctioned the jewelry to the tune of two hundred thousand. Then she hired a lawyer and a forensic accountant. The accountant did some digging and found other hidden accounts and a lot of activity in the Cayman Islands. She had the lawyer contact us and made a deal." Mike stopped to scoop up a forkful of baked beans.

"This barbeque is very good," Rick said, wiping a glop of

sauce off the side of his mouth. "Where did you say you got it?"

I explained where to find Sweet Fire Donna's, in Old Town Alexandria, and some of the other items on the menu that were my favorites. After Mike had cleared at least half of his plate, I returned my attention to him. "Tell us about the deal she made."

Mike swallowed a mouthful of brisket before answering, "She gave us what she knew in exchange for the condo in Boca Raton, the Mercedes she normally drove, and some of the baseball collection she claimed he'd gifted directly to her. They included a signed Mickey Mantle rookie card, and a baseball signed by Barry Bonds. She auctioned the baseball memorabilia, sold the condo, and moved to Cape Cod, where she opened up a clothing boutique."

"Well, Mrs. Matheson seemed to get out of the mess okay," I commented begrudgingly. Perhaps she really was in the dark; however, her cushy life had obviously been bought by her husband's dirty money. That didn't sit right with me.

"Has he ever tried to contact his wife or children?" Rick asked.

"Not that we know of. And she's not Mrs. Matheson anymore. We might have let slip that he was meeting his mistress every Tuesday and Thursday at the Willard Hotel. Since he abandoned her, she was able to divorce him in absentia, and she returned to her maiden name."

"How old were the kids when this happened?" I picked up a rib and began to gnaw it.

"There are two daughters; one was in middle school, the other in high school." He took a bite of cornbread.

Rick sat back and pushed his empty plate away. "Did you get anything out of the mistress?"

Mike shook his head. "We missed her by a few hours. He must have warned her. Three days later, she turned up dead in Philadelphia. Hit and run."

Rick whistled through his teeth.

"Do you think Matheson did it?" I asked.

"No. I think the Serbians did it," Mike replied. "Maybe she knew something. Maybe she didn't. Whatever the case, the Serbs didn't want her talking to us about their business."

"You have some schmutz on your chin." Rick leaned over and wiped the rib sauce off my face.

"Thanks." I gave it another swipe, and returned my attention to Mike, who was staring at me with a funny expression on his face. "Why the mistress and not the wife and kids?"

"We don't know."

"Maybe he took out an insurance policy," Rick suggested.

Mike didn't respond.

"Okay, I'll bite—what kind of insurance policy keeps mobsters off your back?" I tossed aside my dirty paper napkin and picked up another to finish cleaning the slop off my hands.

"Maybe he hid damning information on the Serbians and warned them that, should anything ever happen to his wife and family, it would be released to the proper authorities," Rick explained.

"Who would he leave such evidence with?"

"A lawyer. Trusted friend," Mike said. "We considered the options. But that would also mean Matheson would have to be keeping tabs on his family."

"Is that out of the realm of possibility?" I asked.

Mike shrugged. "Not necessarily, but we never found any connections once he left."

I tilted my head. "You think he doesn't care about the wife and kids."

"If he did care, why abandon them to the FBI?" Rick supplied.

"Maybe he meant to take them." There was no reason for me to defend this guy, but for some reason, my debate skills kicked in, and I played devil's advocate. "Maybe he ran out of time."

Mike shrugged again. "Maybe. But that's pretty cold."

"Yeah, and there was the mistress, too." I gave in. "You still haven't explained why he's attacking you personally. Did you lead the investigation?"

"No. I was one of many agents working the case on the White Collar side."

"Had he ever met you?"

"Yes, we rounded him up during a massage parlor sting. I interviewed him while my coworkers planted a tracker. He found the tracker within a few hours and ditched it. I didn't want to tip our hand so soon, but the ranking agent from the Organized Crime division convinced my boss it would scare him and lead us to the Serbians and Tate, and bring a quick close to the case."

"He remembered you. After he lost all the weight, he realized you two had a similar body type and features. Maybe it's nothing against you personally. You just fit the bill," I suggested.

"I don't know, K.C." He scratched his beard in thought. "This feels personal."

"Personal to you." I pointed an empty fork at Mike. "Not personal to him. What if using your identity is a means to an end?"

"I don't know if I buy that argument. Why a baseball postcard? Once Mike saw the card and realized there was a message, he knew exactly who we were dealing with," Rick said. "This seems to be directed at Mike."

I sat back in my seat and conceded, "Rick has a point."

"Nothing is for sure, until I figure out a way to get in to the park and see if there's something in that stadium, and if so, what it means."

"I checked online today. There are stadium tours. Why don't I take a tour and duck out? If they catch me, I can say I went into the bathroom and lost the group," I suggested.

The moment I mentioned the tour, Mike started shaking his

head. "If they catch you before you're able to get to the seat, you'll never get another chance, and security will get more serious about watching strays on tour."

"He's right. It's risky," Rick agreed.

I disagreed, but I knew it would do no good to argue with the two men seated across from me when they'd made up their minds. Instead, I crossed my arms and pretended to sulkily accept their rejection of my perfectly fine idea.

What I hadn't mentioned—I'd already booked space on Thursday's four o'clock tour, and unless someone came up with a better plan, come Thursday, I would be working my way up to section 404, row N, seat ten on my own. With or without their blessing.

"I can get us in safely and up to where we need to be," Rick said.

Mike fell silent, eyeing Rick.

"Does it involve climbing a fence?" I wiggled my brows.

"Nope," Rick said.

"Calling in a favor?" More brow wiggling.

"Neither. The Korean Embassy has a handful of diplomats arriving this week. We're providing security," he explained.

"The diplomats want to see Nats park?" Mike drawled in a disbelieving tone.

"No." Rick paused, and I leaned forward, waiting for him to clarify. "But their kids do. I can arrange a private tour. That's our in."

Mike's skepticism vanished. "That . . . might work. I want on the team."

"No. I won't risk it." Rick shook his head. "You'll stay here. However"—he turned to me—"Karina, do you have a black pants suit?"

I snorted. "I work in Washington, D.C. Isn't it mandatory? Wait." I grabbed his hand. "Does this mean I get to go?"

Rick nodded. Mike's features turned down.

"Yesss!" I pumped my fist.

Rick ignored me and spoke directly to Mike. "It's low risk. I can send her with one of the guys on a side trip while the rest of my men do their job with the Koreans."

Mike frowned further. "I don't like it. Can't your men do it? After all, they will already be there."

My eyes narrowed, but Rick spoke before I could. "I don't have the manpower. With the delegation in town, my crews are spread thin. It's a two-person job, and I can only spare one man for this little project. We don't know what's up there. There needs to be one person to retrieve, and one person to be a lookout—that will be Joshua. Any more than that will bring undue attention. If security finds Karina and Joshua snooping around, they can simply tell them we thought we saw movement and they're sweeping the stands. Moreover, this mission is need to know. You're wanted for questioning by the FBI, so unless you want me reading in the entire office staff . . ." He let the allusion hang for a moment before continuing, "It's the best you're going to get, and it's my only offer." Rick delivered the explanation concisely and without malice.

I figured it would be how all military superiors delivered mission parameters to the soldiers under their command. I couldn't help the smile that split my face. If I'd been a less nice person, I might have stuck my tongue out at Mike, whose own pinched face looked helplessly furious over Rick's perfectly suitable suggestion. Instead, I asked, "Do I get coms?"

"Of course." He grinned at my enthusiasm.

"She's untrained. Are you planning to have an untrained civilian *pretend* to be one of your *elite* team members?" Mike uttered snidely.

Rick's jaw clenched and his gaze turned to flint as he addressed Mike. "She is *not* untrained. Furthermore, if you didn't want Karina involved, you never should've contacted her in the first place."

*Holy shit.*

Rick's neutrality vanished with that one sentence. Mike's hackles went up, and I was suddenly watching a pair of circling dogs. It was time to shut things down before the two started exchanging insults and Rick decided to toss Mike out on his ear, or Mike decided to hit the streets.

My chair scraped noisily across the tile as I rose. "Okay, then. Mike, while I understand your concerns, this isn't your call. Rick is right. Since *you* can't retrieve the item, it's got to be me. There's no reason to put any of Rick's men in the middle of this. As a matter of fact, Rick, just get me in with the team, and I'll do it on my own."

Both men turned to me and spoke at once.

"Not on your own," Mike said.

"Joshua goes with you," Rick said.

So, I got them to agree on something. "Fine, then Josh and I will do what needs to be done." I checked my watch. "Now, it's getting late. We'll make arrangements to discuss the details of the op tomorrow." I strode over to the island to peruse the takeout containers. "There are plenty of leftovers for lunch, Mike."

"I have some cash in my room." He stood.

I waved off his suggestion. "Forget it. My treat. You can be in charge of KP." I grabbed my purse. "Rick, walk me out."

We didn't speak until we got to the elevator and Rick said, "I'll take you down to ground level, but then I'll have to leave you to walk yourself out."

"Why? You got a hot date?"

Rick gave a deep sigh. "I think your ex has some things he'd like to say to me while you're out of the room. I thought I'd give him the courtesy to allow him to say them."

*Uh-oh. Bad idea.* "While that sounds very chivalrous, whatever

Mike thinks, he can keep it to himself. He no longer has a say in what I do or don't do in my life. I. Am. Doing. This."

"Oh, I know you are. And while it's clear you've moved on, he still cares about you. Deeply. I shouldn't have goaded him," he sighed with regret.

"Codswallop! You're overstating the case." Rick's brows rose high in disbelief, and I continued, "While I agree he cares, I believe it's a simple case of Mike being in the passenger seat rather than what he's used to—the driver's. Obviously, he's not in charge, another alpha male—whom he's always been wary of—is calling the shots, and, per usual, I'm trucking headlong into a new predicament directly of his own making. HA! He hates the entire ding-dang situation." I waited for Rick's response.

"Did you just say *codswallop?*"

I rolled my eyes and the elevator doors opened. Rick put out his arm to keep them from closing.

I didn't move. "So, we're not going to put on a show for the feds tonight?"

The slightest curve drew up his lips. "Would you like to put one on?"

"Listen, you're the one who started down that road. I was just asking."

He removed his hand and the doors closed, but since we hadn't pushed a button, the elevator stayed put. We faced each other. Rick stepped closer, his silvery gaze intent on my lips. My heartbeat sped up—both fear and desire spread through my body. I stepped back and bumped into the wall.

He didn't touch me, but placed a hand on either side of my noggin.

"Do you have c-cameras in here?" I whispered.

Ever so slightly, his head moved back and forth, and then his lips were on mine. Though he touched no other part of me, I felt the heat emanating off of him, and my body turned into a sea of flames. He lingered, nipping and tasting before ending the kiss.

*Uhhhh . . .*

When my brain unscrambled itself, I said, "The feds aren't watching. Who was that for?" Okay, perhaps my brain hadn't finished unscrambling itself.

"Me," he rasped. Then, he moved swiftly to press the button with the outward pointing arrows.

The doors opened.

"Good to know," I sang, sailing out of the elevator. I didn't know if he allowed the elevator to close or continued to watch me as I floated down the hallway. I didn't bother to look back.

*Let him stew on that.*

# Chapter Ten

It turned out there wasn't much for me to plan. Rick sent a text on the bat phone the next day.

**On Saturday, arrive at Silverthorne at 1300 hours. Wear a black pants suit and sensible shoes. You'll be briefed and fitted with appropriate gear when you arrive. Don't be late.**

So romantic. I mean, our last encounter ended with *another* sensational kiss, and this was what I get? Just to yank his chain I sent back,

**Remind me, what time is 1300?**
**1:00 p.m.!**
**Are you sure? Also, what if I don't like briefs? I tend to prefer bikini-style.**

He must have realized I was messing with him, because he didn't respond to my last volley.

****

Thursday morning, I found a text waiting for me on my regular cellphone from a blocked number.

**Give me a call – A**

I didn't know many people whose name began with an A; however, the blocked number led me to believe Amir was trying to communicate.

After dressing for work and sucking down a cup of life-giving brew, I opened my door, planning to trot over to Tim's place, and practically plowed into my down-the-hall neighbor. Jasper had a crooked nose, wore round John Lennon-style glasses, and had receding, white-blond hair that reached his shoulders—today he had it pulled back in a ponytail. At the end of a leash was a large green iguana with spikes down its back—one of many reptiles Jasper housed in his condo.

"Good morning, Karina." He grinned at me.

"Hello." I gave a half-hearted wave.

The iguana flicked its tongue and started to waddle its leathery body my way. At least it wasn't one of Jasper's snakes; however, I wasn't interested in having a close encounter with a lizard today either. I skittered sideways.

"Don't worry about Smaug, he won't bite," Jasper reassured me.

"I'm not worried about him biting me. I prefer not to get salmonella drool on my two-hundred-dollar boots." I took another step away from the oncoming reptile.

"Since Smaug is a domesticated iguana, it would be highly unusual for him to acquire and pass on salmonella to humans. I keep his cage very clean." He bent down and picked up the pet. "See"—he held Smaug at chest level—"he's quite friendly."

I sucked in a relieved breath because the animal was no longer in shoe-attack mode. Smaug blinked, its sharp claws curled around Jasper's hands, and his chin flap flared.

"Are you headed to work?" he asked.

"In a few minutes. Tim asked me to water his plants while he's gone. I'm going to do that before I leave."

The lizard climbed up his chest and found a comfortable perch on Jasper's shoulder. "That's very neighborly of you. I've been trying to find some time to visit my sister out in Ohio. Would you be willing to feed and water my pets while I was gone? I wouldn't expect you to pick them up."

"Uh . . ." Jasper's apartment could've been on an episode of *Wild Kingdom*. While I was perfectly fine with dogs, cats, and hamsters, things that slithered and looked like a handbag were out of my comfort zone. As far as I was concerned, everything in Jasper's apartment belonged in nature. Like, far away nature. Like, down in South America nature. There was also a big difference between caring for a plant and a live animal. "Gee, Jasper, I'd love to help you out, but I'm allergic to the skin that snakes shed," I lied.

"Really? I had no idea people had allergies to reptiles," he said with true surprise in his tone. "They're generally known to be hypoallergenic."

"With the increase of exotic pet owners, there's been a marked uptick in allergies to those pets." I had no idea if what I was spouting held any truth, but I was sticking to my lie like a fly on a frog's tongue.

"I'm terribly sorry. I had no idea." He took a step backward. "Why didn't you ever mention it?"

"Well, Jasper, I know how you love your pets. I didn't want to make a fuss."

He pushed his glasses up to the bridge of his nose. "I'll bear that in mind for the future."

"Great. I appreciate it. Now, I don't want to hold you up any longer. Go enjoy your morning walk with Smaug." I gave Jasper a wide berth and let myself into the calming scent of Tim's pet-free apartment zone.

The first thing I did was Google "*reptile allergies*" on the bat phone. Sure enough, there were known cases. Whew. Jasper was a nice enough guy, he just didn't seem to understand why others wouldn't love his pet choices as much as he did. On the other hand, I thought up that lie pretty quickly and began to wonder if Mike was right when he questioned my moral compass. Then I remembered I was in Tim's apartment to contact Amir because my own apartment had been bugged by the FBI.

"Mike Finnegan can suck it!" I said aloud to the silent

apartment.

Amir picked up on the third ring. "Amir speaking."

"I believe you sent me a text."

"Are you in a secure location?"

"If you're asking am I out of my apartment, the answer is yes." I paced around Tim's chrome coffee table. "What can I do for you, Amir?"

"I assume you sent the recording."

"Um . . ." Rick must have sent some of the footage to Amir, but which one? "To what recording are you referring?"

"The Chinese restaurant."

"Ah. I see. No, I didn't send the recording. But I've been privy to it. Did you find it interesting?"

He sighed. "Do you know where Mike is?"

Hm, what were the penalties for lying to an FBI agent? "You mean at this very moment? No. I don't." After all, he could've been in the shower, bed, kitchen, gym . . . there were any number of rooms at Silverthorne he could be. Maybe he put on his hobo clothes and went out for a latte. I decided to throw Amir a bone. "However, he has made contact with me. Is there a message you'd like me to pass along?"

"He needs to come in. The longer he stays out, the worse it gets. Newcomb is gathering evidence every day," Amir said in a depressed tone.

"Is he still a person-of-interest wanted for questioning, or is there an arrest warrant out for him?"

Amir hesitated.

"Amir?" I began pacing around the glass coffee table.

"Newcomb is asking for a warrant today."

I sucked wind. "On what grounds?"

"Fraud and accepting a bribe."

"You must be joking!" I cried. "A bribe? How on earth is he going to make that stick?"

Amir hesitated before speaking. "We have a tenuous link between Mike and Terrance Matheson. He's wanted for money laundering. It was a case Mike worked. He skipped town before we put the cuffs on him. We never figured out who tipped him off."

I decided not to let Amir know what I knew about Matheson. Instead, I changed tactics. "Did you show Newcomb the footage of the Chinese restaurant?"

"Not yet. It didn't arrive until after midnight."

"Will it change his mind?"

"Doubtful. I'm concerned he might dismiss it . . . or bury it." He mumbled the latter.

I gulped, pausing my steps. "That would be unlawful."

Amir didn't respond.

"Perhaps more people should receive the footage." I paced into the kitchen and turned on the tap to fill the watering can.

"There's a chain of command."

"For you. Not the person who sent the material."

"That's true," he agreed.

"Perhaps Director McGill should see it." I'd interacted with Director Leon McGill during Senator Harper's murder investigation. He'd been fair and willing to listen. Unlike Newcomb, he also didn't hold a grudge against Mike.

Amir didn't acknowledge my suggestion, instead, he warned, "Karina, if you're sheltering him, you could get in big trouble. If Newcomb gets the warrant, you could be arrested for harboring a fugitive."

"You know I'm not," I cried defensively. "You've bugged my apartment and are tracking my phone. What more do you want? *I am not housing Michael Finnegan.*" After all, it was the truth. Maybe I'd left a few things out . . .

"Listen, I don't agree with the bugs and I'm not even sure if Newcomb was cleared to plant them. He's cut me out of the loop." Amir said the last in almost an ashamed tone.

I turned off the water and took a beat. "I see."

"I can still help Mike. Next time you speak to him, tell him I'm on his side. I can help him, but he needs to come in. Soon," Amir urged.

"I'll see the message gets delivered. Anything else?" I asked, wiping drips off the watering can with a paper towel.

"Watch yourself."

"Done."

Back in my apartment, I held the two burn phones in my hand, trying to decide which one I should use. I chose the bat phone.

**We need to talk. Figure something out and let me know.**

As I drove to work, my regular phone rang, and I pressed my Bluetooth to answer. "Hello."

"It's Rick."

Not how I expected to hear from him, but I went with it. "Good morning, sunshine. How can I help you?"

"Are you free for lunch? I thought we could get together again." His voice sounded friendly and natural.

"Yes, that would be lovely. What were you thinking?" I had no idea if I was free, but as soon as I got to work, I'd arrange to make it so.

"I'll swing by and pick you up. Noon?"

"Noon is fine. See you then." We hung up, and I pulled in to my parking space. On the way up to the office, I checked my calendar and found I was booked to attend a luncheon.

I knocked on the side of Rodrigo's cube. "Hey, pal, what are you doing for lunch?"

He swiveled to face me. "No plans. Why?"

"I've . . . uh . . . double booked myself, and wondered if you wanted a free lunch—fundraiser for Congressman Coggswell? It starts at noon."

He tilted his head. "Where is it?"

"Marriott, Metro Center. The food will be good."

"Okay. I'm in. Email me your talking points, and the people I need to schmooze." He spun back to his computer, and I headed to my office.

"Karina," he called, his head stuck out of the side of his cube.

I paused. "Yes?"

"Where are *you* going for lunch?"

"Uh . . ." My brain scrambled for a good answer and decided upon an old standby. "Doctor's appointment. Lady stuff," I added *sotto voce*.

Rodrigo's head disappeared faster than a donut at a cop convention. I assumed I would hear no more from him. He'd be long gone before Rick swung by to pick me up.

My morning consisted of an uneventful staff meeting and busy work responding to emails. At noon, I headed downstairs to meet Rick and was standing at the curb when he roared up in a black 1970 Ford Torino Cobra. There was a little Cobra symbol on the driver's side with the number 429 below it. It was a muscle car that turned heads and liked to suck gas. He once told me it belonged to his father.

I climbed in and pulled the heavy door shut. "I'm surprised you chose something so conspicuous."

"My truck is in the shop. I didn't have time to swing by the office to get one of the fleet cars. Buckle up," he stated in his usual, succinct cadence.

As soon as I snapped the seat belt in place, the big engine growled and we moved into traffic.

"How much gas *does* this thing suck down?" I asked.

"Too much. Where is your phone?"

"I left it on my desk at the office. Hopefully, no one

important will call."

Always one to get straight to business, Rick said, "You'd better tell me what this is about."

I described my conversation with Amir and finished with, "I assume you sent the files."

"We did."

"And you encrypted them, or whatever you have to do, so the FBI can't figure out where it came from?"

"If they dig, the closest they'll get is an IP address in Kuwait." He stopped for a pedestrian in the crosswalk.

"Kuwait?" I shook my head. "Forget it. I don't want to know."

"What do you want me to do about this new information? Pass it along to Mike?"

"I—I don't know." The fact that he asked my opinion surprised me. I pressed my fingers to my temples where a tension headache brewed. "To be honest, I didn't think I'd be dragging Silverthorne into this type of territory. It was one thing to hide Michael when he was simply a person of interest, but now that there is a possible warrant out for his arrest, it puts you in a sticky spot."

"You want me to kick him out?" Rick asked without inflection.

"Not necessarily. However, you're responsible for a company full of workers." I pointed out the obvious.

Rick remained quiet until we rolled to a halt at a red light, then his attention shifted to me. "I'd heard about Newcomb's efforts to get the warrant. It's why I decided to send the restaurant file."

"*You* did?" I blinked. "Does Mike know you sent the file?"

"I told him, I sent the file this morning . . . after I got him to agree it would be a good idea to send it to Amir."

"And he knows about the warrant?"

The light turned green and Rick focused on the road. "No."

"Should we tell him?" I chewed my lip.

Rick took a moment before answering. "Not yet."

"Why?"

"I want to play out our plans this weekend."

"Why?" I repeated.

"If we tell him, I'm afraid he'll bolt before we proceed. He was talking about leaving last night, to take care of this on his own. My instincts are telling me the ballpark is the key to this entire escapade. If he hits the streets now and gets caught, I believe his chances for getting cleared and keeping his job drop exponentially." Rick allowed another group of pedestrians to pass in front of us and turned onto Union Street. "I explained this to him and finally got him to agree."

I nodded. "If we tell Mike about the warrant now, he'll go."

"Yes. Which he'll have to do eventually."

"However, if we find something at the ballpark that can help"—I followed his thinking—"we might be able to turn things in his favor."

"It's my hope." He parallel parked across the street from the Union Street Public House, a restaurant in a renovated eighteenth century warehouse a block off the waterfront.

I glanced over my shoulder and spotted a dark sedan parking farther down the street. "I noticed you didn't bother to lose our tail."

Rick unbuckled his seat belt and turned to me. "Is there something else you needed to discuss?"

"The plans for Saturday."

He removed his aviators and tossed them on the dash. "You'll get instructions on Saturday. Make sure you lose your friends before you arrive." He glanced down at my black stiletto boots. "And remember to wear sensible shoes. Not those."

"Aye aye, Captain." I delivered a salute.

He rolled his eyes and opened the door.

I had a house salad with a crab cake sandwich, and Rick ordered the salmon. He spent the rest of the meal plying me for information about my childhood. He'd met my sister, so I told him about my brother and his wife and adorable daughter who lived in Oregon. I talked about growing up in the D.C. area, and my high school nerd years that I spent playing piccolo in the marching band and, of course, as president of the debate team.

"But you already know about that from my dossier." I tried to deliver my remark in a matter-of-fact tone, rather than an accusatory one.

"The information in your dossier is simply facts and figures about your life, with little to no exposition." He cut a glazed carrot and put it on his fork. "You see, I knew you had a married brother with a child. I didn't know she liked purple nail polish and playing princess and the dragon with her favorite aunt."

"Yeah," I snorted. "Don't repeat that to Jilly. She thinks *she's* the favorite aunt."

He finished chewing and tilted his head. "By the way, how is Jillian?"

I thought about the question for a moment before answering. My sister taught middle school English and lived about twenty minutes from my condo. "I think she's doing well. She took on teaching the advanced English classes, and said she really enjoys working with the students. She's also helping with the spring musical, they're doing *Hairspray*. Her boyfriend moved in, and I'm simply waiting for him to put a ring on it."

"Tony? The paramedic?"

I nodded, impressed that he remembered. "Yeah, he's a great guy."

"I'm looking for another team member with a medical background. I wonder if he'd be interested," Rick mused. "He speaks Spanish. Right?"

"Don't you dare." I pointed at him and said in a teasing, but serious manner, "Tony doesn't need to get embroiled in whatever hazards Silverthorne is involved."

Rick's eyes danced, and his mouth twisted into a smirk. He grabbed my offending finger "I hate to break it to you, darlin', but my company, for the most part, works rather dull jobs. It's only when *you* get involved that things go to hell in a handbag." He released me and sat back with a self-satisfied air.

"Uh-huh." I raised a skeptical brow. "What were you doing in the middle east last year? Syria, I think it was."

"I have no idea what you're talking about," he deadpanned.

"Right," I drawled. "Anytime you're out of the country, I may not know what you're doing, but I'm fairly certain, it isn't picking rosebuds in Kew Gardens."

He leaned forward and opened his mouth, but I interrupted whatever retort he was about to make. "Listen, don't get me wrong, I'm well aware the services Silverthorne provides are necessary. Clearly, I've used your expertise for my own needs. And there is really no way I can *ever* repay you for saving my keister on those occasions." I lowered my voice, placed both my hands firmly on either side of my plate, and said the following with deep sincerity, "However, since Jilly's kidnapping, I've become *very* protective of her. I don't want to see her hurt. Ever. Again. Whether you admit it, or not, you and your men can be put into dangerous situations. You've chosen it. He has not. I'm sure you could throw a bunch of money at Tony to convince him to join you, but I'd appreciate it if you didn't."

Rick's features softened as I spoke, and he reached over to lay a hand on one of mine. "I get it. Tony is off limits. You have my word."

I turned my hand in his and gave it a squeeze. "Thank you."

He raised his brows. "Now what happens if they break up?"

I chuckled. "If he breaks Jilly's heart, you have my permission to hire him, and send him to an outpost in Siberia."

"Done." He released my hand. "Now tell me more about the time you and Jillian entered the family dog in a local beauty pageant."

By the time the check arrived, I realized I'd spilled quite a bit of my juicy childhood tidbits but still knew nothing more about Richard Donovan. He once told me his father died from cancer. He'd also described his father as a bastard. There had been no explanation beyond the cancer and bastard scraps. I wanted to ask him more, but, any time I tried to turn the conversation back to him, he deftly deflected my efforts.

When we got back in the Torino, I asked, "Was this the date I owe you?"

"No," he replied, putting the car into gear. "It was business."

Hm, it didn't feel like business. Well . . . not *all* business. "And will there be a business kiss when you drop me off?"

He searched the rearview mirror. "There probably should be. Our friends in the FBI are still with us."

"So, would you call the kisses big corporate or more like small business?"

He delivered me a side-eye.

"Am I getting billed for them?"

His jaw clenched, his eyes crinkled at the corners, and his fingers tightened around the wheel. Outwardly, I kept my face neutral; inside, I laughed at his discomfort. When he pulled up to my office, I unhooked my seat belt and waited for Rick to make his move.

He continued to stare straight ahead and said without inflection, "I believe we've given the FBI enough to gossip about."

"Oh, poo. Don't be a sore loser."

That got his attention. "Karina—"

"Pucker up." I leaned forward and planted one on his lips. It didn't take long for him to slide a hand around the base of my skull and engage. Once we parted, I said, perhaps a teensy bit breathlessly, "Thanks for lunch."

"You're welcome." His expression was unreadable behind his aviators.

I slid out of the car. "And thank you for helping Mike. You're going above and beyond. I don't know how I can repay you for putting your ass on the line." I shut the door before he could respond.

To my relief, Rodrigo hadn't returned from the fundraiser and the only people to observe my interaction with Rick was our friendly, neighborhood FBI surveillance team.

# Chapter Eleven

Saturday morning, I perused my options regarding "sensible shoes". I liked shoes. Some might call me a shoe-aholic. There were many of them stacked neatly on multiple shoe racks in my closet. Beyond my sneakers, very few of them could be classified as "sensible". I owned three pairs of black flats. Two had a tendency to slip off my heels if I moved faster than a walking pace, and the other left painful blisters within an hour. I should really throw them away, but I'd spent a stupid amount of money on them. After twenty minutes, I found two pairs of shoes that would fit Rick's parameters and be appropriate with my black pants suit. Either a pair of black-and-white saddle shoes that I'd purchased to go with a 50s Halloween costume, or a pair of low-heeled black oxfords in the style worn by women during World War II. I'd bought them for a local hangar swing dance. If needed, I could maneuver and run in either pair. A game of eeny-meeny-miny-moe decided it for me. I tossed the 40s oxfords on the bed next to my suit and headed to the bathroom to shower.

At 12:56 p.m., I rolled in to the Silverthorne parking lot and was met by Josh. He looked me up and down and commented, "I think my great-grandmother wore shoes like that," and escorted me to the armory at the back of the building.

Jin, Sonia Lee, two Silverthorne operatives I'd never met, and Rick stood around the metal table checking their weapons and adjusting shoulder holsters. Everyone wore a dark suit with a white, tailored shirt and looked like Secret Service agents.

Jin introduced the two strangers. "Karina Cardinal, this is Bunkechukwun Akinde." He indicated a short, barrel-chested black man.

"Everyone calls me Bunkie." We shook hands. His hand was warm, and there was a gap between Bunkie's two front teeth when he smiled at me. I liked him immediately.

"This is Max O'Sullivan," Jin said.

Max was of average height with dark hair, green-brown eyes, and a hand rough as sandpaper. "Ma'am." He nodded, then proceeded to shove a Glock 9mm into his shoulder holster.

"Ladies and gentlemen, as you know, Jin is your team leader. I'll turn it over to him," Rick said.

"Last night, you were given a dossier on the subjects we'll be escorting. I assume you've studied them." Jin laid a map across the table and outlined the route we'd take to get to the Korean Embassy, and from the embassy to Nationals Park, as well as alternate routes in case of traffic or street blockages. "We'll park in garage C, where we'll be met by a park representative, Aisha Jordan. Sonia?"

Sonia pulled up a photo on her tablet and showed everyone Aisha's image.

"The VIP tour should take about two hours," Jin continued. "Sonia and I walked the tour route and swept the park with security at oh nine hundred this morning. Threat level for today's outing is low." He went on about other technical details, which I prayed I didn't need to remember because my brain was more focused on *my* job at the park than theirs. "Any questions?"

Everyone but me shook their heads.

After Jin finished, Rick stepped forward. "Sonia, Bunkie, and O'Sullivan, prep and load the cars. You pull out at fourteen hundred."

The three removed larger firepower from the armory walls, along with a couple of duffle bags that were already packed, and headed out to the loading dock.

I watched them go. "So, what do I need . . .?" I turned back to the fellas and found Josh holding a white bulletproof vest. "Oh, no, you're not going to make me wear that."

"You wear it beneath your blouse," he said.

"It gives me a uniboob and makes me look twenty pounds heavier. It's not really necessary. Right? Besides, no one else is wearing one." I'll admit the last sentence held a bit of a whine, but I made every effort to keep from actually pouting. The last vest I'd worn had been heavy, itchy, and there'd been a slight odor. Since a contract had been put out on my head and I refused to allow the police or Rick to bury me at a safe house, we'd come to a compromise when I promised to wear a vest and stay in the van. "I thought this was a low-risk job. Jin said it was low risk."

"The South Korean security detail is low to moderate. We have no idea the risk of your operation. Besides, Sonia and I are wearing one," Jin explained.

I scrutinized Jin and realized his wiry body had gained some bulk beneath his suit. Then I checked Josh. "What about Josh?" I pointed.

"The team has the option to choose. *You* do not," Rick stated with finality.

"It's a new model, ultra-lightweight Kevlar. Only three pounds," Josh said in an encouraging tone.

I ignored him and spoke plainly to Rick. "Josh is my partner on this unknown, risky venture. I believe I'd be more comfortable if I knew my partner was safe."

Rick's cheek lifted in a half-smile. "She has a point. Joshua, go get your vest . . . please." I didn't imagine Rick usually said please when he gave orders to his men.

Josh's face pinched but he didn't argue. He shoved the ultra-lightweight vest at me and stalked out of the room.

Jin's face split into a wide grin.

"Where do I change?" I asked.

Rick and Jin turned their backs to me and stared at the wall of guns.

"Cripes." I removed my jacket and blouse and climbed into the Kevlar. It was much lighter than the one I'd worn before, and there was no odor. Luckily, I hadn't chosen a fitted blouse and was able to button it over the vest. It made my jacket tight across the shoulders and under the arms, but it would do. "Okay, now what?"

Josh came back, buttoning his shirt. His tie hung loose, and his jacket was slung across his forearm.

I beamed at him. "You were right, Josh; this one is much better than the last one I wore. Thanks."

He shot me an irritated glance and began working his tie.

Jin cleared his throat to gain our attention. "Once we arrive, the tour will be led to the one-hundreds level, where we'll visit the Suites and Diamond Club, which is behind home plate. The Diamond Club will have cake and ice cream for the kids to eat. After they finish, the park escort will take the kids around the stadium and then down to the field, where they will be allowed to run the bases. While the kids are eating, you and Josh will go to section 404 to retrieve the package. If you're stopped by security, allow Josh to do the talking."

"Got it." I gave a thumbs-up.

Jin continued, "Once you retrieve the package, you and Josh will return to the team and finish the tour. After we exit the parking garage, you two will return to Silverthorne while we escort the kids back to the embassy."

"Easy peasy." I grinned. None of the men grinned back at me, and Josh was still wrangling his tie. "So, what am I supposed to do when we're with the kids?"

"Keep your eyes peeled for anything suspicious," Rick said.

"And if I see something suspicious?"

"Notify the team, and we'll take care of it," Jin replied.

"Does the rest of the team know about my side job?"

"They know there's another op running alongside this one. They don't know details," Rick explained.

I gave a sharp nod and adjusted my vest.

"Put this on your belt." Rick held the Ruger in one hand and a holster in the other.

"Um, do I have to?"

Rick had practically forced me into getting licensed to carry concealed in Washington—the District didn't allow open carry. Unlike Virginia, which had stupid easy laws for obtaining and carrying a gun, D.C.'s laws were much stricter, and Rick wanted everything to be above board. I never thought I'd have to utilize it.

"You are a Silverthorne Security team member on this op. As such, you will carry appropriate gear," Rick responded in a no-nonsense tone.

"Can't I just take a stun gun?" My go-to weapon of choice.

"No. You'll carry it on your hip." Rick demonstrated. "Do not bury it in your bottomless purse."

There was no arguing with him, and I held up my jacket to allow him to clip it to my belt.

Josh yanked out the knot on his tie a second time, and I felt bad for him. Some men required a mirror to do it properly.

"Here, Josh, allow me."

He remained stock still, while I straightened the mangled tie and whipped it into a half Windsor knot.

"That should do it." I tightened the knot in place and gave it a final pat.

"Thank you," Josh murmured.

Jin picked up a small box from the table. "This is your earpiece."

"Great. I've been meaning to ask, what have you done with Mike? Did you cuff him to the plumbing? I can't imagine he'd sit idly by." I tucked the tiny wireless communication bud into my left ear. "Testing. Hello? Do you read me?"

"Loud and clear, K.C.," Mike's voice said in my ear. "I'll be monitoring the op from here."

I stared at Rick and whispered, "You let him into tech ops?"

Rick shrugged. "He's got top secret security clearance."

"I can hear you, K.C., and see you," Mike said.

"See me?" I glanced around the room, spotted a camera in the corner, and held up the peace sign.

Jin held out a South Korean flag lapel pin. "Camera. We all have them."

"Ooo, spy stuff. Very cool." The back was bulkier than a normal lapel pin and Jin had to help me adjust it properly. "Where is your camera?"

He pointed to the pen sticking out of his breast pocket. "Wireless, 1080p resolution."

"There's a camera in there?" I got nose-to-nose with Jin's pocket and could barely see a tiny hole where the camera lens must be. "I'll never look at ballpoint the same way again."

Jin checked his watch. "Time to load up."

We pulled out of Silverthorne in three vehicles. Bunkie and O'Sullivan headed up our caravan in a black Ford SUV, an exact copy of the one Josh and I were in. Jin and Sonia drove in between our two vehicles in a gray, extra-long SUV. The three cars followed closely all the way up Massachusetts Avenue into the Northwest section of town—an area also known as Embassy Row. We passed brownstone, brick, and marble buildings, all with an assortment of country flags proudly fluttering in the breeze. Bunkie turned into a circular driveway in front of a five-story rectangular building. Compared to the variety of buildings we'd passed, the Embassy of the Republic of Korea looked rather plain with its boxy granite architecture. Jin and Sonia exited their vehicle.

"Should we get out?" I asked.

Josh shook his head.

A woman came out front, spoke briefly with Jin in Korean, and went back into the building. A few minutes later, she returned, herding five children of differing ages. They were dressed in navy-blue uniforms with gray overcoats. All had shiny black hair, except for one girl who wore bright blue streaks in her shoulder length mop. The six of them remained quiet as they piled into the SUV. Sonia shut the door, got in, and we were off. In the background, I could hear snippets of the children speaking in their native tongue.

I said to Josh, "I thought Jin was Vietnamese."

"His mom is Vietnamese, and his father is Korean," Josh replied. "He speaks seven different languages. Sonia is second-generation Korean American, and she speaks it fluently. That's why they're leading the team."

"Wow, seven languages." I was impressed. "Which ones?"

"English, Vietnamese, Korean, Japanese, French, and Tagalog."

I counted on my fingers. "That's only six."

"Thai," Jin supplied in my ear. I'd forgotten they could hear our conversation.

I covered my earbud and leaned closer to Josh. "Can you give me a rundown on the kids? And who's the woman with them? Nanny? I wasn't privy to the dossier."

"Tech ops, this is Josh. Take me off VOX."

"Roger that," a disembodied voice said in my ear.

I continued to keep a hand over my earbud and whispered, "What does that mean?"

"Only tech ops can hear our conversation instead of the entire crew," he explained as we came to a stoplight. "The woman is their interpreter and guide. She's also an undercover agent of their National Intelligence Service. The boys are Yu-Jun, age eight, Woo, age ten, and Seo-yun, age fourteen. The two girls are

Choon-hee, age ten, and Gi, age twelve. Their parents are all ministers in the National Assembly—the Korean legislative branch. They're in town for a special event at the Korean Cultural Center."

"Got it."

"Any other questions?" The cars rolled forward.

I thought about it for a moment and felt like a bit of a fraud sitting amongst these highly trained operatives. "Maybe tech ops should take me off VOX, too."

"You're fine." Josh smiled and wheeled the car around a corner. "You can hear everyone, but the only team members that can hear you are Jin and me. Tech ops, this is Josh. Return my relay to VOX."

"Roger, returning to VOX," said the same disembodied voice.

Our caravan turned onto the wooded glen of Rock Creek Parkway, and I remained quiet, listening to the men discuss the route over the coms. Traffic moved at a normal pace. We slipped under the Kennedy Center for Performing Arts and were soon coming up on the backside of the pillared Lincoln Memorial, onto Independence Avenue, where traffic was denser, and the lights slowed us down until we reached I-395. Once we exited the highway onto South Capitol Street, it was smooth sailing to the ballpark. O'Sullivan led our convoy into the covered parking garage with no problems.

The park's representative, Aisha, a petite black lady with a pixie cut and the enthusiasm of an excited Jack Russell terrier, waited for our arrival with a clipboard in hand. She spoke so quickly the interpreter had difficulty keeping up. Although, I could tell by the kids' reactions to Aisha's explanations that they understood some of her English. When we got to the Diamond Club, we found a big cake with the Nats logo sitting at the bar, along with a handful of sundae dishes, and two members of the waitstaff. The kids excitedly climbed onto the stools. I stood by the door, trying to look official, and waited for Josh to give me the sign to make our move. He and Jin were across the room in conversation, but the kids had gotten so loud, I couldn't hear what they were saying.

Someone tugged on my sleeve, and I found the twelve-year-old with the blue streaks at my side. "Toilet?" she asked.

Bunkie stood nearby and said, "It's down the concourse on your right."

Bunkie hadn't been read in on my special op with Josh. I looked around for Sonia, to pawn this duty off onto her, but she was nowhere to be found. The tween's brown gaze was a bit desperate, and I waved at her to follow me. In the bathroom, I checked the stalls to make sure they were empty . . . because that seemed like a bodyguard thing to do. They were. It wouldn't have mattered; after I checked the first one, Gi darted past me and slammed the door shut. I washed my hands and waited discreetly by the exit.

"Cardinal! Where are you?" Josh barked over the general buzz into my earpiece.

I stepped out of the restroom to answer him. "Bathroom. One of the girls had to go."

"Sonia should've taken her. We need to move." He sounded a bit agitated.

"I couldn't find Sonia. Relax, it'll just be another minute," I assured him.

Only it wasn't.

When I walked back into the bathroom Gi was still in her stall, and I heard quiet crying. *Uh-oh.* "Um, Gi? Are you okay? What's wrong?" I tapped on the metal door.

She sniffed and said something in Korean. Although I didn't speak the language, I recognized the panicky tone.

I debated my options. I didn't know if I had the right to kick the door in to help her, or if it would cause an international incident. "I'm sorry, Gi, I don't speak Korean. Can you tell me in English?"

The soft weeping turned into a loud sobbing.

It was time for reinforcements. "Uh, Houston, we have a problem. Gi is locked in a stall crying. I don't understand what she's saying."

"I'm sending Sonia," Jin said.

A moment later, Sonia swept into the bathroom and hissed, "What did you do?"

Taken aback, I put up my hands. "Nothing. She went in there and started crying."

Sonia spoke in a softened tone to the sobbing girl, and Gi calmed down enough to get out a hiccupping response.

"What did she say?" I whispered.

Sonia grimaced and covered her ear. "She's got her period. Apparently, this is her first time."

"Oh, how awful. In a foreign country, out in public. Poor thing," I said sympathetically.

Sonia and I stared at each other until she broke the stalemate. "Do you have anything?"

I turned my palms to the ceiling. "Josh told me to leave my purse in the car. You?"

Sonia shook her head.

There was a dividing wall between the toilets and the sinks. I trotted around to the sink side. "There's a machine on this side. Have you got a quarter?"

She came around the wall and stared helplessly at the machine. "No, only credit cards."

This was what happens when women weren't allowed to carry their purses. "Uh, gentlemen, I need someone to bring a quarter to the ladies' room ASAP."

"This is Josh. I'm on it."

"I'll meet you by the door," I said.

He strode up, wearing his impatient face. "What's the problem?"

"Gi got her period."

Josh dropped the quarter in my hand and departed without further comment.

I handed the pad over to Sonia and discreetly retreated to the sinks while she talked Gi through the directions. A minute later, a miserable Gi shuffled out. Her shoulders drooped and she kept her head bent down while she washed her hands.

I didn't want the other kids to tease her or have the rest of her tour ruined. I told Sonia to translate for me. Smiling at Gi, I said, "Congratulations, Gi! You're now a woman. What an exciting time you have entered." Sonia translated, but all I got was a head shake from Gi.

Not knowing how her culture handled the entrance to womanhood, I decided to change tactics, and instead commiserated with her about my first time. I was at an outdoor concert with my family, wearing white, no less. I had to stand in line, and when I finally got to the bathroom, it had stained my pants. My sister loaned me her sweater, and I tied it around my waist the rest of the night. Gi perked up as Sonia translated my tragedy.

"Really?" Gi said.

I nodded. "I was so embarrassed. However, by the time I got out of the bathroom, it had gotten dark, and with my sister's sweater, no one noticed. But while I was dealing with it, I missed a couple of my favorite songs."

My story seemed to cheer her up, and by the time we left the bathroom, she walked upright with a lighter step.

Josh intercepted me on the way back to the Diamond Club. "Time to move, Cardinal." We entered a nearby elevator. Our coms went scratchy, then silent. As we rode up, he asked, "Did that really happen to you?"

*Cripes!* I'd forgotten we were on coms while I was in the bathroom. "Yup. And I don't want to hear another thing about it."

The doors opened, and I took off down the concourse to section 404. Josh's long legs soon caught up, and we walked through the passage that delivered us out onto an overlook together. A true bird's eye view of the field.

"Wow, this is way up here." Gripping the cold, metal safety rail, I leaned over.

Josh surveyed the area. "It looks clear. Go on up."

I climbed the steep stairs all the way to the top, row *N*, and crossed to seat ten. "There's a manila envelope in a plastic bag. Taped to the underside of the seat."

"Retrieve the bag and return to Joshua." Rick came through loud and clear.

"Just a minute. There's something in here." I pulled a seat down and sat, opening the envelope. Out slid a little, gray flip phone. "It's a phone and what look like financial statements." I stuffed the papers back into the envelope. The phone gave a shrill ring.

"Don't answer it!" more than one person shouted in my ear.

*Too late.* "Hello?"

"You're not Agent Finnegan," a nasal voice said.

"No, I'm not," I agreed, watching Josh tear up the stairs two at time.

"Who are you?"

I winked at Josh as he strode down the aisle toward me. "A courier. Who are you?"

"The man with a rifle scope pointed at your head."

My heart dropped. "Now why would you want to shoot the messenger?" I asked in a placating tone.

The next thing I knew, I was thrown to the ground. Josh knelt above me, his weapon drawn, searching the stadium. "We may have a sniper situation. Repeat, sniper in the area."

The coms went crazy. I pulled out the bud and put the phone to my ear. "Still there?"

"I see you brought company," he said over the whine of a fire engine in the background.

"My bodyguard doesn't like people who threaten my life."

The voice chuckled, but I could barely hear him over a second siren. "Tell him to put that silly gun down. Get the phone and those papers to Agent Finnegan and have him give me a call."

"Wait—"

The line went dead.

"Hello? Hello? He hung up," I said to Josh.

"Stay where you are. Jin, O'Sullivan, and Sonia have the subjects on lockdown. Bunkie is on his way up here." His features were set and his gaze searching . . . searching.

"He's bluffing. I don't think he's here."

Josh didn't respond. He and Bunkie were communicating on the coms.

I tapped his leg. "Josh, I heard a fire engine. Did you hear one?"

"What? No, I didn't. Keep your head down." Distracted, he pushed my face down to the dirty concrete.

"Josh! Geroff!" I swatted his hand from my head. My gun was jammed against my hip, and my shoulder, which took the brunt of the fall, would be bruised for more than a week. I was struggling like a turtle to right itself, but with Josh hovering above me, his feet tangled around mine, I couldn't get any traction. "He's not here!"

Josh finally gave me his attention. "How do you know?"

"I heard multiple sirens, a fire engine, maybe an ambulance in the background . . . on the phone." I stuffed the earbud back in. Jin was giving directions to the other team members. When he took a breath, I cut in, "Did anyone hear sirens around the stadium? Ambulance or fire engine sirens. Anyone? Jin, did you or Sonia?"

"No," Jin replied.

"Ask Max and Bunkie," I barked.

I heard Jin ask the two men. They replied in the negative.

"He's bluffing. Wherever he is, at the current moment, had a mess of sirens nearby. There haven't been any fire engines in the area. If he's watching, it's on a webcam or something he's purposely placed to keep an eye on this area. Maybe motion activated." I grunted, got a foot loose, and shoved Josh away to get to my knees. Not an easy task considering how tightly packed the seats were to the row below. "He doesn't want to shoot me. He wants me to deliver the package."

Bunkie popped out of the passage, gun drawn.

"Oh, for crying out loud, tell him to stand down," I snapped, using Josh's shoulder to rise to my feet.

Nobody listened to me. Josh and Bunkie got in front and back of me and made me walk down the stairs into the concourse hunched over, like an emergency presidential evacuation. Once we got under cover, they gave me some breathing room, however Josh gripped my elbow and we moved at a fast clip toward the elevators. Jin was on coms giving directions to the rest of the team to get the children safely to the SUVs. Our coms went scratchy once we got into the elevator, and we could no longer hear the others.

I stood between the two men. "Why are we evacuating the kids? Don't they get to finish their tour and run the bases?"

Josh shook his head. "Security has locked down the stadium and are exiting all civilian groups. Our protocol is to evacuate the subjects and return them to the embassy."

Now that things got hairy, the kids were no longer "the kids", they were subjects. Great. I felt guilty they hadn't been able to finish their tour. We hustled to meet up with the rest of the detail in the parking garage. They had already started to roll out. Bunkie literally hopped onto the moving vehicle's running board. Once he climbed in, the two SUVs sped off at a fast clip. Josh and I got into our own SUV at a slower pace.

I couldn't help the "oof" and grimace that went along with it as I reached for the seat belt.

"What's a matter? K.C., are you hurt?" It was the first time since we'd left that I heard Mike's voice on the coms.

I let out a hiss, twisting to lock the belt in place. "I'm fine. Just a bit banged up from being knocked off my feet." I removed the gun from my hip and shoved it in the glovebox. "I have the package and directions from Mike's nemesis. Will discuss further when we get back to base. Cardinal out." I removed my earbud and dropped it into the cupholder.

"Yes, she removed it," Josh muttered.

The initial adrenaline rush receded, leaving behind throbbing aches. My shoulder, hip, and knee were letting me know that the next few days would be painful. I pulled my pants leg up to find a swelling purple lump on the outside of my right knee.

We came to a stoplight and Josh glanced over at me. "You going to survive, or do I need to read the last rites?"

I rolled my eyes. It was such a Josh thing to say. No apologies coming from that section. "Ask Rick to have a priest meet us at the office," I suggested.

The arrow turned green. Josh snorted and spun the steering wheel. "You'll be fine."

# Chapter Twelve

Josh and I had removed our vests, returned the weapons to the armory, and were now gathered around the kitchen island with Rick and Mike reviewing the materials laid out in a line from end to end. Bank statements with Mike's parents' information on them—annuities, checking and savings accounts, and a money market account. Another group of financial papers Mike identified as belonging to his brother-in-law's architecture firm.

The phone had been dropped into a plastic baggie and whisked away upon our arrival by a red-haired, narrow-faced fellow who I'd never met before. Nobody bothered to introduce us. I assumed he was an elusive tech ops guy by his pale computer tan. Mike scolded me for putting my fingerprints on the phone, possibly destroying evidence. I highly doubted a man this smart would've left fingerprints behind. Pointing this out, I turned to Rick to see if he'd back me up. He merely shrugged and said his men would check it out.

"That's a lot of your family's private information, Mike. How could he have acquired all this? How long would that take?" I sat on a stool, pressing an ice pack to my shoulder.

Mike put down one of the pages. "Clearly, he's been working on this for a while. Matheson was a financial genius. It's why he got away with his crimes for as long as he did."

"Do you think he hacked into these records?" I asked.

He rubbed his beard. "It's not out of the realm of possibility," he mused.

Rick stared hard at Mike. "Banking systems are some of the

most challenging institutions to hack. They make a lot of money and pay for top-of-the-line encryption services to keep people out." Mike didn't respond, and Rick's phone interrupted our discussion. "Donovan. Yes . . . I see. Have you figured out who and when?" Rick went silent for a few minutes, listening and nodding. His frown intensified and the worry lines between his brows deepened.

It took a moment for me to realize Josh and Mike were staring at my fingernails drumming on the countertop. I whipped my hand away and moved the ice to my knee. Rick stepped into the hallway to continue his phone conversation out of earshot. Mike studied another bank statement.

Josh opened the fridge and held up a water. "Want one?"

Mike and I shook our heads. Josh cracked his open and drank deeply.

Rick returned and planted his palms on the counter. "That was the head of security at the stadium. After the evacuation, I asked him to check their monitoring systems. It seems their security cameras were hacked."

"When?" I asked.

Rick kept his eyes on Mike as he answered, "Six weeks ago. An entire week of footage has been erased."

"So, we have a vague idea when Matheson planted the materials," Mike murmured.

"And how he has been monitoring the section since then," I added.

"Yes, and yes," Rick confirmed.

"Can you get street-cam footage of the surrounding area for the week the stadium cameras went dark?" I asked him.

Rick's face remained passive, but Josh's nostrils flared.

Mike shook his head. "Silverthorne would have to get a subpoena to request it."

Seeing as Rick's company had acquired real-time footage of

local street cams when my sister had been kidnapped, I knew they could do it. Obviously, it hadn't been done through legal channels. I rolled my lips inward and said no more.

"Besides," Mike continued, "traffic cams usually only retain twenty-four to seventy-two hours' worth of footage." He turned back to Rick. "Do they know how the system was hacked?"

"One of their staff members used a variation of 'password12345' for his login credentials. Once the hacker got into the system, he was able to plant a keylogger on an admin machine. Then, it was only a matter of time before an administrator typed in their credentials and password."

Mike grimaced. Josh shook his head.

I was incensed. "Seriously? He's in security, for crying out loud! Every idiot knows you don't use 'password12345'. Even my grandmother is smarter than that!"

"Apparently, he wasn't part of the security staff. He's a kid out of college they hired to the marketing department." Rick tucked his phone into his back pocket. "You said Matheson was a money launderer. Did you know he had these types of skills? Was he under investigation for hacking as well as laundering?"

Mike's head swiveled back and forth. "No, he wasn't. Either he's working with someone or he took time to learn the skills during the past four years while he's been on the run."

"Which one do you think it is?" Rick prodded.

Mike squinted into the middle distance. "Matheson is smart and one to take risks; he's also already familiar with computers. He wasn't known for playing well with others. My guess would be he developed the skills. They would be valuable to someone on the run. He's the type of guy to take advantage of an opening. Maybe he got lucky."

Josh put down his water. "What did stadium security say about our little side trip to section 404?"

"They're not happy about it." Rick rubbed a hand through his cropped hair. "They've realized we used the Koreans as cover to acquire the materials. They want to know what was in the envelope."

An unexpected chill washed over me. My face was all over their security footage. It wouldn't take long for the FBI to connect the dots between me, Silverthorne, and my purpose for being with them today.

*Hell!*

At this moment, they could be on their way to the offices with a search warrant to root out Mike and take all of us in. "Uh, Rick," I interjected, my leg bouncing anxiously, "what happens when the stadium folks call law enforcement to report the hack?"

"Top executives have called for an emergency meeting"—he checked his watch—"starting in half an hour with head of security and the chief technology officer. They may not report the incident at all."

"I don't understand. Aren't they required to report it?" I looked between Rick and Mike for clarification.

Mike crossed his arms and went into lecture mode. "Not necessarily. Companies don't always report breaches to us. Even when they do, sometimes it's not until later, after they've patched the problem and beefed up their security. When a company wants me to dig into a hack or data breach, they have to give law enforcement permission to access their files and other sensitive materials. Many companies don't necessarily want us in there. Oftentimes, they will work with the cyber security companies they're already paying to fix the problem."

"They don't want to get caught up in a media storm, either," Josh put in. "It's bad for business."

My mouth dropped. "Are you telling me companies keep hacks quiet, to—what—keep the egg off their faces?"

"Every day." Mike nodded. "You've got to see it from their point of view. A publicly traded company that gets hacked can see their stocks take a dive within hours of it going public with the news. They would lose millions. Data breaches, where personal data was stolen, is generally reported. The FBI encourages it. But, if they establish nothing was stolen from the stadium, like . . . let's say . . . account information of their season ticket holders, then they don't have to report it."

I couldn't believe it. "Holy crap, that's scary."

"I know." Mike picked up one of the papers.

"When will we know something?" I asked, tossing the partially melted bag of ice onto the counter. "Is your security friend going to call and tell us what happens in the meeting?"

Rick shook his head. "I can't count on it."

I let out a deep sigh. "Then Mike has to move out of Silverthorne."

Mike's head popped up from the piece of paper he'd been studying. "She's right. If the FBI gets wind of this, they'll track K.C. right to your facility." He laid down the statement "I believe it's time I reach out and lay my cards on the table."

"Without knowing what all this means?" Josh indicated the counter full of materials. "What was the purpose of today's op? A mission in futility? No way. We need to call this Matheson guy." Mike began to shake his head in negation, but Josh plowed on. "Find out what his game is. Record the call. See if we can trace the call and at least identify his location."

With a final, definitive head shake, Mike responded, "I've gotten you buried too deep into this mess. If Newcomb gets a warrant to search your building, who knows how far his tentacles will reach?" He turned to Rick to make his point. "You've got staff members who aren't even in the country that he might go after."

Rick's jaw clenched and he crossed his arms but didn't respond.

Mike continued, "Newcomb is vindictive enough to have all

your security clearances pulled during an investigation. Your company may never recover."

"Jeez, Rick, he's right." I rubbed my temples in an effort to keep the rising headache at bay. "It's time for Mike to go. We can't risk your company. I'll contact Jessica Williams. She can make arrangements for you to come in. If she can't represent you, she'll know who can." Jessica was the lawyer I'd used during Senator Harper's murder investigation. She was sharp as razor wire and knew how to weave through D.C.'s bureaucratic red tape. Mike and Director McGill were familiar with her.

Mike went pale as I spoke, but his jaw was set, and he nodded along with my plan.

"Not yet." Rick's tone was firm and unyielding, his face dispassionate.

"What do you mean, 'not yet'? We have a window of opportunity here. Half an hour, by your own words. If that window closes, we might not even know. You're putting everyone at risk." Neither my features nor my delivery was dispassionate. "I won't let you do it." I slammed my hand onto the counter for emphasis.

"Uh-oh, boss, you'd better take her seriously. She's talking with her hands," Josh drawled.

Mike outright laughed and Rick's mouth definitely twitched upward. My own mouth pinched up tighter than a frog's ass, and my face burned.

"We're done with the phone." The pale-faced tech ops kid stood in the doorway, holding up the baggie. He pushed his glasses atop his nose and continued, "No tracking or listening devices found. The only fingerprints were Cardinal's. One phone number has been programmed in it."

Rick took the phone from him. "Bring up a laptop."

The kid nodded and disappeared.

I snapped my fingers as it came to me. "He's the tech ops

disembodied voice in my ear. What's his name?"

"Angus," Rick answered.

"Where'd you get him? He looks like he's fourteen," I commented.

"He's twenty-three," Rick explained. "We hired him straight out of MIT."

"Impressive. However, we need to get back to our discussion about what to do with Mike." I picked up my melting ice bag and took it over to the sink.

"You know, I'm right here." Mike pinched the bridge of his nose. "Furthermore, there's no 'we'. This is my decision. It's over. I'll call Jessica."

"Mike, you can do what you want, but in my opinion, unless there's been a data breach, I doubt Nats stadium will report it." Rick continued his argument, "I think you should make the call. Allow us to record it and see if we can get a trace. From what I see here"—he indicated the swath of papers—"you're either being threatened or blackmailed."

"Hm, I hadn't thought of it that way." I tapped my chin in thought. "Rick is right. If you're being blackmailed, it could help your case."

Mike put his arms akimbo and surveyed the room. Rick's gaze remained neutral, I nodded encouragingly, and Josh said, "What have you got to lose, man?"

Mike's curiosity won out. "Fine. We'll call him."

He reached for the phone, but Rick stopped him. "Hold up, Angus is coming back with the tracing software."

Ten minutes later we were seated around the table—Angus behind a laptop at the head of the table, Rick and Josh on his right, with Mike and me on his left. A USB cable was plugged into the phone and the computer. Mike pressed the redial button.

Our quarry picked up on the third ring. "Agent Finnegan, I assume."

"Matheson," Mike replied.

"So, you *do* remember me."

"You're hard to forget," Mike said drily.

"I liked the girl you sent. Very pretty, but she looks a little uptight. Does she unwind in bed and turn into a wild sex kitten or is she a bit of a cold fish?" the money launderer taunted.

"What do you want, Matheson?" Mike growled.

"I want to take everything away from you. Just like you took everything away from me." He said the words so simply, it took my breath away.

"I don't know what you're talking about. You made your own bed," Mike replied.

"My wife divorced me, took the kids, and made sure I'd never be able to see them again."

"You abandoned her."

"I was planning to send for them when I got settled," Matheson snarled.

"What about your mistress? Were you planning to send for her, too?" Mike mocked.

Rick frowned and shook his head at him.

"She was nothing." Matheson went on the defensive. "Just a romp in the sheets."

Mike pressed a finger to his temple. "What do you want?"

Now the crook got down to business. "You've seen the bank statements?"

"I've seen them."

"With a few keystrokes, I have the capability of bankrupting your ageing parents. And, with a few more keystrokes, I can make it look as though your brother-in-law is embezzling from his own company." That nasal voice crawled up my skin. "One phone call and the IRS and law enforcement will be all over him like flies on shit."

Mike sucked wind, and his facial features blazed in anger. I put a restraining hand on his tense forearm. Rick and Angus shared a look. Angus shook his head and made a stretching motion with his hands.

"You still there?" Matheson asked.

"Your point?" Mike ground out.

"My point is, I've got you by the short and curlies. I need you to do something for me, and you'll do it, because not only is your own life in the toilet, but you'll also bring down your family with you if you don't," he stated gleefully.

"What are you expecting me to do?"

"I want The Baseball," Matheson said in such a way you could hear the capital *T* and *B* in his tone.

Mike's face twisted and he shook his head. "I can't. It's locked up in evidence. My credentials have been revoked. You saw to that when you started this game. There's no way I can get it."

"I have faith in your abilities, Agent. Use the girl. She seems capable."

Mike paused a moment. "Why do you want it?"

"It's my ticket to freedom," Matheson said.

I wrote down *ticket to freedom?* on a yellow notepad someone had left on the table.

"One point two million wasn't enough?" Mike responded.

"The baseball will keep me from looking over my shoulder for the rest of my life."

I added *looking over shoulder* to my previous note.

"I want something in exchange." Mike paused, but Matheson didn't speak, and he continued, "All the files you have on my family."

Silence.

Had Matheson already hung up?

The *V* between Mike's brows deepened. "Matheson? Take it or leave it."

"Done. You have forty-eight hours. Text me when you've got it." Matheson ended the call.

"What's 'The Baseball'?" I used finger quotes.

"Matheson had a baseball signed by the 1961 Murderer's Row," Mike said.

Josh's jaw dropped and Angus's eyes rounded to fifty-cent-piece size. Rick's features remained passive, but he sat back in his chair, crossing his arms.

Unfortunately, I was clueless. "Would someone care to explain that statement to me?"

"In 1961, the Yankees hit a record 240 homeruns. They held that record until 1996, when the Orioles hit 257," Josh explained.

"Doesn't count. The Orioles had the benefit of the designated hitter," Angus argued.

"I agree," replied Josh.

*"Guys!"* I leaned my elbows on the table. "Who or what is Murderer's Row?"

Josh started counting off on his fingers. "Yogi Berra, Mickey Mantle, Roger Maris—"

It came to me in a flash. I snapped my fingers and pointed at Josh. "Oh, yeah! From that movie by Billy Crystal. The M&M boys duking it out to beat Babe Ruth's homerun title. Maris won, but his title had an asterisk because the season was longer. I can't remember the name of the movie."

*"61*,"* Angus and Josh said in unison.

Josh continued, "What that film failed to establish, since it only focused on Maris and Mantle, was the depth and magnitude of skill and talent across the entire team. The 1961 team is considered by many to be the best Yankee team in history."

"Who else signed the baseball?" I asked.

"Johnny Blanchard, Elston Howard, and Bill Skowron," Mike supplied.

"Hm." I frowned. "I've never heard of them. I don't

remember those names from the movie."

"It doesn't matter if you remember them or not. There's no way I can acquire the baseball," Mike snapped, shoving away from the table.

I watched him pace around the counter. "Where is it?"

Mike's gaze turned to slits. "Buried in a high security evidence warehouse in Sterling, Virginia."

"How much did he pay for the ball?" Angus asked.

"He won it in a poker game, but it's estimated it would go for $2.4 million at auction. Possibly more," Mike replied.

Josh let out a whistle between his teeth.

"Did you make the trace?" Rick interrupted our baseball discussion.

Angus shook his head. "He used VOIP with 256-bit AES encryption. He knows what he's doing."

"What's VOIP?" I asked.

"Voice over internet protocol. You probably know it as WhatsApp or Skype," Angus explained.

I frowned. "I don't understand. He was using Skype?"

"No, he encrypted the calls using a dark web interface with 256-bit encryption software," he clarified.

"So, this encryption software, it's hard to break? Even with time?" I made a *give me more motion* with my hands.

"Impossible without an encryption key. NSA and other intelligence agencies use 256-bit encryption," Josh supplied.

Rick sat back in his chair and pushed his hands through his hair.

"GODDAMNIT!" Mike swiped an arm across the counter and the papers went flying. I'd never seen him so angry and frustrated. "He's right! I'm boxed into a goddamn corner. If I turn myself in, he's going to ruin my parents and my sister, and he'll be in the wind before this gets straightened out. It'll be months, possibly years, before it gets fixed, and I'll be behind bars giving all my money to a lawyer. *Fuck!*"

"Now, Mike, calm down." I left my seat to pick up the papers. "There's got to be some sort of avenue we can take. Maybe you've got friends in the department that could get the baseball. Rick, Josh, and I could set up a sting operation. We'll figure something out."

He snatched the papers out of my hands, balled them up, and got in my face. "KARINA, ARE YOU DEAF? THERE IS NOTHING TO BE DONE! I'M SCREWED, AND NONE OF YOUR CRACKBRAINED SCHEMES ARE GOING TO FIX IT!"

"Hey, now," Josh said.

Both he and Rick had risen from their chairs when Mike started shouting at me.

Rick moved quickly to my side and said in a firm tone, "I think you need to take a break, man. The stress is getting to you."

My hands shook and I clasped them together. Mike and I had certainly fought while we were together and he'd lectured me about past exploits, but I'd never seen him completely lose his shit in quite this fashion. The tightness around his eyes revealed strain. He put a hand to his temple, and I had a feeling he suffered a tension headache.

Mike's gaze darted around to find a roomful of frowns. He dumped the crumpled papers on the counter and quickly exited the kitchen without another word.

I drew in a deep breath and let it out.

Rick touched my elbow. "Are you okay?"

"Fine," I said in a clipped tone. Then I squatted and snatched up the rest of the papers, feeling Rick's concerned gaze on me the entire time. I didn't look him in the eye. I knew if I did, he'd see how much Mike's tantrum had rattled me. I slapped the mass of papers on the counter. "I need to clear my head, too." My voice sounded high and pitchy. "Can someone take me down to the gun range . . . please?"

"I'll take you," Josh offered.

# Chapter Thirteen

The acrid scent of gunpowder hung heavy in the air. Josh had me retrieve the Ruger from the armory, and I'd burned through three clips. The first clip had been utter crap, barely hitting the target, if at all. Then Josh told me firmly, but kindly, that I needed to stop firing in anger and to focus. All seven rounds of the second clip made it onto the target, but it was during the third clip that calmness descended, and an idea came into my head on how to get Mike out of this mess. The last three bullets hit dead center. I laid my weapon on the little shelf and removed the earphones and safety glasses while Josh pressed the button to bring my target toward us.

"I've got it," I announced.

Josh held up the paper. "Not bad, Cardinal. You're improving."

"Listen"—I pulled the paper down so he could see me—"I've got the answer. I know what to do about Mike."

"Uh, Karina, I hate to tell you, but I think Mike was right. It's time he cut his losses." Josh gave me a look of pity. "And, as much as Rick cares about you, he can't continue putting the company in danger of prosecution by keeping him here."

"You're right, but if he can wait just an itty-bitty-bit longer"—I pinched my thumb and forefinger together—"everything will work out. For Mike, Silverthorne, Rick, you, me, Angus, Buckie, Shep, Murgatroyd . . ."

"You're just naming a bunch of names now, aren't you?"

"C'mon, let's go find Mike and Rick." I grabbed his hand.

"Whoa, there, Princess." He pulled me back. "You just gonna leave your weapon sitting there?"

My palms went up. "It's not mine, it's Silverthorne's, and Rick usually tells me to just leave it there. Why? What should I do with it?"

He tilted his head and gave me a funny look. "Rick's never had you police your brass?" He indicated the shell casings on the floor.

I gave him a wide-eyed shrug. "Nope. I've offered, too. Should we do it now?"

Josh rolled his eyes. "I'll get the broom."

I swept while Josh held the dustpan. "Josh, can I ask you a question?"

"Shoot."

"Does Rick go on a lot of dates?"

He took the loaded dustpan and dumped the brass in a recycling bucket at the back of the room. "Dates? No."

I digested that tidbit. "When was the last time he had a girlfriend?"

Josh laid down the dustpan and scrutinized me. "Not for quite a while."

"What did you mean when you said 'as much as Rick cares for me'?"

"He's very protective of you. I've never seen him treat another client the way he treats you."

"How's that?"

He folded his arms. "Why don't you ask him?"

"If you haven't noticed, communication isn't Rick's strong suit. He's a mystery to me. I can't figure him out."

"And *I* can't figure out which one of the two of you is the bigger fool."

"Gee, thanks. That clears everything up."

Josh rolled his eyes and said in a dismissive tone, "Help me reload the magazines."

Once we finished, Josh checked the Ruger to make sure it was empty and handed it to me along with the magazines. "Take these upstairs to the weapons room."

I stuck the magazines in one pocket and the gun in the other. It did nothing to enhance the lines of my dress slacks. After dropping off the firearms, on the way back to the elevator, I noticed a couple of people standing in the doorway to the gym where my self-defense lessons were held.

Elbowing Josh, I asked, "What's going on down there?"

He lifted a single shoulder. "Some of the guys must be sparring."

"Do they often gather around like that?"

"Depends on who it is. Want to go see?"

The crowd drew in a collective breath. A moment of intuition flashed, and I took off down the hall.

"Excuse me." I squeezed past Bunkie and came upon a sight that I'd hoped I'd never see.

Rick and Mike, wearing foam-coated helmets, chest guards, and gloves—not puffy boxing gloves, something thinner and more compact—circled each other on the blue padded mats that were at the center of a room otherwise filled with state-of-the-art exercise equipment. Mike made a move, Rick countered, and within moments the pair was wrestling on the ground, and it looked as though Rick had the upper hand. Mike did a squirrely quick move to disengage and they both popped back up onto their bare feet. Their T-shirts were soaked in sweat, contributing to the general gym stink of unwashed socks and evergreen air freshener.

"How long have they been at it?" I asked Bunkie.

"About twenty minutes."

The pair re-engaged in grappling and throwing kicks and punches while ducking and dodging. This time, Mike wrestled

Rick into some sort of hold with his legs and one of Rick's arms. After what seemed like forever, but was probably no more than fifteen seconds, Rick made a jerking move, and Mike's hands slipped free. In a flash, their positions reversed, and Rick now held Mike in a chokehold.

"This is enough," I mumbled. Putting a thumb and forefinger beneath my tongue, I gave a shrill whistle that echoed off the concrete walls. All eyes turned to me, and Rick released Mike. "Hey, jackasses, showtime is over. Shower and meet in the kitchen in ten minutes. I've got a plan." I pushed my way past Bunkie and Josh. "And for the love of all that is holy, can we get a pizza delivered or something?"

I strode back to the elevator, and huffed impatiently, as I waited for Josh to catch up to me. When he did, he swiped his card and tapped the elevator code but didn't join me when the elevator arrived. Instead, he told me, "I'll meet you up there in a few minutes."

I found Angus still sitting at the head of the table behind his computer with a pile of bank statements at his elbow. "What are you doing?"

"Writing code to monitor the VOIP in case he uses it again. I might be able to locate it if I can gather enough data." He didn't bother to look up as he tapped away on his computer.

"Uh-huh." I didn't speak computer, and I could formulate no educated question that might gain clarification. My stomach grumbled. "Is there a pizza delivery place in the area?"

He didn't answer, and I wondered if he'd even heard me. I didn't bother to repeat myself, instead turned to my phone to seek answers.

"Here we go," Angus said. "Dino's Pizza. What kind do you want?" He flipped the computer toward me.

I trotted over and we ordered a handful of pizzas.

Rick arrived first. He wore jeans and a fresh royal blue T-shirt with the Silverthorne logo on it. It was a good look; the shirt brought out the blue in his gray eyes. He was reading something on his phone. "How was the firing range?" he asked, tucking the phone into his back pocket.

"Edifying." I crossed my arms and delivered a grim stare at him. "What's the word from the head honcho at the stadium? Are we about to be invaded?"

"Their own people are taking twenty-four hours to investigate and run diagnostics on the breach."

That sounded like good news. "So, they don't plan to report it yet?"

"Correct."

I changed tactics and asked, "Want to tell me what the hell that little show in the gym was all about?"

Mike popped around the corner in jeans and a black sweatshirt, his dark hair gleaming wet. "What did I miss?"

"Nothing. I think Karina was just about to chew me out." Rick's cool gaze looked amused.

"What? Why?" Mike trotted over to the fridge for a bottle of water.

"What do you mean, 'why?' What did you two think you were playing at?" I snapped.

"Just blowing off some steam, K.C. Relax," Mike said in a tone that set my teeth on edge.

My lips rolled in, and I stared at the stark white ceiling, counting backward from twenty in silence.

"Have you eaten yet?" Mike asked. "You seem a little hangry."

"She just ordered pizza," Angus replied helpfully.

"There's some fruit in the fridge. Why don't you get her an apple?" Rick suggested.

"I'm. Fine," I gritted out. "Now if everyone would stop worrying about my eating habits—" It was, of course, at that moment my stomach decided to betray me by letting out a wheezing grumble, like a whale in heat, belying my statement. "Oh, hell, gimme a damn apple, and take a seat around the table. I've got a plan." I stomped over to Mike, who'd tucked his head into the fridge.

He placed a shiny red apple in my palm but didn't release it immediately. I glanced up to find him staring at me, his mouth working. Finally, he murmured in low tones, "I'm sorry about earlier. I lost my head and took it out on you. That wasn't cool."

I gave a sharp nod, and he released the apple. Once we were all seated, I munched on my snack and outlined my scheme. "First of all, Angus, is there anything you can do to safeguard Mike's parents' and brother-in-law's assets? Put up a firewall? Freeze the money?"

"I've been thinking about that—"

"Only the government or court order can freeze the money," Mike interrupted Angus.

I glared at him. "I've been frozen out of my own bank account for improperly inputting the wrong password too many times. I'm sure there's *something* that can be done. Angus, continue."

"I've got a solution that can safeguard them. I just need to spoof the number and . . . here, it's easier if I just show you." He hooked a Bluetooth earpiece around his ear, typed on his computer for a minute, and then we heard a buzzing tone like putting through a phone call.

"Hello," a woman answered.

Mike jerked and made to rise, but I grabbed his arm and put an imperious finger to my lips in a shushing motion. Rick held his palms outward and mouthed, "Wait."

"Good evening, ma'am. This is Cooper from PDX Bank. Am I speaking with Mrs. Finnegan?" Angus asked in a southern drawl.

"Yes, it is," she replied.

"Ma'am, we've noticed questionable activity on your accounts that end in—" He reeled off the last four numbers of each account that Matheson had identified in his paperwork. "I believe your ATM card has been compromised."

"Oh my, really? Let me check my wallet. Wait just a minute." It sounded as though she put the phone down, and we waited quietly for her return. "Cooper, are you still there?"

"Yes, ma'am."

"My ATM card seems to be missing." Her voice sounded distressed.

Mike's forearm stiffened beneath my hand.

"Don't you worry. It's no problem, ma'am. I'm gonna fix you right up." He laid on the syrupy southern friendliness. "I'll need to transfer you to our fraud department. Tell them your card has gone missing and ask for a replacement. Ask them to replace your husband's card as well. Just to be safe."

"Yes, okay."

"And, ma'am, I recommend after you report the missing card, go into your online bank account and change your passwords. Just to cover all your bases."

"Thank you, I'll do that." She sounded relieved. "You've been very helpful, Cooper."

"That's what we're here for. I'm going to transfer you now. Please stay on the line." Angus typed in some numbers on his computer and ended the call.

"Where did you send her?" Mike asked.

"To her bank's fraud department," Angus replied in his normal voice.

"Is that it? It seems too easy," I said.

Mike pressed his fingers to his eyes. "Let's hope you didn't trip an alarm that tipped off Matheson."

Angus made a funny little cringe, as if he'd not thought of that.

I plowed on, "Well, it's done. There's nothing we can do to change it. Now can you do the same thing for Mike's brother-in-law?"

Angus adjusted his glasses. "That's going to be a little harder. His accounts are commercial business accounts, and, after looking them over, I can't be sure that Matheson hasn't already started moving money to implicate your brother-in-law."

"Pizza's here." Josh entered the kitchen, carrying three large pizza boxes and a two-liter of diet soda.

Everyone congregated at the counter. As we organized plates, food, and drinks, Mike, Rick, and Angus started a rabbit hole discussion about accounting, embezzlement markers, and tax law implications. I allowed them to run around their debate, like squirrels chasing their tails, while I polished off two slices of pizza and sated my appetite.

Finally, I broke in, "Boys, boys, enough. This isn't a problem we can solve right now. Let's table it for the moment and move to the next item on the agenda."

Mike turned to me. "There is no way in hell we can get that baseball. I'm not getting it. You're not getting it." He pointed across the table at Rick, Josh, and Angus. "And they're not getting it. Period."

"You're right, Mike. No one will access the vault, or whatever you FBI people call it. We don't need to." Now I had everyone's attention. "We don't need it, because we're going to fake it."

Mike started shaking his head. "He'll know. Or he'll figure it out. Then where does that get us?"

"Just. Listen. Before you go dropping bird bombs all over my idea," I groused, rubbing my sore shoulder. Up and down my entire left side, I ached. Maybe firearms practice hadn't been such a good idea after all. "All we have to do is make it look authentic enough at the handoff. In the meantime, I'm hoping Rick has some sort of tiny RFID tracker thingy." I delved into my handbag in search of some ibuprofen.

Rick frowned in thought. "I think I see where you're going with this. You want to plant a tracker in the baseball?"

"Yes. Then Angus can track him back to his lair, and hopefully, we can call in an anonymous tip and send your FBI friends in to go get him." I pulled out a tiny travel bottle of painkillers and shook it. No pills rattled inside. "I'm hoping they'll find the money, or a computer, or some other evidence of what he's done to set you up. Easy peasy." I tossed the bottle back inside my purse. "Is there some ibuprofen around here?"

Mike set his drink down hard and glared at me. "How are you going to do this, K.C.? You don't even know what it looks like."

Rick retrieved a bottle from one of the kitchen cabinets and handed it to me.

"Thanks." I twisted the lid and shook two tablets into my hand. "I don't know *exactly* what it looks like. It's a baseball. You've seen it. How hard can it be? We get the right kind, rough it up a bit, cut the strings and put in the tracker, close it up, and slap some signatures on it. Bam! Fake baseball."

Mike poured more soda into my empty glass. "I saw it *once*, and that was four years ago."

I wasn't to be deterred by his lack of confidence in my plan. "If this is such a famous ball, there must be photographs." I swallowed the two pills and chased them with the diet soda. "Didn't the FBI photograph it before putting it into the evidence warehouse?"

"I suppose," he confirmed.

"Voila." I flicked my wrist. "We'll go off the photos."

"Where, pray tell, do you plan to get the photos?" His voice oozed derision, and he leaned the chair back on two legs.

"I planned to ask Amir for them, in exchange for turning you in," I said in velvety tones.

The chair slammed down. Rick let out a bark of a laugh.

Angus's eyes ping-ponged between the three of us.

"Mike," I said kindly, "having you at Silverthorne has gotten too risky. We have enough evidence that you've been set up. It's time to call Jessica and make a deal to turn you over to McGill. In the meantime, Silverthorne and I will fake the ball and hand it over to Matheson. Once we track him to his secret evil lair, we call in the calvary. FBI shows up, and huzzah! they catch the bad guy and his paraphernalia. You're off the hook. Everyone goes home happy. The crook goes to Club Fed."

No one spoke. Angus wiped his hands and opened his laptop.

"Rick, back me up." I looked to him for assurance. "This is the right play. Even if the stadium guys take twenty-four hours before contacting the police, the noose is tightening. We've got to turn over our evidence to the FBI."

Rick chewed his pizza thoughtfully, contemplating my suggestion. "It's not that easy, Karina. Once we turn over the evidence, the FBI is going to want to ask us a lot of questions. There might not be time to put together your sting operation."

"Hm, I hadn't thought about that." I took a drink of soda. "Maybe we should wait until the handoff."

"Then how are you going to get the pictures of the baseball?" Josh was quick to ask.

"We might not need them," Angus interrupted. "I found an interesting article about that baseball, and there are some good photos here." He turned the machine around for us to see.

Four photos of the 1961 Murderer's Row baseball lit up the screen.

"When were these taken?" Rick asked, shifting the computer screen in his direction.

"The article is dated 2006. I imagine around that time," Angus replied. "The ball was purchased at auction for $200,000."

I let out a low whistle. "Who purchased the ball?"

Angus adjusted his glasses. "Some dude named Drago

Petrovic."

Suddenly, Mike came out of his shocked stupor and grabbed the computer. "Petrovic? You sure about that?" He scrolled down the article.

"Said so in the second paragraph," Angus supplied. "Why?"

"Drago Petrovic is a Serb involved in organized crime. Matheson was laundering money for him. Petrovic is probably the person he won the baseball from in a poker game. Ha!" He clapped his hands together. "That's why he needs the ball. It's Drago's price to get the Serbian mob off Matheson's back. That's what he meant when he said it was his ticket to freedom." He jammed his forefinger on the notepad where I'd written *ticket to freedom*.

I was glad Mike's little epiphany seemed to cheer him up, but . . . "Uh, that's great. It doesn't exactly help our little sting operation. Does it?"

Mike deflated a little. "Well . . . I'm not sure."

"It's a good piece of the puzzle," Rick said thoughtfully, wiping his hands on a napkin. "We know that Matheson is likely in the area and will remain here until he's able to give the Serbs what they want—the baseball. Once he hands it over to them, he's in the wind with his million dollars. That means we've got time. Not a lot. But it gives us something to work with."

My head bobbed along with Rick's explanation. "Great. So, where can we get one of these"—I shifted the computer screen so I could see it—"American League baseballs with red stitching, and a stamp that says . . . *Reach*?" When I glanced up from the computer, I found blank faces staring back at me. "Come on, Josh, you're the baseball nut. Where do you find old baseballs?"

His palms turned up. "eBay?"

"That's using your noggin." In ten seconds, I had eBay up and was searching for American League baseballs from the 1960s.

"Yes, here they are."

"The only problem with using eBay is the shipping. It could take days for a ball to get to us," Angus pointed out.

I wasn't deterred. "We'll pay extra to have it expedited. Or maybe we'll find one locally and pick it up." With determination, I opened half a dozen auctions on different tabs and began checking the shipping locations. "Ha! Right here in Landover, Maryland. It even has a Buy It Now button. It's only forty bucks. I'm going to contact the seller and see if we can arrange a pick-up." I typed a quick message and clicked Send. "Now we wait." I shoved the computer back to Angus. "Can you print out the photos from that article so we can see the baseball better?"

"Absolutely. I'll try to enhance them, too." Angus went to work.

I glanced back and forth between Josh, Rick, and Mike. "What's next?"

Mike glared at me. "You know, I haven't agreed to any of this. Neither has Donovan, for that matter."

We both turned to Rick. I delivered what I hoped would be my thousand-watt smile.

Rick wadded up his napkin and dropped it on the empty plate in front of him. "If you can acquire the ball, I'm willing to let it play out. If not—"

I didn't allow Rick to get any further. "See? There you go. Decision made. We'll keep you under wraps for a little longer."

We heard a ping, and Rick pulled his cellphone out of his pocket. He read a text and frowned. "It seems the FBI is here."

# Chapter Fourteen

My heart plummeted. Mike paled. Josh and Angus went on alert.

Rick pressed a button and put the phone to his ear. "Talk to me . . . uh-huh. . . .just sitting? Nothing else? You're sure? . . . Okay. Keep an eye on it." He hung up.

We all waited on tenterhooks. I found myself leaning forward, my hands gripping the edge of the table.

"We believe it's Karina's surveillance," Rick explained.

"My car is parked in the garage. How did they know I'm here?" I shook my head in confusion.

"Maybe they don't. Perhaps they're simply hoping to acquire you here," Mike suggested.

"So that's it. Just one car?" I thought about all that had happened since I arrived at midday. "Good Lord. How long have they been parked out there?"

"Since you arrived, I've been running regular perimeter checks. They must have shown up within the hour." Rick placed his phone on the table. "Angus, why don't you head down to tech ops and print out the photos of the baseball?"

Angus closed up the computer and exited. I got up, gathered the empty plates, and took them to the sink.

Josh rose and started sorting out the leftover pizza. "This bottom box has half a pizza inside. Do you mind if I take it down and give it to the guys in tech ops?" he asked.

"No problem." I placed the last dish in the dishwasher. "No. Wait a minute, Josh." I glanced over to the table. Rick concentrated on his phone. Mike was hunched over with his head in his hands, staring at the pile of bank papers. "I'm tired of playing ostrich. I think it's time I had a little chat with the FBI."

Mike's head popped up. "Whatever you're thinking, it isn't a good idea."

Rick's brows rose, intrigued. "Go on."

"Why don't I take them a little gift?" I pointed to the pizza.

Everyone's gaze went to the red-and-green pizza box.

"What for?" Josh asked.

"I'd like to feel them out," I said. "See if I can get a beat on what they know."

Mike's head shook. "You're out of your depth, K.C. They're trained agents."

"Look, if I go out there, it'll accomplish two things." I held up two fingers. "First, they'll be put on notice that they've been made, and perhaps they'll leave. Two, I might be able to ascertain if they suspect something about Silverthorne."

"It can't hurt." Josh backed me up.

Mike continued shaking his head and said, "It's not a good idea." In hopes of finding an ally, he looked to Rick, who was scrutinizing me.

"I don't know that I agree with you, Mike," he said, thoughtfully rubbing his five o'clock shadow. "I've seen Karina in action. She can be very charming when she wants to be. And she's fairly wily with words. I believe it's worth the risk to see if any intel can be obtained."

Mike slammed his fist on the table. "NO! I forbid it!"

I knew the laughter that burst out of my mouth only sought to further anger Mike, but I literally could not contain it. And it kept coming. I bent over, clutching my stomach. After a minute or two, I straightened, wiping a tear from my eye, to find Mike's face red as a circus clown's nose and his jaw clenched tight. Drawing in a few calming breaths, I responded, "Michael

Finnegan, what on earth"—another snicker slipped out—"makes you think you have the right to forbid me to do anything? Even when we were dating. Were you ever able to control me? You can yell and bang your fists all you want." A very unladylike snort slipped out. "We are *not* together. If you ever *had* a say in my life, you certainly don't *now*."

"Karina," Josh said in a warning tone.

I'd gone a step too far, but my own emotions were on edge, as well. We were doing this for him, and, frankly, I may have still been smarting from his earlier outburst and the sideshow in the gym. So juvenile. Mike rose, and I expected him to blast me or possibly throttle me with his bare hands. Instead, he stormed out and we could hear the door to his room slam shut.

For two seconds, I thought about following him.

"Leave him," Rick advised. Per his usual man-of-mystery schtick, he showed zero emotion whatsoever about our outbursts. "I'll take you down to the first floor. Jin will meet us there, fit you with a camera, and show you to the surveillance vehicle."

I nodded. "Sure thing." I scooped up the box and headed to the elevator before anyone could rethink the plan. Mike's door was closed when we passed by.

The elevator doors closed, and Rick turned to me. "I'll give you the same advice my first handler gave me. Get in, get out. Don't answer questions. Don't get cute. Mike is right, you'll be dealing with trained agents. Feel them out. Watch the body language. Don't engage for more than a few minutes. If anything seems off, leave immediately. If you're out there more than five minutes, I'm sending Joshua to come get you."

"Okey doke." I glanced away from that intense gaze.

"I'm serious, Karina. Walk. Away."

My head bobbed. "Yup. Understood."

He turned to stare at the closed doors. "And you might want

to think about giving Mike a break. He's still in love with you."

I sputtered, trying to think of a comeback. The elevator doors opened, and there stood Jin.

He outfitted me with the same camera I'd worn to the stadium. He tucked something under my collar. "Audio. We can hear everything, but we can't communicate."

"No coms?" I asked.

"They shouldn't be necessary," Rick replied.

Jin escorted me outside of the Silverthorne gates and pointed to a black sedan. It was parked between two streetlights deep in shadow. I swung my hips and sauntered down the block carrying the pizza box as if I were a cocktail waitress. The government plate on the front of the car was a dead giveaway, and I mentally rolled my eyes. He must have seen me coming. I could see the outline of his head and shoulders. The single agent slunk down in his seat.

*Tap, tap, tap.*

He didn't glance up.

*Tap, tap, tap.*

Finally, the window rolled down. "Can I help you?" Red hair peeped out from beneath the knit cap he wore.

"Why, Mr. Keller! This *is* a surprise. I was expecting an FBI surveillance team, not a tax investigator. What brings you out on this cold night? And all by your lonesome?" I asked in a sweet-as-pie tone.

"I was . . . just . . . uh . . . in the neighborhood." He looked distinctly uncomfortable.

"Did Agent Newcomb assign you to be here?" I probed.

Keller blanched and swallowed.

"Well, I thought you might be hungry. The boys and I ordered pizza, and when they told me there was an agent sitting outside, I thought to myself, 'I'll bet he's hungry.' You see, when I was dating Mike . . . you remember, my *ex-boyfriend?* Anyway, when we were dating, I remember him telling me about some rather boring stakeouts, and I thought, 'This pizza might be able to brighten up his evening.'" I shoved the box into the window, so Keller was forced to take it.

He stared at the box, seeming unsure if he should accept it. "Uh. That's very . . . kind."

"You're wondering if I've drugged it or something, aren't you?" I gave a tinkling laugh. "I assure you there's nothing wrong with it." I opened the top, scooped out a slice and took a bite. "See? Mm, yum."

"Thank you." He placed the box on the passenger seat.

"I assume that you've not yet found Mike?" I took another bite and chewed.

"I can't talk about the case, Miss Cardinal," he said irritably.

Swallowing, I answered, "You don't need to tell me. The very fact that you're sitting here says it all." I frowned. "Speaking of, I'm confused as to why *you* are here. FBI personnel a little thin? Or could it be that this little stakeout is unsanctioned by either the IRS or the FBI?"

"On second thought, that smells delicious. Maybe I will have a slice." He scooped one out and took an enormous bite.

"What are you and Newcomb up to, Mr. Keller?" I asked in low, throaty tones.

Something must have gone down wrong because his eyes went wide, he put a hand to his neck, and he leaned forward as if trying to vomit. I whacked him on the back and a big ole wad of pizza shot out of his mouth and smacked against the steering wheel. He coughed and cleared his throat a few times as the half-chewed bite slithered between his legs to the floor.

I leaned close to his ear. "You need to be more careful, Mr. Keller. Don't take such big bites."

He grabbed a water bottle from the cupholder and gulped.

"So, what *are* you doing here? Playing at being Elliot Ness?

I'm hardly Al Capone."

He glared at me and wheezed, "I could ask you the same thing."

"Taking self-defense lessons and eating pizza with friends." I indicated the pizza box.

"And how do you pay for those services, Ms. Cardinal? Neither your credit cards nor your bank accounts show any charges from Silverthorne."

I'll admit, I wasn't surprised that they'd done a dive into my accounts, but it still threw me off. "I beg your pardon?"

"I imagine you're screwing the boss, Donovan." His eyes narrowed. "Or maybe the big blond. Hell, maybe the entire crew. Do you get these 'self-defense' classes in exchange for your services?" he jeered.

I balled my fists and bit my tongue so I wouldn't rise to the bait and smack the shiznit out of him.

He continued, "You'd better watch yourself. You wouldn't want an IRS audit complicating your life right now. Would you?"

My own gaze turned to slits. "I'm wondering, Mr. Keller, what's the name of your boss? It might be a good idea for me to have a bit of a chat with him."

"I don't believe that's necessary." He turned the ignition and the car roared to life. "It's time for me to head home anyway. Thanks for the pizza." The window slid up, and Keller made a speedy exit.

****

"Mike!" I banged on his door. Jin had removed the tech gear and put me on the elevator. "Damnit, Michael, open up. This is important."

The door whipped open, and Mike stood in front of me wearing a barely controlled mien. "Yes, *Karina?*"

Rick magically appeared at my side as I spoke. "Why was there an IRS bean counter out front conducting surveillance?"

The irritation disappeared to be replaced by confusion. Mike cocked his head. "Who?"

"The same red-headed geek who searched my apartment with Newcomb and Amir. I don't understand. Do IRS investigators have the authority to place surveillance on me?"

Mike frowned and turned away.

Pushing the door wide, I followed. "Mike?"

"It would take a number of steps, and a vast amount of evidence of tax fraud for them to take those steps."

"Could he be part of an FBI joint task force?" Rick leaned against the doorjamb.

"What *exactly* did he say?" Mike sat on the bed.

"Not much. He threatened me with a tax audit. And when I asked who his boss was, he started shaking like a chihuahua in Siberia without a coat and beat a hasty retreat." I failed to mention that Keller had also called me a whore. I figured Mike had had enough shocks for today, and I didn't feel like explaining why Keller thought I might be a whore . . . to either man.

Mike shook his head. "It doesn't add up."

"Excuse me." Angus appeared behind Rick with an open laptop on his arm. I swear the Silverthorne guys walked around in soundproofed shoes. "You got a response from the seller on eBay. He says he's willing to meet to give you the baseball."

I skipped over to Angus and drew him into the room. He placed the computer on the desk for me to read the message.

"K.C., I don't think you should—"

"Too late." I cut off Mike's protest and pressed the Buy It Now button, completing the sale. Then I sent the seller a message requesting we meet at a Starbuck's in Landover tomorrow morning at nine thirty. "It's done. Now we wait and see if the seller can meet me. Thanks, Angus."

"No problem." Angus adjusted his glasses and left with the laptop.

Mike's brows were turned down and his lips were moving but nothing came out. His hands shuffled imaginary papers.

"Mike? What's going on in that head of yours?" I sat on the bed across from him.

"It's not adding up. The bugs planted in your apartment, an IRS investigator following you around. Either more has happened—quite a bit more—that we don't know about, or Newcomb and Keller have gone off book and are performing unauthorized surveillance on you," Mike explained.

"You said Newcomb was dirty. You just couldn't prove it." Rick pushed away from the doorway and took a seat at the desk.

"Yes, but now he's brought in an IRS agent. Why? It's risky," Mike pondered.

"The kid is young. Late twenties. Maybe he's hoping to move up in the world—work for the FBI as an agent, and he thinks cracking this case will get him there," I suggested. "Newcomb could be holding the carrot."

"Maybe," Mike sighed and drew a hand down his exhausted features.

"Well, he's left for the night." I checked my watch. It read ten past nine. Was that all? So much had happened, it felt as though it should be midnight. "I think it's time I head home." I got up and squeezed Mike's shoulder. "Get some rest. Tomorrow will be better."

On my way out, Rick quietly said something to Mike that I couldn't make it out. He met me at the elevator.

"Do you think the baseball scheme is going to work?" I asked, entering the elevator.

He pressed the first-floor button. "I think it's been four years since Matheson has seen the ball. I think he's so desperate to live a life without looking over his shoulder, he's going to want the baseball to work as much as we do. Our next step is going to be how to make the handoff."

"I should do it. Mike will be exposed if we put him out on the street. I know we'll have to turn him in soon, but I'm not willing to have him arrested without more on Matheson. We need Matheson to go back to whatever hole he's hiding in so we can send in the FBI to catch him there."

Rick's face turned severe. "I'm not comfortable sending you in. I'm thinking about having one of the men do it."

"Josh?"

He left the question hanging until we'd reached our destination and the doors opened. "Perhaps."

"Why don't you send me in with Josh as back-up? Matheson has already seen me. He knows I courier things for Mike. I think he'll be less skittish if a girl does the dirty work than if big hulking Josh does it." We walked together toward the loading dock.

"You make a fair point." He held open the door to the armory for me. It closed behind us and he took my elbow.

I glanced back at him with raised brows.

"Just because I haven't stomped around and yelled at you, doesn't mean that I'm not concerned for your safety. I have reservations about your plan."

His comments surprised me. "You don't think my plan will work?"

"There are many aspects that could go sideways. What if Matheson brings the Serbs and the baseball leaves with them?" he asked.

My shoulders sank. "I—I guess I hadn't thought about that."

His questions continued. "What if Matheson sends a cutout?"

Confused, I frowned. "What's a cutout?"

"The same thing we're doing. Sending someone else to make the exchange. It's a term we use in intelligence."

*A CIA term, you mean.* I tucked that morsel of information into my memory banks to analyze at another time. "You think Matheson won't show to collect the ball? I . . . don't . . . know. If the Serbs are really after him, would he risk losing it to a cutout who might double-cross him? How many people around here can he trust?"

"Who knows? We're only going on assumptions regarding his reasons for wanting the baseball. Not that your plan doesn't have merit. But you can be impetuous, and you don't always think of all the scenarios. That's my job—to think beyond the initial plan, because I've been in the field when the best-laid plans are shot to hell by a single fly in the ointment." His tone was gentle but deadly serious.

"Why didn't you bring this up earlier?" I asked defensively.

"Because Mike's stress levels are so high right now, and I don't need him stroking out. And, as I said, your idea has merit—"

"*If* everything goes according to plan," I finished the thought. "Yes."

My face scrunched. "Well, I guess the question to ask is, what *can* we control? The fake ball . . ."

"The meeting place," he stated emphatically. "It's imperative we control the meet."

"Then we do the best we can with what we've got." I looked down at the mild hold he still held on my arm.

He didn't release me. "Why did Keller call you a whore?" That silvery gaze bore into me.

I debated claiming ignorance or concocting a lie, but I was too tired to do either. A windy sigh escaped me. I explained how Josh and I put on a show to get rid of the bug in my bedroom. There was absolutely no change in his expression as I relayed the story. "And just so you know, Josh was a very unwilling participant. Embarrassed beyond belief."

A smile spread on his face, brightening his features, and he let out a ghost of a laugh. "I can imagine."

I decided to take advantage of his good mood. "Let me ask

you something. Earlier, you mentioned your first handler. What exactly was your job before Silverthorne?"

Immediately, his features shuttered. "It's getting late." He released my arm and moved past me.

I wasn't allowing him to get away with it this time. It was my turn to grab him. "Rick?"

He paused without looking at me.

"Are you ever going to tell me about yourself? Your family? Your past?" I gripped harder. "Hell, your present?"

His hand remained flaccid in mine and he stared into the middle distance. "There are things I can't tell you. You know that . . . or you should."

I released his limp fish. "Yes. I guess I do. In some ways, you're no different than Mike." I strode around him, shoving the door to the loading dock so hard it slammed against the wall with a resounding crash.

"Karina." His voice was soft.

I increased my pace, practically running to get to my car. He caught up as I fumbled in my pockets for my keys.

"Karina!" he barked.

I jumped and spun to face him. "What? What is it you want from me, Rick? Because this game you're playing is confusing the hell out of me."

His jaw flexed in frustration. "It's not a game."

"Isn't it? One moment you're kissing me senseless, the next you're telling me to be nice to my ex because he still has feelings for me. Almost as if you're hoping we get back together. Jesus! Why did I bring him here? Why did you let me?" My Irish was up, and my hands were in full action.

"You asked," he said quietly.

"So what? Why are you helping me? Why have you ever helped me? Is it only about paying off my credit on Rivkin's bounty?" I practically screamed the last sentence at him.

"It's not about the money! I care about you, damnit!" he roared.

I didn't believe Rick had ever raised his voice to me. I jerked back and we both took a beat to calm down.

"Josh once said you have a soft spot for me. Is that it? Like an affection for a family pet?" I spoke in cool tones.

"You're hardly a dog, Karina," he said with an inscrutable expression.

"That's not an answer."

He drew in a deep breath. "I'm not in a position to give you the answers you want."

Once again, my hands went up. "What the hell does that *mean*? Who *is* in the position to give me the answers? Are you expecting me to pump your men for it?"

"That's not what I meant. I can't get into it . . . right now. It's important to compartmentalize. Can we, please, table this discussion until after this mission is over?"

I snorted. "Compartmentalize. Fine, yeah." And then I delivered one of the most lethal lines a woman can say to a man during an argument: "Whatever."

"Karina—" His voice caressed me, making me angrier.

I put up a hand to stop him, then dug into my purse to find my keys.

"Your keys are on the dash," he whispered softly.

*Of course.* I'd left them in my car in case one of the Silverthorne guys had to move it out of the way. I whipped open the door and threw myself and my bag inside. Bessie sputtered to life. Rick remained beside the car, his gaze drilling into me. Ignoring him, I glared straight ahead. Finally, when he didn't make a move, I slid the window down and, without taking my eyes off the SUV in front of me, intoned, "You gonna open the garage door? Or should we wait until the exhaust fumes take us out?"

He put a hand on the window frame and leaned down. "We'll

talk more when this is over, and Mike is out of my building."

I refused to respond.

He tried again. "Please drive safe."

I gave a sharp nod.

A sigh whispered across my hair and his hand finally disappeared. The oversized garage door clanged upward, and I made my escape.

# Chapter Fifteen

The baseball purchase couldn't have gone smoother. The seller was in his sixties and told me he had to move his ailing father into an assisted living home. He came across the old ball when he was cleaning out his father's house. I told him my boyfriend liked to collect old baseball paraphernalia.

At half past ten, I parked in front of the Silverthorne offices bearing a four-pack of coffee and in much better spirits than when I'd left the previous evening. Having a night to think about my behavior toward Rick, I decided he was due an apology. Rick never pretended to be anything but what he was with me. I knew his job included a lot of stuff that was confidential. Probably even national security level confidential. Replaying the events of the day as I lay in bed, I'd also realized Rick had shown me a great deal of respect. He'd kept his concerns about my plan to himself, discussing them with me in private, out of earshot of Mike and the team, sparing me any embarrassment. He'd delivered his viewpoint without condescension while also admitting my ideas held merit. Actions quite different from those I'd experienced from Mike. Finally, he was right about discussing "us" *after* Mike's case wrapped, and Mike was out of Silverthorne. Having my ex in the middle of things made it awkward. Rick's earlier comment about compartmentalization may have been on target. I planned to pull Rick aside and tell him all of this.

Angus waited at the door to let me in. He wore a flannel shirt and ripped jeans and looked like a high school dropout.

"Good morning!" I chirped. "Take your pick. That's a

caramel macchiato, the two in front are plain coffee, and this is a chestnut praline latte."

"Which one are you drinking?"

"I prefer the chestnut praline, but I'll be fine with the macchiato."

His hand hovered for a moment before zoning in and scooping out the macchiato. "Did you get the baseball?"

"Yup. It's in my purse. Is there someone at Silverthorne who can forge the signatures?" That little piece of our puzzle hadn't occurred to me until this morning. My own artistic skills were negligible. I was hoping Rick had someone in his arsenal that was a skilled forger or at least willing to give it the old college try.

"I've been working on it and made some samples for you to see," Angus said.

"Great. Is everyone up there?"

He shook his head. "Mike is exercising in the gym. I think Rick is meeting with a client. Josh is—" He frowned. "I'm not sure where Josh is."

I was surprised Rick had a client meeting on a Sunday, but I guessed security was a twenty-four-seven job. "Let's pop into the gym to check on Mike."

Angus led the way. The coffee lent a new aroma to the gym scent. It might have been an improvement. Mike was alone and dripping wet as he worked with the rowing machine.

"Coffee?" I held up my three-pack.

He grabbed a nearby towel and wiped his face. "Did you get the baseball?"

Ah, straight to business. "In my purse."

His face seemed a little less drawn today and the circles beneath his eyes not quite so deep. I was starting to get used to the growing beard. "Angus has been working on his forging skills," he said cheerfully. The extra sleep seemed to have improved his temperament, and I assumed he'd come around to the scheme.

I nodded. "He told me."

"I'll come up with you and get a shower." Mike rose from the machine. "Is one of those plain coffee or are they all girlie flavors?" He gave me a nudge and a wink.

I gave a put-upon sigh. "The front ones are plain. Sugar packets are in the center."

"Thanks." He took his coffee and two sugar packets, and we all trooped to the elevator.

On the second floor, Mike ducked into his room; Angus and I made our way to the kitchen. A dozen brand new, signed baseballs sat in a bowl on the kitchen island; two in particular were singled out, resting next to half a dozen eight-by-ten glossy photos of the real baseball. I set the coffee on the table and went to look at them.

"These are good." I picked up one, rotated it, and compared it to the glossies. "The coloring looks good. What did you do to fade the signatures and age the ball?" I put the baseball down and checked out the other one.

"They're each done with a different approach." Angus leaned his forearms against the opposite side of the island.

I held the balls side-by-side.

"Once everyone is in here, we can choose the best forgery," he suggested.

"Sounds like a plan." I set them down and took a deep drink of coffee.

Angus received a text and excused himself, leaving me alone in the kitchen to twiddle my thumbs. I retreated to my phone to answer emails. Once those were complete, I checked my horoscope, then moved on to a news app to see what was going on in the world. The Pope was planning a visit to Mexico. An Iranian nuclear scientist was killed in a convoy bombing, and the Iranians were blaming Israel. Three Americans in Venezuela, working for an American oil company, had gone missing. The World Economic Forum was being moved from Switzerland to Singapore. My finger scrolled past all of the bad news searching for something good. I finally found it—firefighters were able to extinguish the brush fires in Australia.

"Where is everyone?" Mike asked.

I held up a finger. "Just a minute."

Mike glanced over the baseball forgeries while I finished the article.

"Well, you smell better. You look better, too." He wore fresh jeans and a sweatshirt with NAVY emblazoned across the front. I wondered if Josh gave it to him. "Did you get good sleep?"

"I did." Mike found some cereal and poured it into a bowl. "Want some?"

I shook my head. "The forgeries look very good to me. What do you think?"

"I agree. Angus did an excellent job." He brought his breakfast over to the table and took a seat. "Where is everyone?" he asked again.

"Angus was here earlier and said Rick was meeting with a client." I shrugged. "He wasn't sure about Josh. I'll text them and see what's going on." I shot off a quick text.

**Where are you guys? I've got the baseball. Mike and I are in the kitchen.**

"You seem to be calmer. Have you accepted the plan?" I asked.

"Sure. As long as Matheson shows up to the meet, we're good to go." He sounded chipper. Almost too chipper. I surveyed him as he spooned a load of flakes into his mouth. Something was off, but I couldn't put my finger on it.

"Have you decided how to approach McGill?"

He swallowed and shook his head. "Still giving it some

thought."

"Guys?" Angus stood in the doorway with his ever-present laptop.

I swiveled around. "Hey. We were wondering where everyone went. Did you hunt down Josh?"

"Rick wants to speak with you. I have him on a video call." Angus placed the laptop between Mike and me and pulled up a video conferencing platform. His fingers flew across the keyboard typing in the secure passcode, and a moment later Rick popped into view.

He wore military fatigues and tactical gear and seemed to be in a large warehouse or airplane hangar. Clearly, he *wasn't* in the building.

"Rick! Where are you?" I asked.

"I'm out of the country." He sat down on a large crate.

Mike and I shared a look of concern.

"I have a team that was providing protection services for a group of technicians securing the final shutdown of an oil refinery in South America. At midnight, I got a call that a manager and one of my men had disappeared. We suspected a kidnapping or possibly an arbitrary arrest by local authorities."

Mike put down his bowl and went into FBI mode. "What have you found?"

"At two this morning we received an encrypted email with a photo and directions to 'stand by' for further instructions."

"What do they want?" I asked.

"We're assuming money. But we've not been contacted since the initial email," Rick replied.

"Has the State Department been notified?" Mike asked.

"Yes. We spoke with them immediately after we got the email. However, the embassy and consulates were closed last year due to the unrest. They have to work diplomatic channels through the Swiss. It's a bit time consuming."

While the two men ping-ponged a Q&A session, something was scratching at the edges of my brain. Something I'd seen . . . or read. Something that had to do with kidnapping.

"If you get a ransom demand, State will never pay. They don't negotiate with these groups. Do you have kidnap and ransom insurance for them?" Mike asked.

Then it hit me, and I sucked wind. "Oh my God, you're in Venezuela. There was an article in the news." I whipped out my phone and pulled up the world news site I'd been searching earlier. "Yes, here it is. The article said three men went missing. They worked for Talley Group, an American refinery company that shut down when all American companies were required to close operations and pull out of Venezuela due to the government instability and . . . increased violence." I looked up from my phone to find Rick frowning deeply.

He delivered a flavorful curse. "It's in the papers? Which one?"

"Uh"—I scrolled to the top—"Reuters. It went up about an hour ago."

He leaned closer to the camera. "Does it provide names?"

"No. It said three men." I glanced up from my phone. "Who's the third?"

Rick looked over his shoulder to answer someone out of the camera line, and then returned to us. "One of the Talley Group. He was shot and left on the side of the road."

I'd gotten to know a handful of the Silverthorne guys. One, in particular, was fluent in Spanish, and though I was definitely *not* his favorite person, he'd always been professional. A bad feeling came over me and my gut clenched.

"Has the K&R insurance company provided you with a negotiator? If you need a reference, I've got—"

I interrupted Mike. "Who was kidnapped? Which one of the Silverthorne guys?"

Rick didn't answer.

I leaned closer to the camera. "Was it Hernandez? Did they get Hernandez?"

Rick took off his helmet and ran a hand through his hair.

Fear, anger, and frustration coursed through my veins. "Omigod!" My hands fisted in frustration. "Not Hernandez. We can't let those bastards take down Hernandez. What can I do? What can I do?" My eyes zoomed manically around, as if the answer would appear from thin air. Then, my brain engaged into gear and it came to me. "Of course, I know what I can do to help. I know congressmen and senators. I can make some calls. I know the chair of the Senate Foreign Relations Committee. I'm friendly with three members on the committee. I'll start there. Then I'll move on to the House," I babbled, scrolling through the contacts on my phone.

"Karina, stop!" Rick barked at me.

My head jerked up.

"Mike, talk to her," he said sharply and left our field of vision. All we could see were corrugated metal walls, crates, and the rear of a ratty, blue pickup truck.

"K.C." Mike laid a hand over my phone. "Relax. This can take time. Rick knows what to do. He's working the proper channels with State and the K&R company. If the money gets paid, or State finds the proper pressure point to put on the government—"

"What are you talking about? Venezuela is a disaster!" I hissed at him. "Don't you know anything? Their government is sliding into dictatorship, there are two governments competing against each other, and the illegitimate dictator controls the military. We don't have an embassy or working consulates down there. What can the State Department do?"

Rick returned to his seat as I finished my little tirade.

"K.C., calm down." Mike patted my hand.

I delivered him a deadly glower. "Did you just tell me to calm down?"

He snatched his hand back and, in a reassuring manner that bordered on condescending, continued. "It's going to work out. You have to realize—the two men are no good to the kidnappers if they're dead. If it's money they want, the insurance will pay. It's only a matter of time. Back me up, Donovan."

Rick's mouth twisted and he rubbed the scruff on his jawline.

"What? What's that look for?" I pointed at the screen. "I don't think he can 'back you up', Michael. Richard Donovan, *tell me what's wrong.*"

He cringed. "I found out the Talley Group allowed their insurance to lapse two months ago, and the guy they took has diabetes."

"Well, that doesn't sound good," I said. "Will the company pay his ransom out of their coffers?"

"Hold on a sec." Rick leaned out of the frame and we could only see his leg. When Rick came back into the picture, he said, "Listen, things are happening, and I don't have much time. The main reason why I called was to tell you I brought Joshua and a handful of other operatives down with me. Jin, Sonia, and Bunkie are still on the Korean delegation job. The only person available to work with you for the handoff is Angus. If you can delay Matheson, do so. Jin and Sonia have been read into the current plan. They will put the Koreans on the plane tomorrow at noon. They'll be available after that."

"What about the stadium? Aren't we on a clock ourselves, here?" I asked.

Something was happening. A man in full combat gear carrying a rifle walked behind Rick. Someone else threw a heavy duffle bag into the back of the pickup truck and hopped in after it.

He nodded. "Right, I forgot to mention I spoke with my contact. It looks as if the stadium is keeping things internal.

There's no indication they'll reach out to the FBI to report the breach. Time is on your side. Wait for Jin and Sonia" The latter sentences were delivered in a brief staccato manner.

Distinctly, from off camera, we heard Josh holler, "Boss, the intel is confirmed! Time to roll out."

"Be in touch." Rick closed the lid on his computer, and our screen went black.

Crossing my arms, I sat back in my chair. "That didn't look like a diplomatic route to me. So, I shouldn't be worried?" Sarcasm dripped like honey from my mouth.

Angus simply folded the computer shut and said quietly, "I'll be back in a few minutes."

*Smart boy.*

I continued to stare at Mike for answers.

His face turned grim. "It's an exfil. Their—"

"A what?" I interrupted.

"An exfiltration or extraction. They're going to get them out. Their client has a life-threatening condition. They can't wait for the diplomats to meander their way into a deal, nor can they be positive the company will pay his ransom," he supplied. "They probably have assets on the ground and intel providing a location."

"How long can the Talley guy go without insulin?" I asked, figuring if anyone knew, it would be him. Mike had grown up with a father who was a diabetic.

He cringed. "It all depends on how they're traveling—if they're being driven or forced to walk—how many calories he's burning, what they're being fed—"

"*If* they're being fed." I gnashed my teeth.

"Yeah." Mike frowned.

"How do they know the company won't pay the ransom?"

Mike shrugged. "I'm not there. As far as we know, they haven't delivered a ransom demand yet. When they do, negotiations may take too long."

"What are the odds for success?"

Mike shrugged again. "I don't know. Depends on where they're being held. City. Country. Mountains. They all carry different risks." The next words were spoken in a whisper and a touch of pity. "If they don't succeed, it's highly unlikely the government will send troops or agents to get them."

"So, they're on their own?" My voice got a little pitchy, and I gulped back a rising sob.

"K.C." He placed his arm around my shoulder. "Donovan and his men are some of the best."

"How do you know?" I whispered.

"By their reputation. They've been trained for this. I trust that they know what they're doing, and you should, too." He gave me a squeeze.

I rubbed my temples. Mike was right. I'd seen the Silverthorne guys in action. However, Josh, Hernandez . . . Rick, they were all important to me, and my emotions were sending my mind into dark places. "I need the bathroom. I'll be right back."

His arm slid off.

I headed to a place where I could have some privacy and get my thoughts in order, because, right now, the rising panic I felt for Rick would help no one. I cared about all the Silverthorne guys, however seeing Rick in this sort of danger was a direct blow to my solar plexus. I needed a moment to shake off the dread and anxiety building there. It was time for me to take a page out of Rick's playbook and "compartmentalize." While Rick's fate was out of my hands, we could still do something about Mike's fate.

I splashed cold water on my face, patted it with a towel, and stared in the mirror. "*Cardinal!* Get your shit together," I hissed.

By the time Angus returned to the kitchen, I'd subdued my anxieties—well, more like, I stomped on them like one does a cockroach, with little bits oozing out the side—and was back in mission mode. Mike and I had both agreed upon which baseball should be replicated with the one I'd gotten from eBay.

"This one is the winner." Mike held it aloft like he was presenting the Nobel Prize.

Angus laid his computer on the counter, plucked the ball out of his hand, and tossed it in the air. "I thought so, too."

"Any news?" I asked.

Angus's gaze zipped back and forth between Mike and me.

"I get it. Mike explained it all to me. It's an exfil. Any news from the team?" I repeated.

He shook his head. "It'll be hours before we know. They've gone deep into the mountains." I swallowed down that jolt of fear and transferred my attention to what Angus was saying. "The boss suggested we do the exchange at a location that is public, but not very crowded." Angus brought up a map on his laptop. "He wants it during the daytime with avenues for escape. We want Matheson to have a comfortable escape route. We'll turn on the tracker as soon as the baseball has left the location."

"Speaking of the tracker," I said. "I'm concerned it's going to make the baseball lumpy, and thus identifiable. Thoughts?"

"I've put trackers in both the balls." He held out the ball in his hand. "Did you notice?"

"You already put the RFID in?" I plucked it from him, and Mike picked up the one on the counter. We examined the ones in our hands, then traded.

"Wow. Okay, now I'm *really* impressed."

"Yeah, K.C. is right. I had no idea you'd already put them inside. Nice work." Mike gave Angus a hearty football coach-style back slap.

"Now all you have to do is make contact with Matheson." I waggled the phone we'd retrieved at the stadium.

Mike nodded. "Let's do this."

Angus plugged the cell into his computer to try to trace the call, then Mike pressed the redial button and left it on speakerphone.

"Agent Finnegan, I presume," Matheson answered. "Have you got it?"

Mike leaned in and answered, "I do."

"See, I knew if you put your mind to it, you'd figure it out," he said in a such a smarmy manner, I wanted to reach through the phone and slap him. "How did you do it?"

"I sent in the girl with a borrowed badge," Mike replied. "When and where do we meet?"

"Tomorrow. Ten. There's a trash can in front of—"

"Forget it. No dead drops," Mike interrupted. "It's a handoff. I want to make sure you hold up *your* end of the deal."

Matheson remained silent. I fiddled nervously with my earring.

"Lincoln Memorial?" Mike suggested.

"No," was Matheson's abrupt reply.

Mike ground his teeth. "It's got to be a public location. Pick something."

More silence. The earring fell out into my hand.

"FDR Memorial. Nine. In front of Eleanor. Bring the phone." Matheson hung up.

"Did you get anything?" I asked Angus, hooking my little silver filigree earring back in its hole.

Shaking his head, he adjusted his glasses. His own phone lit up and made a dinging noise. Angus checked the message and closed the computer. "I'll be back."

I gave Mike the once-over. "It looks as though it's you and me for the exchange."

"And Angus."

My brows went up. "Angus isn't a field operative. Are you planning to stay in the van with him?"

"Nope," he stated firmly.

"I didn't think so." Pacing around the island, my mind worked the options. "Do you still have your hobo clothes?"

He nodded. "I do, but we're going to have to dirty them up a bit."

"So, what's the plan? Are you the hobo . . . or am I?"

Mike leaned against the counter, and I came to a halt next to him. He stared into the middle distance, his brain formulating and discarding the options. Finally, a sigh escaped him. "You'll have to make the handoff. I'll be nearby as a homeless person."

"You'll be exposed." I chewed my lip. "Do you think it's necessary? Matheson isn't dangerous. I can make the exchange and meet you back at the van."

Very slowly, his head moved back and forth. "Forget it. I *do not* want you out of my sight."

"When does McGill enter the plan?"

"Soon."

# Chapter Sixteen

Monday morning, I called in sick to work. My sleep had been practically nonexistent, so I didn't have to fake a ragged, worn-out voice. There still hadn't been any news from Rick and the exfiltration team when I'd left around five on Sunday. Both Angus and Mike tried to reassure me that no news wasn't necessarily bad news. Later, I realized that we might not be told if the mission was a success until everyone was home safely.

After a shower and two cups of coffee, my eyes were open, and my brain began functioning. The bat phone rang while I was styling my hair. I took it to the back of my closet and softly answered, "Rick?"

"Cardinal? It's Jin."

I put a hand to my heart. "Jin? What's wrong?"

"Nothing is wrong. I'm calling to express my concern," I sighed and Jin continued, "I thought Rick told you to push the exchange with Matheson until this afternoon, when Sonia and I could participate."

"Matheson wasn't in a helpful mood," I said drily.

"That's not what Angus told me."

"He's wrong." I began sorting through a stack of jeans in search of my favorite pair—a faded blue denim that had softened through many cycles of wash and wear. "We barely got Matheson to agree to a public handoff. He wanted a dead drop. Tell me, what's going on in Venezuela?"

"I have nothing to report," he said.

I paused my search. "What do you mean 'nothing to report'?"

"There is no update."

"Jin, what does that mean? Did the mission go sideways? You must have something. It's been almost twenty-four hours." I worked to keep the alarm out of my voice.

"They were moved into the mountains. The terrain is rough, and it takes time. The team went radio silent. As far as we know, everything is fine. There's no need for you to worry." Jin's reply was delivered in his normal, even-keeled tone that gave nothing away.

"Are you worried?" I asked.

"I am not."

The tightness across my shoulders refused to ease. "At what point do we get worried? At what point should I begin calling my friends on the Senate Foreign Relations Committee? At what point do we shake the trees or send in more guys to go get the guys who went to go get the original guys?" I babbled.

"Rick and the team are fine, until I hear something different. In the meantime, I need you cool and centered. Since Sonia and I won't be there, Mike will be relying on you."

"In other words, I need to dig deep to channel my innermost Mr. Miyagi?"

"Something like that." His tone lightened, and I imagined he gave one of his small grins.

I closed my eyes and drew in a breath. "I hear you. I'll concentrate on the mission at hand today." My refocused attention returned to jean pile. "Was there something else you needed?"

He paused. "No."

"Good luck with the Koreans." Finally, I hit on the right pair of denims. I gave a yank and was miraculously able to remove the jeans without having the stack tumble over.

"Gi gave me a gift for you," Jin said in matter-of-fact tones.

"Really?" I said distractedly, sorting through sweaters.

"I've left it at the office."

"Mm-hm." I laid the phone on a shelf and held up a dark green V-neck sweater, trying to decide if it was an appropriate outfit. What *did* one wear for some shady shit with a federal fugitive?

"Cardinal. Karina! *Are you listening to me?*" Jin squawked.

"What?" I retrieved the phone. "Sorry, I was trying to decide what to wear to the meeting. Do you think a forest-green sweater is nondescript?"

He took a beat. "I think it's a thirty-five-degree day with snow in the forecast. You'll be wearing a coat the entire time. Find something warm that fits comfortably beneath your dark peacoat and allows you a full range of motion," he said in clipped directives. However, he broke with his bossy attitude and continued in a softer tone, "It's cold. You should wear a hat."

"Good point." I tossed the sweater onto the floor next to the jeans. "What were you saying before?"

"You have good instincts. If something doesn't feel right, get out." Jin had been the first Silverthorne guy to help me learn to trust my own instincts, even when others were shooting them down.

"I appreciate your concern, and I'll follow your advice. But I'm not worried. Matheson has never been violent. We have what he wants. We'll make the exchange. No problem."

"It's never that easy. Remember Chichén Itzá?" Jin brought up a bit of a sore subject. "I read the after-action report."

"That was different," I said defensively. Jin referred to an exchange we made for my neighbor and a forged Egyptian death mask. "It was night, in a foreign country, and we were exchanging a person. This is just a flash drive and a baseball."

"There's no such thing as 'just a' when making an exchange. Be on the alert," he lectured.

"Yes, of course."

We said our goodbyes. I poured myself one more cup of coffee before collecting my things. I tossed the bat phone, Mike's burner, and my own phone into my handbag, and grabbed my coat off the couch where I'd left it last night. As I shrugged into the coat, I realized what I'd done. I put down the handbag so I could dig out my own phone and leave it on the counter. Irritation swept over me. Behind my TV lay the sneaky little bug left behind by Newcomb. Squinting, I gave some serious thought to ripping it out, and handing it over to Mike, so he could pass it along to McGill with my regards. Then I thought better of it, and a Grinch-like smile spread across my face as I hit upon a better idea.

# Chapter Seventeen

The Franklin Delano Roosevelt Memorial is like none other in D.C. First off, it isn't a single statue, like Jefferson or Lincoln, nor is it a wall or pillars like the Vietnam and World War II Memorials. The FDR Memorial is a sprawling monument over seven acres of prime real estate on the southeast side of the Tidal Basin along the Cherry Tree Walk. When the cherry blossoms are out, the beauty of it can't be beat.

Built with red granite from South Dakota, the meandering memorial was set up into four distinct outdoor areas the designer called "rooms". Each room represents FDR's four presidential terms, and, throughout the memorial, Roosevelt's words are etched into the granite blocks. Before entering the first room, you're greeted by a life-size bronze statue of Roosevelt sitting in his wheelchair, wearing a suit and fedora. Not original to the monument, disability rights advocates lobbied and raised the funds to have a depiction of FDR in his wheelchair created and placed there. Other statues include representation of the Great Depression with a group of men standing in a breadline, while another man sits next to his radio listening to Roosevelt's legendary fireside chats. A larger-than-life statue of Roosevelt with his dog Fala is depicted in the third room. In the fourth room, a statue of Eleanor Roosevelt—the only statue of a First Lady at a presidential monument—stands next to the emblem of the United Nations as the first United States delegate to the UN. All of the rooms have water features that also represent Roosevelt's terms. The room depicting his term during World

War II has a chaotic, crashing waterfall with the granite blocks in a jumbled pile. Etched across one is FDR's famous quote: "I hate war."

Very few tourists were at the memorial on this Monday morning. The leaden skies created a dreariness and the scent of snow whispered in the air. Angus had a wide choice of parking spaces. He pulled our Silverthorne van, full of tech goodies and lots of hot coffee, into a space along West Basin Drive. The boys insisted we arrive two hours early.

We crammed into the back of the van to discuss reconnaissance.

Angus held a handful of minicameras in his hand. "I'll do a perimeter check. Then I'll move through the memorial, planting these as I go, so I can monitor the exchange."

Mike closed the door behind Angus and turned to me with an expression I'd seen before. It was one he used before dropping some sort of bombshell in my lap.

"What's up?" My gaze turned to slits.

"I've made a decision."

"Uh-huh," I said warily.

"I'm taking Matheson. Here. I'll arrest him now," Mike stated succinctly.

"Uh, that's not the plan. What happened to following him back to his lair? What about the stuff he has on your family?"

Mike shook his head. Placing his elbows on his knees, he leaned toward me with a serious expression. "We'll find his lair through interrogation. If I bring him to the FBI, I'm the conquering hero. It's the best way."

"Uh, Mike, I'm not an operative like the Silverthorne guys, or an FBI agent. The only thing I'm packing is my little pink stun gun." I pulled it out of my pocket to show him. "Additionally, I'm not sure what Angus's skills are besides computer stuff."

"We won't tell Angus," Mike said. "Well . . . not until we grab

Matheson," he amended.

I shifted uncomfortably on the metal stool. "I'm not thrilled about keeping Angus in the dark. What if Matheson doesn't show? Or is prepared for an ambush?"

"I think the odds of Matheson showing up are fifty-fifty. If he does, I can't allow this farce to continue. I want you to stun him as soon as he gets close enough," Mike said, as if it were the easiest thing in the world.

"I wasn't really planning on allowing him to get close enough," I mumbled. "And what if there are people around? This is exactly why we're meeting in public. To avoid such confrontations."

"If the setup is inauspicious or too dangerous, I'll say, 'it's too cold out here.' That will mean you should make the exchange and let Matheson go. If I say, 'time to warm up', that's the signal to go ahead and stun him. I'll move in for the arrest."

I pulled back, crossing my arms. "Can you arrest him? Are you still an agent?"

"I haven't officially been removed from duty. So, yes. I can arrest him."

"Do you have your badge? What about restraints? Do you plan to use my belt?"

He pulled his badge from an inside coat pocket and flashed it at me. "I borrowed some zip ties from Silverthorne."

Well, if it's one thing Silverthorne has plenty of, it's zip ties . . . also duct tape. I mashed my lips together in frustration. His latest brainstorm changed the entire plan. "What happens if I decide it's a no-go? After all, I'll be the one in the line of fire. If my instincts are shouting 'hell no!' at me, what do we do?"

"If you see a danger that I'm missing, you can use the same code words." He put his palms up and grinned at me as if to say "no big deal."

I scrutinized him. This was out of character. Mike was a

details guy. The way he sprung the change of plans on me, after Angus left the van, made me wonder how long he'd been working on this new twist. My gut told me he'd been planning this from the beginning, and that he'd been placating all of us by pretending to go along with the original idea. Yesterday, when he was eating cereal, it was there right in front of me, but I couldn't grasp it.

Tapping my chin, I asked, "Did Rick's unexpected out-of-town trip make it easier or harder for you to put your secret plan into action? Did you agree to a morning meeting, so you didn't have to hassle with convincing Jin to go along with it?"

Mike stared down at his boots. "Karina, I just can't allow him to walk away. He's been on the FBI's wanted list for years. It would be a dereliction of duty if I didn't make an effort to capture him. The only reason we're allowing him to return home is for *my* benefit. None other."

He kind of got me with that dereliction of duty crap. And he was right, we were following the ball home for his benefit.

I sighed. "Fine. We'll capture him right here."

"I knew you'd understand." He took my hand in an old and comforting manner, giving it a gentle squeeze.

The door slid open, and I snatched my hand back.

Angus seemed not to have noticed our "moment". "The room which Matheson has chosen is at the end of the monument and provides a variety of escape routes. It's likely why he chose it."

He climbed in, making quarters tight, and began pointing to a variety of spots where he'd place the cameras on the map. Angus went on to advise Mike which bench would provide the best angle to see me at Eleanor's statue as well as most of the entrances and exits. He also strategically placed tiny cameras around the memorial, so we'd have eyes on all directions. Then he outfitted us with our wireless coms.

Mike took his last gulp of coffee and gave me a hard look.

"Are you ready for this?" He was asking if I was ready to take down Matheson.

"Yes. Let's do it." We shook hands.

He closed the door and shambled—in his dirtied, worn jacket, over-large black cargo pants, and the silly, dreadlocked cap that covered most of his face—through FDR's rooms to the bench Angus had indicated across from Eleanor's statue. We watched him shuffle, with shoulders hunched, in and out of the camera frames.

Meanwhile, Angus and I had some time to kill. While Angus adjusted his cameras, zooming in and out, and checked on other tech stuff, I gazed aimlessly around the electronics van. Have I mentioned I wasn't very good waiting around?

I picked up a small black thingy, about as wide as my palm, with a slot and a USB port. "What's this?"

"External hard drive."

I put it down. "What are all those for?" I asked, pointing to a rack of tightly rolled cables hanging from zip ties.

Angus glanced over his shoulder. "Cables."

"Duh. What are they for?"

"Plugging stuff in," he stated.

I could see I wouldn't get anything further from Angus on the cables, so I reached into one of the cubbies to draw out a small case. "What's in here?"

"Don't touch that," Angus snapped.

"Why? What is it?"

"A very expensive drone. Hernandez will be upset if you break it."

I shoved the case back in place and drummed my fingers against the table. Angus stared pointedly at them.

I moved to fidgeting quietly with my earring. "Do you ever feel as though you're part of the Scooby-Doo gang and this is the Mystery Machine?"

He peered at me over his specs. "Which one am I, Shaggy or Fred?"

"You're Velma because you're the nerdy, smart one with the glasses."

"That would make you Daphne, the helpless, flighty redhead," he deadpanned.

I tapped my chin in thought, then shook my head. "Nah, I'm Shaggy because I fall ass backward into these little adventures, but somehow manage to play a dumb-luck role in capturing the bad guy."

Angus's mouth scrunched and his body shook as he struggled to hold in his laughter.

"It's okay. You can laugh." I patted him on the shoulder.

He let loose.

"I can't believe I'm saying this, but you're right," Mike said over the coms. "Does that make me Scooby in this scenario?"

I'd forgotten we were on a party line. "No, you're not Scoobs. Initially, I'd say you're Fred, but I think that role goes to Josh, even though he isn't with us today. Mike, you're the law enforcement officer who always comes at the end to pull off the mask and wrap things up," I replied.

"Has anyone ever told you you're a bit of a nut?" Angus asked.

"But you love me anyway," I sang.

Angus rolled his eyes. "It's half past eight. Time for you to get out there. Here is Matheson's cellphone."

I shoved it in my pocket. "Admit it, you're going to miss having me here to entertain you in the Mystery Machine."

At a loss for words, Angus simply shook his head in disbelief.

"Just get out here, K.C.," Mike said in a warning tone.

"Okay, bossy boy. On my way."

Angus slid the door open, and I left the van to begin my own leisurely stroll to the meeting spot. There were all sorts of nooks and crannies to explore throughout the memorial. I spent a good fifteen minutes allowing my fingers to play over the bronze tactile reliefs created by the designers for disabled persons to "feel" the monument. A large sign blocked the first barren waterfall. Apparently, the pump room had flooded, destroying the mechanics, and all the waterfalls were turned off until Congress appropriated the money to have it fixed.

"Bummer," I murmured.

"What?" Angus asked.

"The waterfalls are broken. They are my favorite part," I replied.

"Where are you?" Mike demanded.

"Still in the first room. I love this place."

"Get your butt over here. The exchange is happening soon. I want eyes on you before then," he said rather snippily.

"Tsk. Fine, I'm coming." I trotted through the next two rooms with my hands in my pockets to keep the stun gun from banging against my thigh. Finally, I descended the wheelchair accessible ramp to the place where Eleanor Roosevelt stood in her special cove. I spotted Mike immediately.

He lay on a bench, opposite of where I stood. A family with two small children romped near the empty waterfall feature. An oblivious father read tidbits aloud from a brochure while the mother scrambled after the toddlers to keep them from playing too close to the pool of nasty, black water at the base of the empty falls, while occasionally glancing nervously at the nearby homeless man.

"I've got something. Jogger coming your way," Angus said in my ear.

The jogger, wearing all black spandex and a red hat, ran through the area without stopping and turned down a path to the Tidal Basin.

"Negative. He's moved on," I murmured.

One of the toddlers shrieked and scampered in the opposite direction of his family toward Mike. The mother spoke sharply to her husband. He came back to Earth, tucked the brochure away, hurriedly scooped up the escapee, and whirled him around in the air. The child whooped with glee, and the family soon departed, leaving Mike and me alone. The first snowflakes drifted from the heavens, and I pulled my coat tighter around my neck.

"Someone is coming from the east," Angus warned.

A girl wearing a red parka and a pink-striped knit cap came up from the Cherry Blossom Walk at the far end of the memorial. She wore a Bluetooth headset and was playing with her phone.

I turned an admiring gaze to Eleanor's statue and hissed, "He's late."

"Only five minutes. Give it time," Angus soothed.

Matheson's cellphone vibrated in my pocket. "Hello."

"Where is Agent Finnegan?" Matheson asked.

The girl in the red parka worked her way closer to where I stood, and I moved in the opposite direction, turning my back to her. "He sent me. Where are you?"

"Nearby. Do you have it?"

"In my backpack. Do you have the drive?"

"The girl in the red coat," Matheson replied.

I spun around.

She stood five feet from me and stared intently. The Bluetooth was still in her ear, and I noticed an attachment I'd never seen before. A camera. White-blonde hair peeked out from under the hat, and her bright blue eyes peered starkly from her unlined, unmade-up, pale face.

"He's sent a cutout," Angus said quietly.

Rick's instincts had been correct about the cutout. Matheson wasn't taking any chances. A glance past the girl's shoulder revealed Mike, still lying on his side with a hand tucked into his pocket, no doubt wrapped around the Glock 9mm he'd borrowed from Silverthorne.

"It's too cold. Let it play out," he whispered in my ear.

"Let me see the flash drive," I told both the girl and Matheson.

The girl waited a moment, then gave a slight nod. She pulled her hand out of her pocket and held a Mickey Mouse USB drive.

"Where is the baseball?" Matheson demanded.

I swung the backpack off my shoulder, took out a small laptop—provided by Angus—

and placed it on the steps at Eleanor's feet. "First, I check the flash drive. If it's legit, you get the ball."

The girl's gloved hand closed around Mickey. My brows rose as I waited patiently for Matheson to give her the go-ahead.

"That wasn't the deal," he ground out.

"Do you think Mike is stupid enough to trust you? For all I know, that's an empty drive, and thus worthless. Or it could be some sort of virus that's going to fry the computer," I stated firmly.

Matheson took a moment. "Show her the ball. Then you check the drive."

I scrutinized the girl in front of me. Her fine-boned features and lithe figure didn't seem threatening, but I knew looks could be deceiving when it came to fighting skills. I figured I could take her and, if all else failed, I had the stun gun.

"Okay." I held open the backpack and pointed to the baseball resting inside so she could see it.

"What the hell is that? It was in a case!" Matheson screeched.

Someone in my ear sucked some serious wind, but I'd been ready for him to question it. "FBI must have bagged it separately. I left the ball inside the FBI's evidence bag where I found it." A pièce de résistance of Angus's doing which Mike properly marked and we'd spent time aging. "I was given no direction to recover a case as well." I closed the backpack and returned it to my shoulder. "Are we doing this?"

"Fine," he replied begrudgingly.

The girl's hand reopened. I took the drive, jammed it into a port, and waited for it to load. Clicking on the drive's icon, documents began filling my screen. I selected one. It looked like one of the papers I'd seen strewn across the counter at Silverthorne.

"Happy?" Matheson asked sarcastically.

"Thrilled." I retrieved the FBI evidence bag with the fake ball and passed it to blondie, who gave it a once-over, then stuffed it inside her parka. I let out the breath I'd been holding. Clearly, she was no expert on baseball memorabilia. She quickly retreated in the same direction from whence she appeared.

"Don't try to follow her," Matheson grumbled menacingly. "I will shoot her if I see anyone following."

I snorted. "Whatever, dude. She's not my type."

"Tell Agent Finnegan the same. Also, he'd better get used to his homeless getup. It's either that or a prison jumpsuit for him." Matheson hung up.

Goosebumps prickled the back of my neck. "Mike, you're blown. Matheson knew it was you," I said, tossing the laptop into the backpack. "He threatened to kill the girl if we follow."

"Damnit!" Mike rose and watched the last of her hat disappear from sight.

"I can see what you're thinking, Mike. Don't do it." A bad feeling came over me, and I suddenly felt very exposed. "Angus, quick. Direct us to your cameras. I want to pick them up and get the hell out of here."

# Chapter Eighteen

I drove the Mystery Machine steadily through the Washington streets with Mike at my side in the passenger seat. It was a cumbersome vehicle with blind spots the size of a city bus, and unwieldy on the narrow D.C. streets. The windshield wipers, which needed replacing, swiped intermittently to clear the lightly falling snow.

In the rear, Angus hunched over the computer, monitoring the baseball. "He's still weaving through Southeast D.C. Going in circles. Either he's looking for a parking spot or he's watching for a tail."

"Or he's passing it off to the Serbs as we speak," Mike mumbled.

"He threatened the girl's life, Mike," I said quietly so Angus wouldn't hear. "It wasn't prudent to follow her. Do you think he was bluffing?"

Mike didn't respond; instead, he pointed and said, "There's a spot."

I pulled into an illegal parking space in front of a fire hydrant along Constitution Avenue. "Are you sure about McGill?"

"No," Mike sighed. "But we've run out of options."

I shoved the shifter into park and left the motor running. "Meeting in front of the Vietnam Memorial seems . . . sketchy. Explain to me, again, why McGill didn't want you to come into the office."

"I told you, he said he had concerns about a mole. Probably the same one that tipped Matheson off four years ago." Mike stared out the windshield. "I trust the director, and I can only hope he trusts the materials we sent to him."

"How do you know McGill isn't the mole?" I couldn't help asking about the elephant in the room.

"McGill was working in San Francisco, in a different department, when we went after Matheson the first time," he said with assurance. Then, he checked his watch and twisted to look over his shoulder. "I need to move. Angus, what's he doing now?"

"Looks as though our baseball is going for a ride. He's just gotten on I-295," Angus said.

I drummed my fingers on the steering wheel. "Then I suppose it's now or never."

Mike opened his door and made a jerking motion with his head. I checked the side mirror for a break in the traffic and hopped out, joining him on the sidewalk. The snow fell in big, fat flakes. I caught one on my glove and watched it instantly melt.

Mike leaned close and whispered, "Remember the plan. If you don't hear from me within the next hour, contact Jessica on my behalf. Have Silverthorne monitor and call in Matheson's final location. I didn't mention it, but there's a reward for his capture."

"Understood." I handed him Matheson's cellphone. "I'm sorry your plan to capture Matheson didn't work. Rick told me, before he left, he thought Matheson might send a cutout."

"I considered it, too. I had hoped for better luck." He jammed his hands into his pockets. "Remember the distress signal. 'Cardinal, it's over.' If all is clear it's 'K.C., talk to me.' Got it?"

I nodded sharply. "Got it."

He leaned in and gave me a peck on the cheek. "Thanks for all your help. I couldn't have done it without you. I owe you one."

"Let's hope it worked. Good luck." I watched him lope off toward the western end of the black memorial wall engraved with the names of service members who lost their lives during

Vietnam.

A D.C. police cruiser nosed its way down Constitution Avenue. I swung into the driver's seat. "We'd better get a move on before local PD starts questioning why we're illegally parked. Where is Matheson now?"

"Still on I-295," Angus answered.

I dropped Mike's burn phone into the cupholder for easy access, saw an opening, and put my foot to the floor to enter into traffic.

"Whoa!" Angus yelped. Electronics slid around and Angus grabbed onto the rack of cables to keep from falling off his little stool. "Jesus, slow down there, Danica Patrick!"

"Sorry." I cringed. "Forgot I was driving the big rig. It won't happen again. Are you okay?"

"I'll be fine, but one of the drones fell out. Hernandez is going to be pissed if it broke," he groused.

"Aw, crap. Did it break?" I pulled to a halt behind a bright green tour bus unloading its passengers.

"No. It looks fine."

Inwardly, I sighed with relief, but Hernandez's name brought the Silverthorne plight to the forefront of my brain. "Angus? Have we heard anything from the exfil team?"

"Not yet. The baseball just got onto the beltway," Angus said, referencing Interstate 495.

"Which direction?" I checked my blind spot and cautiously moved into the center lane to go around the bus.

"South," he called. "Toward the Woodrow Wilson Bridge."

"Okay. He's headed to Virginia. Let me know if he gets off the highway before crossing the bridge."

Twenty minutes later, the metal gate opened for the van to pass through. I drove around back to the garages and pulled into the second bay. I shifted into park, and Mike's burn phone started its annoying, high-pitched ring.

"This is it." With unease, I answered, "Hello."

"K.C., talk to me!" Mike's voice boomed.

Finally, one weight lifted from my shoulders. "It's good to hear your voice. What do you know?"

"Apparently, the director has been very concerned about my safety for a few days now. I think the Chinese restaurant recording turned the tide. They've been making inquiries at hospitals and checking travel manifests in an effort to find me." His voice sounded almost effervescent.

"Great!" I turned and gave Angus the thumbs-up sign. "So, Newcomb wasn't able to get an arrest warrant? What did you tell the director about your undercover investigation?"

"Director McGill has had some rather harsh words with Agent Newcomb. Still, he's not thrilled about my off-the-grid investigation. However, with my concerns about a mole during our initial investigation, along with his own, it seems he's willing to cut me some slack." His voice quieted. "I'm fairly sure it's contingent on my ability to capture Matheson. So, I could really use some help. What have you got?"

"Hang on, I'm going to join Angus in back." I went around to the van's side door and climbed in. "Okay, I'm putting you on speakerphone."

"Tell me some good news, Angus," Mike said.

"He took a trip on the beltway and got off heading north on Route 1. He turned left into the neighborhood of Del Ray," Angus answered.

"Has he made any stops?" Mike asked.

"Nothing but red lights and stop signs." Angus adjusted his glasses. "Wait, he's taking a right on Mount Vernon Avenue."

I watched the little red dot cruise up the avenue. "What's your plan, Mike?"

"McGill is putting together a team . . ." Mike's voice cut out.

"Mike? Hello?" I picked up the phone and spoke right into

the microphone. "Hello? We lost you."

"I'm back. I was saying, the director is putting a team together now."

"He's turned left off Mount Vernon, into the neighborhood." Angus zoomed in on the map. "I think . . . this might be it. He just turned in to a driveway, and it looks as if he's parked. I'll text you the coordinates."

"Thank you, Angus," Mike said with genuine relief.

"Is there anything else I can do?" I asked.

"No. You've done a good job. Go home and get some rest," he said in a reassuring tone. "I'll tell Donovan to bill the FBI for his expenses when he returns."

The air hung silent, and no one dared speak the words rolling through our thoughts.

*If he returns.*

"Roger that. Take care." I went to press the end button. "Oh! Wait! One last thing. What's the deal with Newcomb? Where is he now?"

Mike paused before answering. "It would seem Agent Newcomb and Investigator Keller have driven up to Baltimore today. Apparently, they had intelligence that I would be meeting someone at the Fells Point today, at noon."

I couldn't help the laugh-snort that escaped.

"K.C.?" Mike drew the letters out. Angus gave me a sideways glance, but neither of us said anything as I waited for Mike to continue. "You wouldn't happen to know anything about that, would you?"

"Whatever do you mean?" My voice pitched high with innocence.

"Never mind," he mumbled. "Talk later."

****

*3 hours earlier in Karina's apartment*

I dug out my own cellphone and laid it on the counter.

Irritation swept over me. Behind my TV, lay the sneaky little bug left behind by Newcomb. Because of it, I was currently juggling three different phones, often leaving behind the one that meant the most to me. The one with all my contacts, access to email, social media, etc. Squinting, I gave some serious thought to ripping out the bug and handing it over to Mike so he could pass it along to McGill with my regards. Then I thought better of it, and a Grinch-like smile spread across my face.

I took all the phones out of my purse and dialed the bat phone with the one Mike had given me. The bat phone rang three times before I answered, "Hello? Mike, is that you?"

I then proceeded to hang up Mike's phone and have a one-sided conversation right next to my television.

"What do you mean you're in Baltimore? What are you doing there?"

Pause for dramatic effect.

"I don't understand. You need me to do what?"

I checked my nails, examining a chip in the polish on my ring finger.

"Yes. I suppose so. Fells Point Tavern? What time?"

I switched the phone to my other ear and checked my right hand for chips.

"Yes, I can be there by noon."

No chips on my right hand.

"Don't worry. I'll be careful. See you later. And I expect a full report . . . Mike? Hello? Damnit, he hung up on me."

At that point, I reached behind the television and yanked the bug from the socket.

# Chapter Nineteen

I tossed the magazine aside and strode into my bedroom only to pull up short, because I really had no reason to go there.

You'd have thought having Mike's issues straightened out would've provided relief and lowered my stress levels. To a certain extent, it did. However, by the time I'd left Silverthorne, there'd been no word from Rick and his team down in South America. I'd have liked to stay and wait for communication, but Angus hadn't been overly welcoming. He'd ignored my subtle overtures to remain—dismissing both my proposal to keep an eye on Matheson's whereabouts for him and my offer to bring him lunch. Either his social skills were nonexistent, and he didn't understand my interest in staying, or he simply wanted me out of his hair. In either case, Angus kindly escorted me to my car and, with a weird chuck on my shoulder, told me what a good sport I'd been.

I think his exact words were, "The guys were right. You're not just a pretty face. You can be downright useful for a civilian."

Before leaving, I'd wrung out a promise from him to let me know the moment they had word about the team in Venezuela.

I'd stopped at a Panera on the way home to pick up a soup and salad for lunch. During the drive, I'd convinced myself that Angus knew more than what he'd been telling me, and if it was good news, there'd be no reason for him to hustle me out the door. Therefore, when I arrived home, I found I had no appetite for the food and shoved the to-go bag in the refrigerator for later. After ten minutes of pacing and leaving a slightly panicked voice mail on Jin's phone, I'd talked myself off the ledge of anxiety and tried to quiet my mind by reading *People Magazine.*

It didn't help. The clock on my nightstand read 11:58. I went back out to the kitchen to locate the bat phone and found the black FBI bug sitting on the counter next to my purse.

My eyes narrowed. "Stupid bug."

I stomped into the guest room and pulled my toolbox out of the closet. The pink-handled hammer lay on top.

*Wham! Wham! Wham!*

Plastic fragments and electronic bits flew in different directions as the hammer decimated the listening device. It was as if I could hear Mike's sardonic voice in my ear saying, "Feel better?"

"Yes," I said aloud to imaginary Mike. Then, I scooped the pieces into a Ziploc bag and dropped it into my purse. "I feel much, much better. Thank you."

12:04 read the microwave clock.

The little voice in my head began to speak. *Why should Mike get all the glory? I played a role in finding Matheson. Why shouldn't I get to watch the takedown? Who is Michael Finnegan to pat me on the head and tell me to go rest in my bed like a swooning 1700s debutante?*

I'll admit, the "compartment" in which I'd stuffed my fears about Rick and crew was not going to stay locked up tight if I remained home alone. The only way to keep that overstuffed, filing cabinet from bursting open would be to *do* something.

I'd memorized the street address Angus sent to Mike. Del Ray wasn't that far from where I lived.

Fifteen minutes later, I found street parking a block from where Matheson was holed up in gray-and-white Cape Cod-style home. The Del Ray neighborhood was filled with houses built during the 30s, 40s, and 50s. Farmhouses and bungalows were interspersed with brick Colonials and Tudor-styles. Its convenience to the Pentagon and train stations into D.C. make it a desirable if pricey location to live for government workers. Thousand square foot homes ran in the $900,000 to $1.5 million range and rarely stayed on the market for long. A dusting of snow covered the grass and shrubs, giving the neighborhood a nice winter wonderland feel, but the temp was high enough to keep it from sticking to the street and sidewalks. I considered this the perfect snow—pretty without involving shoveling.

The curbs were low to the ground. I easily rolled the passenger side tires onto the curb, turned off the car, and climbed into the passenger seat. Parking this way gave me a better visual angle of the perp's house. I didn't see any activity and figured I'd beat the FBI. Not knowing how long it might take them to raid the joint, I'd smartly brought along my lunch and proceeded to lay my picnic across the dash next to a pair of binoculars. Agave lemonade sat in one of the cupholders while an origami lotus blossom resided in the other—the gift Gi made for me.

By the time I finished the soup course, things began to happen. A black SUV and two dark sedans with government plates rushed up the street and screeched to a halt in front of the house.

"Aaaannnddd here we go, boys and girls." I took a sip of lemonade.

Agents dressed in black bulletproof vests with bright yellow FBI letters slapped across the back exited the vehicles. Two had shotguns, the rest carried handguns. I counted eight in all. Neither Mike nor the director were among them. Four went around back, three went through the front, and one guy stayed near the SUV with a walkie-talkie in hand. I rolled down the window and stuck my head out, listening for gunshots, or even shouting.

Nothing.

The vehicles remained in the road, but there was no sign of the agents.

A man in khakis and a black jacket walked past me carrying a

7-11 sack and messing with his phone. There was a slight hitch in his gait. A hiccup. My brows drew together, and I focused the binoculars on him. He'd gone about twenty yards before he noticed the vehicles in the street. When he looked up from the phone he came to a hard stop. He made a tentative step backward, then a quick pivot. The sack dropped to the ground, and he took off, glancing over his shoulder as he ran down the sidewalk.

My jaw dropped at his precipitous actions. I couldn't be positive, but my Spidey sense went on high alert. He was of similar height to Mike, with a pointy chin and a brown-haired, receding hairline. A watered-down version of Mike. And he was headed my way. Cursing myself for leaving the stun gun at home, I realized I had no weapon except the binoculars. When he drew near, I did the only thing I could think of—I threw open the door.

My actions caught him off guard, and the man was too close to course correct. He crashed into the car door at full tilt, bounced off, and landed on his butt. The impact slammed the door shut, and, by the time I got out of the car, he was back on his feet.

Recognition flared across his features. Those beady eyes turned to slits, and he hissed, "You!" His hands took aim at my throat, and he came at me.

Putting my defense training into use, I deftly dodged to the side, placed my hands on his back, and bending him forward brought my knee toward his gut. However, my aim was too low, and I nailed him right in the fruit basket.

The following events happened in almost instantaneous succession. The gunshots I'd been waiting to hear finally occurred. The first one spanged off a nearby parking sign, and the next one splintered my back window. The man I attacked, grabbed his junk, and crumpled to the ground. Out of the corner of my eye, I spotted a white vehicle driving unhurriedly down the street. A long black rifle barrel stuck out of the passenger window. Realization hit me like a punch from Mike Tyson. The shots weren't coming from the FBI ahead of me, but behind, and I was in the line of fire. Letting out a screech, I dove through the open car door, and slithered down onto the floorboard, doing my level best to cram myself beneath the dash. Glass exploded above me. I covered my head with my hands and squeezed my eyes shut.

An engine revved. Tires squealed. More gunshots, different kinds—maybe handguns. Yelling. Then the sickening thud of metal against metal. Another thud. A weird creaking sound. The man on the ground next to my car moaned.

Someone from afar shouted, "MOVE! MOVE! THE POLE IS COMING DOWN!"

Then a cracking crash, and the zipping of electrical sparks rent the air.

I wasn't sure how long I stayed there, jammed in my little hidey hole, shaking and whimpering, before I heard my name.

"Karina? Karina? Are you okay? Fuck! I can't reach her. Move him out of the way." Strong hands grasped my forearms. "Karina! Talk to me!"

They say the olfactory system is our strongest sensory system. The mix of his leather coat and sandalwood soap filtered through to my brain before the voice.

"Rick? Is that you?" I allowed him to drag my arms up. Unfolding myself and tripping out of the car like a new foal, I followed my arms into his embrace. "Rick?"

He crushed me to his chest. "Jesus Christ. I thought . . . I didn't want to think."

"What are you doing here?" I mumbled into his neck.

A breath of laughter ruffled my hair. "I should be asking you the same question. Mike said he told you to go home."

"I did go h-home . . . it was b-boring. And n-nobody . . . tell me wh-what happening . . . with you or M-Matheson." I wasn't sure how much Rick caught; my voice shook along with my body. Actually, I wasn't sure I was speaking in coherent sentences.

"It's alright. I've got you. Deep breaths. Come on now, *pequeña ave*. You're okay." Rick proceeded to croon platitudes over my head and rub my back. The leather from his coat crimpled against my ear.

I followed his instructions and began to concentrate on breathing. In. Count to five. Out. Slowly, the shaking dissipated.

"That's better." His arms loosened, and I was able to step back to assess what was happening around me.

The man I hit with the car door, whom I assumed was Terrance Matheson, moaned, his hands around his family jewels as Jin sat him upright against my car.

"Oh, my nuts," he moaned, his eyes closed tight in pain.

Jin pulled a pair of flexi-cuffs out of an inside pocket of his dark brown, pin-striped suit. After assessing Matheson for a moment, he took pity on him and cuffed his hands in front. Then he stood above his captive, at parade rest, his gaze trained on the action happening at the far end of the street.

The white SUV, that I'd seen in my periphery, had crashed into a maroon sedan parked on the street. Both vehicles were now crushed beneath a wooden utility pole, and heavy black wires lay in the middle of the street. The FBI agent, who I'd seen outside with the walkie-talkie, was on the ground. Two of his comrades hovered over him, giving first aid. Bystanders gathered on their porch stoops and front yards. Three agents were trying to access the occupants of the SUV, while another shooed the bystanders back into their homes. The last agent was in the front yard of Matheson's house, speaking animatedly on her cellphone.

A fire engine, followed by an ambulance, roared up the street, halting before getting too close to the electrical wires. Two police cars arrived on scene.

"Jin, why don't you go liaise with the FBI? I'm not sure they're aware we have their suspect," Rick directed.

Without a word, Jin took off down the street.

"Holy schmoley. What the hell happened?" I murmured.

Using two fingers, Rick pointed out each area as he dispassionately described the incident. "When we arrived, someone in the SUV was shooting at your car. The agent you see on the ground returned fire. The gunman turned his sights on the agent and shot him twice. Additional agents came running out of the house, fired back, and hit the driver. The SUV swerved, slammed into the parked car, and both vehicles plowed into the telephone pole."

"Hey, Matheson." I kicked his foot, his eyes popped open, and he groaned. "Who was shooting at you?"

He grimaced. "Serbians. They must have found out the FBI was on to me."

Rick's gaze narrowed at the groaning heap at his feet. "Who tipped them off?"

"Someone on the inside. I never knew his name." Matheson squeezed his eyes shut, slid to the ground on his right side, and curled up in a fetal position. "Oof."

"Better?" I asked.

"I need ice," he whined.

"You should be thanking me," I suggested. "If you hadn't run into my door, one of those bullets would've taken your head off." I indicated the parking sign that sported a new bullet hole right where Matheson's head would've been if he hadn't collapsed to the ground after I'd kneed him.

Matheson didn't see; his eyes were shut tight again. "Thanks, lady," he muttered sarcastically.

"Whose house is that?" I indicated with my chin. "The blonde's?"

"Nooo. It's in foreclooosure." He drew out his Os like a dying calf.

I had no idea empty houses were such a magnet for squatters. "Is the blonde helping you? Is she the one with the computer skills?"

His head rocked back and forth. "No, no. Daughter of my mistress. She needed money for college. I gave her fifty thou to make the exchange."

I scrunched my nose and frowned. No one had told me his mistress had a kid. Poor thing. "Would you have shot her?"

"No," he grunted. "I didn't want you to follow. You did anyway. You're better than I thought."

"We put a tracker inside the baseball."

He let out a primal groan and cried, "You ruined it."

I figured Matheson deserved to wallow in his misery, but apparently Rick didn't care for his dying calf impression. "It's a fake, you dumb shit. Stop with the theatrics already."

Another fire engine arrived, along with more police. Red lights strobed off the surrounding houses like a warehouse rave. At the end of the block, two black government sedans parked perpendicular to the street, effectively cutting off traffic. Police began cordoning off the area with crime scene tape. More people from neighboring blocks gathered to ogle and gawk.

We watched as Jin initially got the wave-off from a police officer, but after a bit of discussion, the officer changed his tune and escorted Jin to the FBI. A conversation with a pair of agents ensued, along with finger pointing in our direction. A moment later Jin, escorted by three agents, strode our way. Two of the agents were men of average height—a bald African American and a fiftyish man with salt-and-pepper hair. They followed behind Jin and a blonde with a ponytail and aviator glasses. She reminded me of the actress Mary McCormack. We'd met before.

Her name popped up from my memory banks just as they arrived. "Agent Reinhart, right? I believe we met during the Naftali Rivkin incident."

She eyed me. "Karina Cardinal."

"You remembered." I grinned.

Neither of us put out a friendly hand. Much like our last meeting, a bunch of crazy shit had just gone down, with me in the midst of it. Come to think of it, Silverthorne had been at our prior meeting, as well. Additionally, Rick still held a strong arm around my waist, and I would've had to step out of his comforting embrace to shake her hand. I was still unsteady and using Rick as my crutch.

"It's not a name to easily forget," she replied.

I made the introductions. "You've met Jin, and this is Rick."

"Yes, I remember them, too." Reinhart gave a brief nod, removed her shades, and crouched down to get a look at our captive. "It's Matheson. Get him up. Put him in Agent Lewis's vehicle."

I guessed she wasn't up for introducing her colleagues, and I didn't press the matter. The two male agents each took an arm and helped Matheson get to his feet. The money launderer bleated pitifully.

Agent Reinhart's attention returned to me. "What happened to him?"

I shrugged. "Wasn't watching where he was going. Ran into my car door." In *sotto voce*, I added, "He might need some ice for his doodads."

Jin coughed. Rick's arm tightened around my waist.

Agent Reinhart slipped the shades back on. "We'll need a statement."

"No problem, Agent," Rick responded.

"Hope you weren't planning on using your car any time soon. A crime scene investigator will need to tag and photograph it." She smirked.

I'd been dreading it. Avoiding it. For the first time, I turned to see the destruction of Old Bessie. The rear and driver's side windows were destroyed, and glass peppered the seats. My salad seemed to have exploded; lettuce interspersed with the glass and seemed permanently fused to the windshield. Bullet holes skimmed across the hood. I could only imagine what the door and front panel of the driver's side looked like. The passenger headrest was torn to bits. Foam spewed out of the tattered gray cloth. A hole the circumference of my thumb marred the glovebox. My heartbeat raced.

"Jesus," I murmured.

The glovebox—centimeters from where I'd cowered beneath it.

It started with a ringing in my ears that got louder. Someone said my name—maybe Agent Reinhart. My hands felt heavy, and I couldn't lift them. Then the tunnel vision began. Blackness loomed around the edges. My head seemed to fill with air. I'd felt this one other time, and I knew what was coming.

From far away, my voice said, "Rick?"

****

My extremities tingled as I came back to consciousness. The ringing receded. Then I was aware of light from behind my closed lids. It felt as if I were on a rocking ship. One arm wrapped beneath my knees and another around my back. The leather creaked against my arm.

"I'm taking her to the hospital. Jin, hand me her purse." Rick's voice reverberated against my ear.

"I can have the paramedics check her out," Reinhart offered.

"Forget it. They're trapped in there, and they'll be dealing with your agent and the car beneath the pole. My vehicle is around the corner. It's not blocked in. Yet." He hitched me up and started moving.

"We're going to need to question her," Reinhart called.

"Later!"

I forced my eyes open and whispered, "Wait."

His jaw was set, and his long strides didn't stop.

With each jarring step, the brain fog subsided. I tried again in a firm tone, "Rick, stop."

He finally looked down at me, but his steps didn't falter. "Karina?"

"Back with the living. Sorry, that was a particularly useless thing for me to do."

He kept walking.

"You can put me down."

Ignoring my suggestion, he continued his pace. "You're bleeding from your head. You may have a concussion. I'm taking you to the hospital to get checked out."

"I'm bleeding?" I touched an area around my side part that felt sore and pulled my fingers away to find them covered with congealed blood. "Did I fall down? Didn't you catch me?" I asked in an accusing tone.

"I caught you," he reassured. "I'm afraid you were grazed by a bullet." We arrived at a black SUV, one of the Silverthorne fleet vehicles. "Can you open it?" He leaned down, so I could reach the handle.

I obliged. With the door open, he gently placed me in the front seat and put my handbag at my feet. I grabbed the sleeve of his jacket to stop him from closing the door. "Rick. Stop. It's just a superficial cut from a piece of glass."

That was when I noticed more shards rooted in my coat sleeve. I plucked one off and flicked it to the ground. Rick grabbed the hand that I'd used to flick the sliver away and rotated it. Scratches crisscrossed the flesh, and there might have been some tiny crystals embedded in there, too. "Okay. I'll go. But only"—I held up a finger—"if you give me a debrief on the way there."

"Deal." He slammed the door and strode around to the driver's side. "What do you want to know?"

"Wait." I peered over my shoulder. "Where's Jin? Isn't he coming?"

"He's staying behind with the FBI. I'll have him take care of your car. If they release it." He mumbled the last. The SUV roared to life.

"Not sure there's much to take care of, except to get it to a junkyard," I sighed, buckling my seat belt. "It may be time to get a new car."

We pulled away from the curb. "I support that idea 100 percent." Rick spun the wheel, making a three-point turn, and drove in the opposite direction of the crime scene.

"Yeah, yeah." I waved a hand at him. "I've been out of my mind with worry. Tell me what happened in Venezuela. Did everyone get home safely?"

"Hernandez has a broken leg with a compound fracture, a broken collarbone, and a couple of cracked ribs."

"Jeez. I'm glad he's alive, but, wow. It'll take months to recover from those injuries. What about the Talley guy?" I reclined the seat two notches and let go of the tension in my shoulders. It was such a relief to be in his company again, even if it wasn't under auspicious circumstances. I felt as if I could breathe again.

"Our client went into a diabetic coma," Rick stated grimly.

"Oh, good Lord." My head rolled to the left. "Did you get him to a hospital in time? Will he recover?"

"Joshua delivered hydration and insulin as soon as we were able." Rick stopped at a red light. "A Navy hospital ship is docked off the coast of Colombia, helping Venezuelan refugees. We were able to get the men onboard for medical assistance."

"And?"

He didn't respond. The light turned green and the SUV pulled through the intersection.

"Rick?"

"We don't know if he's suffered brain damage or other permanent damage to his organs," Rick replied in a hard tone.

"They stabilized him, and Talley shipped him to a hospital in Houston."

Knowing how Rick took the world on his shoulders, I had no doubt he blamed himself for the entire incident. I slumped down and asked in a small voice, "When will you know?"

"Within the next forty-eight hours."

I knew they weren't helping, but I couldn't stop asking questions. "Where is Hernandez?"

"Still aboard the ship. They had to operate on his leg. I left Joshua behind to keep an eye on him."

I shook my head, staring into the middle distance. The anxiety of the last twenty-four hours had me asking, "What took so long? Why didn't Angus or Jin report to me this morning? Was I not to be informed?"

Rick's fingers clenched tight, but he replied in a level tone, "Our SAT phone was damaged, and I didn't have a secure line to contact the office."

"I see. Why didn't you call from the ship?" I made an effort to keep all semblance of an accusatory tone out of my voice.

His fingers relaxed. "I didn't go aboard the ship."

My brows scrunched together in confusion. "I don't understand. You just said Hernandez and the Talley guy were taken to the ship."

"With Joshua," he clarified. "I didn't go."

I let that hang for a few minutes before asking, "I'll bite—where did you go?"

"I had to drop off a package to some DEA agents in Panama City." He let out a yawn.

"What kind of package?"

No answer.

"Drugs?"

"No."

I waited. "C'mon. Clearly, you made a deal with DEA. Intel?

Did they help you retrieve Hernandez and the Talley guy?"

Rick gave me the side-eye. "Did Angus say something to you?"

"No. I live in D.C. I know how the politics work. What did you have to give the DEA?"

"I helped them capture a Columbian drug lord." He mic-dropped the statement.

I sucked wind. "Which one?"

"I can't say."

That didn't stop my questions. "Was he on your way to the rescue? Or a side mission?"

"On the way."

"I see." I looked him over. Really looked. His eyes were taut and red-rimmed, his face drawn with a weariness about it that I hadn't noticed before. He hadn't shaved, and his impeccable posture transformed into a slouch. My heart contracted and I whispered, "When was the last time you slept?"

He took a pair of sunglasses out of the cupholder and slid them on his face. "I got about twenty minutes on the flight home from Florida."

"When did you land?"

"An hour and a half ago."

Cripes. He'd just returned home from hell and . . . "Wait a minute." I jerked the seat upright. "How did you end up here?"

His jaw flexed. "I ended up here because Michael called me in a panic when he couldn't locate you. He said you'd gone dark, and he was worried you might have a new hairbrained scheme surrounding Matheson that might get you in trouble. Clearly, he wasn't wrong."

I deserved that and shrunk lower in my seat. "I was only watching from afar. It's not my fault Matheson slipped out to the 7-11 for lunch without anybody knowing."

"Why didn't you answer your phone?"

"I left my cell at home. Why didn't he call me on the phone he gave me?" My voice was a bit pitchy and defensive.

"He did." The two words dropped like anvils.

"Really?" I snatched the bag at my feet and dug around until I found Mike's phone. "Oh. It's dead. I forgot to charge it." I grimaced. "Why didn't *you* call the bat phone?"

"The bat phone?"

"The one you gave me."

"I did."

"Uh . . ." I located the second phone and checked. There were four missed calls and half a dozen texts. "Oops." I slid farther down and whispered, "It was on vibrate."

"Luckily, you had it turned on. We were able to track your location."

"Well, that's convenient." I dropped my chin down low.

"Yes. It was," he said in a no-nonsense tone. "Jin and I raced across town, only to find you in the midst of a shootout at the O.K. Corral. I'm fairly certain, I lost a year off my life in the moments it took to get from my car to yours." He paused then murmured, "I thought you'd been shot."

I gulped and said in a timid voice, "Uh, sorry?"

"The thing is,"—he shook his head in disbelief—"Jin and I did nothing. You'd already incapacitated the bad guy. I have a feeling you would have been just fine even if we hadn't shown up. It's uncanny. You're like a cat with nine lives," he snapped.

"Well . . . now you understand how worried *I've* been about *you*." I wanted the declaration to come out with sharp self-righteousness. Instead, it came out as a bald statement.

We came to a halt behind a line of cars, and his hands tightened around the steering wheel, again. "You needn't have worried."

I straightened and my chin came up. "What if I said those exact words back to you? Would it have stopped you from worrying?"

"No," he breathed.

Turning to stare out the passenger window, I said, "I tried your compartmentalization thing, while you were gone. I don't think I'm very good at it. When I wasn't running possible scenarios of how our meeting with Matheson could go sideways, I was dreaming up all sorts of horrible deaths scenes *you* might be facing. I have a colorful imagination and some of them were fairly gruesome."

He didn't respond.

"You and the rest of the boys, of course," I amended.

The snow started up, and Rick flipped on the wipers. The flakes were small, no longer floating like their fat counterparts, the wind blew them at the windshield like an industrial fan.

"I'm not used to having someone worry over me," he said quietly.

I drew in a sharp breath. Ahead of us, the light turned green.

"Your hand is bleeding again," he commented, then eased forward as the line of cars moved.

I glanced at my left hand resting on the console; a trickle of blood oozed down my thumb. "I must have scraped off a fresh scab when I was searching through my purse." I reached into a side pocket of my handbag, pulled out a tissue, and wiped away the sticky fluid. "Speaking of . . . could we *not* go to the hospital? There's an urgent care clinic a mile away. I don't think I need stitches, and they can do it if I do," I pleaded.

"You might need an MRI." Rick let out an enormous yawn.

"Don't be ridiculous. It's just a cut from a piece of glass. They poured down on me like the fountains at the Bellagio."

He sighed. "You're going to continue to argue with me about this, aren't you?"

"I'm going to get out at the next red light, and call an Uber to take me home, if you don't take me to the urgent care place."

He didn't seem to have the energy to argue further. "Fine."

I grinned. "Turn right at the next light. It'll be three blocks up on the left."

"Please use the bat phone to contact Mike."

"Didn't anyone call him?"

"I told Jin to do it," Rick said through another yawn.

"Then he knows." I stared out the window.

We came to a halt at a stop sign. I could feel Rick's eyes on me. The SUV didn't move forward.

"What?" I turned to meet his stare.

Rick didn't respond. The car behind us honked.

"Fine!" The horn honked again, this time longer, in irritation. "I'm calling. I'm dialing the phone. Just go!"

We jerked ahead, and Rick's mouth curved upward.

The phone went directly to voice mail. "Hi. It's me. Hip hooray, your bad guy was captured. I didn't see you at the scene, so I figure Leon is either hiding you for safety, or he threw you into a hole, and you're being interrogated with a rubber hose by one of your own. Either case, I'm fine. There was some broken glass at the crime scene, and I'm headed to urgent care with Rick. I'm in good hands. Talk later."

"You got off easy." He smirked.

"Yeah, well, normally I don't, so I won't look that gift horse in the mouth."

# Chapter Twenty

Three hours later, Rick and I entered my condo complex. The elevator doors opened and out trotted my neighbor Mrs. Thundermuffin, with her leashed cat. She wore a brown 60s throwback fur hat, a blocked, multicolor leather coat that ended at her calves, and a pair of golden combat boots. Long ago, I'd determined I wanted to be Mrs. Thundermuffin when I grew up. She liked to put on airs of a slightly dotty eccentric, but I'd come to realize it was an act, and there was quite a bit more going on behind that innocent blue gaze of hers.

"Hi, Mrs. Thundermuffin, I didn't know you'd returned from Florida." I leaned down to give her a light hug and air kisses.

"Got in last night. Brr. I think I should've stayed another week." She pulled her coat tighter.

"How is your sister doing?" I asked.

"She's . . . doing okay." Mrs. Thundermuffin's hesitant response didn't surprise me. Last summer, she flew down to Mexico to rescue her thief of a nephew from an artifact forger and his thuggish brothers and ended up being held hostage herself. Craig, the nephew, was currently doing time in federal prison on multiple charges. She took in my bandaged hands. "What happened?"

"Oh, nothing. Just some broken glass. Have you met my friend Rick Donovan? Rick, this is Mrs. Thundermuffin."

They shook hands.

"Call me Milly. I believe we've met before."

"Yes, ma'am." His drawn face barely pulled into tight smile, and I realized he was dead on his feet.

"Well, we don't want to keep you and Mr. Tibbs from your walk." I pressed the elevator button. "The snow has started falling again. You'd better get out there before it sticks to the sidewalks."

"Come by for tea and we'll catch up." Her combat boots squeaked across the vinyl tile as she headed to the front doors.

I pressed the button for the fifth floor and checked my watch. "See? I told you urgent care was better. If we'd gone to the hospital, we'd still be filling out paperwork. And . . . I didn't even need stitches." The attending doctor had cleaned my head wound and used medical glue. He'd plucked a bunch of slivers of glass out of my hands, then the nurse cleaned and bandaged them. I checked out with instructions for taking care of the wounds and directions to use ibuprofen or acetaminophen for pain. Really, the bruises on my shoulder and knee from Josh's takedown at the stadium were more tender than the new injuries.

Rick blinked and rubbed his eyes. "Was your neighbor walking a cat? On a leash? In gold combat boots?"

I grinned. "Yes. That was Mr. Tibbs. Stick around. Maybe we'll run into my other neighbor, Jasper, walking his lizard on a leash."

"You've got some colorful people living here."

"Someday, I'll tell you the story about the guy who dropped acid and ran down our halls buck naked because he thought he was being chased by a dragon."

His eyes closed tight, and he shook his head. "I'm not sure I want to know." Rick followed me to my apartment and waited in the doorway while I turned off the alarm. "I'd better get back to the office and check in."

"What? Oh, um . . . would you mind coming in for a few minutes? I'm . . . I'm not ready to be alone. Just for a little bit."

I knew two things. First, when he wasn't demanding updates from the medical staff about my injuries, Rick had been on the phone for a good portion of the time we'd been at the urgent care clinic and was up to date on Silverthorne's activities. Second, he was such a good guy, he wouldn't deny my direct request after such a traumatic event.

"Sure." He shut the door and shrugged out of his coat.

"Can I get you something to drink? Water? Soda? Wine?"

"Water."

I poured him a glass, took it into the bedroom, and set it on the bedside table. Rick stood in the doorway with his arms akimbo and a quizzically raised brow. "Karina?"

"I need to lie down for a few minutes, or I'm going to drop on the floor. Can you lie next to me?" I patted the bed. "This isn't an invitation. I just need . . . a warm body nearby. You know, for . . . comfort. Feel free to leave after I fall asleep."

"Sure." He unlaced and toed off his Timberland boots and stretched out on his back.

"Thanks." I curled on my side, facing him, and drew up the soft chenille blanket at the foot of my bed.

My plan worked. It only took eleven minutes for Rick to fall asleep. He breathed deep and evenly, and his face was slack in vulnerable repose.

"Rick?" I said in a normal tone.

Nothing.

I pulled the soft blanket up to his chin, closed the blinds, and silently left the room. Though I was fatigued, it was nothing compared to what Rick must have endured in the past forty-eight hours. The poor thing was practically a walking zombie, and, frankly, I was worried about him falling asleep behind the wheel. My own brain still hadn't stopped spinning from the day's events, and likely wouldn't wind down until later tonight. There was no way I'd get to sleep.

I figured I'd catch up on anything I'd missed and called Jin.

He answered on the third ring. "Go for Jin."

"Hi, Jin. Just wanted to let you know I'm fine. We're back at my place, and Rick is taking a nap. He's not near his phone, so if there's an emergency, call me and I'll wake him. Is there anything going on?" I turned on the TV to a twenty-four-hour news network and left the volume on low.

"Nothing I can't handle. I'm still on scene."

"Any word on the Talley guy or Hernandez?" I dropped the remote on the couch and plopped down next to it.

"Angus said our Talley man is awake. They're running tests to evaluate the damage. I haven't heard from Josh on Hernandez's condition."

"Be sure to send my best when Josh calls."

"What about you? What's the verdict? Concussion?" Jin asked.

"Nothing like that. I didn't even need stitches. They patched me up and sent me on my way."

A reporter came on with the graphics "FBI Bust" on the lower part of the screen. I recognized the Del Ray neighborhood as the camera zoomed in on the downed telephone pole. "What do I need to do about my car? Is the FBI taking it in for evidence?"

"They're still processing the crime scene. I removed your CDs and EZ Pass transponder, so they won't be stolen. Is there anything else I should get?"

Jin was so efficient. What would I do without him? "There's an emergency kit in the trunk. You'll find a button in the glove box to open the trunk. Also, there should be an ice scraper under the driver's seat. Oh, and I left Gi's lotus flower behind. If it's not damaged, can you get that for me?"

"Yes, I'll take care of it," he assured me.

"Thanks, Jin. I'll contact the FBI to find out when I can fetch the car."

"You'll need to have it towed. I checked under your hood.

Some of the bullets penetrated the transmission and engine block. If you . . ." A siren drowned out what he was saying, and I only caught the tail end. ". . . your insurance company."

I sighed. "You're right. I'll do that as soon as we get off. Can you take some photos and send them to me?"

"Will do. Also, Mike wants you to give him a call."

No surprise. Mike had left two messages while I was at urgent care. "Yes, I'll do that. How are you getting back to the office?"

"Sonia's here. She'll take me back."

"Okay, thanks again."

I poured myself a glass—a very full glass—of cabernet before making my next call.

"Karina? Is that you?"

"The one and only." I stretched out with my feet on the coffee table.

"What the hell were you thinking?" Mike admonished.

I took a long drink of wine and realized how lucky I'd been that Rick, and not Mike, found me in Del Ray. Had Mike been the one to discover my presence, he would have rained down recriminations all over my head. Which I probably would have deserved. And then he would have disregarded my wishes and shoved me into an ambulance. Not that I thought Rick approved of my methods, but he simply had a different manner of dealing with my antics. Frankly, Rick was more willing to give me the benefit of the doubt.

"K.C.? Are you there?"

"I am. And I will only remain on the phone if you change your tone and your accusatory manner."

"Fine," he ground out. "Would you please tell me why you found it necessary to go over to where Matheson took the baseball?"

"I simply wanted to watch the takedown. How was I supposed to know it would turn into a shitshow?" I replied, full of innocence.

"How would you know . . ." I could picture Mike shaking his head. "Never mind. Donovan told me you had a head wound. Are you okay?"

*Et tu*, Richard? "I'm just fine. A piece of glass cut my scalp. It wasn't deep. The doctor used medical glue." I touched the hardened adhesive. "I think my biggest concern is how I'm going to shampoo my hair."

"What about your car? I heard it looks like Swiss cheese."

Another long swallow. "I suppose I'll be getting a new one. I've got to call the insurance company when I get off with you. Do you know if the FBI plans to take it for evidence?"

"I don't know. Let me write a note to find out." There was a pause while he presumably wrote himself a note. "Did you really knock Matheson down with your car door?"

I swirled the wine around the bulbous glass and drew in the bouquet. "I really did."

"You know, there's a reward for his capture."

"Excellent. Where's my check?" The news network had transitioned to a story about an earthquake in Indonesia. I flipped to a local news channel where they were reporting the weather. It took me a moment to realize Mike didn't respond to my comment. "Earth to Mike. I was kidding."

"I wasn't joking. I'm writing another note to see what I can do."

My eyes widened in surprise. "Wow. That would be great." I sipped more wine. "Tell me about Newcomb. Did he enjoy his trip to Baltimore?"

"What did you do?"

I couldn't help the malevolent chuckle that escaped. "Nothing illegal. I simply had a conversation—with myself—near the bug he planted."

Mike gave a snort. "Whatever you said, it kept him out of our business. Keller is cooperating with us. Apparently, Newcomb made a call when he realized they'd been sent on a wild goose chase."

"What kind of call?"

"The kind you make on a disposable phone. Keller sent us to the trash can where Newcomb dropped it. There was only one call made on it."

My feet dropped off the coffee table, and I sat up. "Don't tell me . . . he called the Serbs."

"Bingo."

"Wow. Just . . . wow." My feet went back up onto the coffee table. "What happens now?"

"OPR is investigating him."

*OPR? Where have I heard that acronym?* "That's your internal affairs, right?"

"Right. We found a computer at his home and a numbered account in the Caymans with transactions going back for years. Oh, and he also didn't have permission to bug your apartment or monitor your phone."

"Sounds as though you found your mole." I held my glass up in a silent salute.

"I'm facing some disciplinary actions myself, but with McGill's help, it looks as if I'll get off with a slap on the wrist."

"Good for you."

"I owe you, big time."

I stopped sipping my wine, and my voice became serious. "One day, Michael Finnegan, I'll come looking for that favor, and I expect you to pay up."

He gave a hearty laugh.

"I'm not kidding."

The laughter stopped.

"Gotta go. Bye," I said and hung up.

Before calling my insurance company, I checked on Rick. It

didn't look as though he'd moved an inch. His arms were still crossed over his chest, breathing was deep and even, and his face was slack, at peace.

The call to my insurance company took the better part of an hour. A very nice lady named Vera with a midwestern twang gave me plenty of sympathy for my bullet-riddled car. I emailed her the photos Jin had texted to me. But, because of the age of the car and the damage to the transmission and engine block, Vera said the insurance company would call it a total loss. She chirpily assured me that a paltry check for three thousand dollars would be coming my way in the coming weeks. Then she kindly arranged a rental car for me.

Around seven thirty, I rustled up a salad and grilled cheese sandwich for dinner. Rick slept on and, since I hadn't heard from Jin, I saw no reason to wake him. I spent the next two hours responding to emails so there would be less to catch up on at work tomorrow. After the emails, I flipped to HGTV. By ten, I could barely keep my eyes open.

Rick had turned on his side and slept peacefully. I brushed my teeth, put on a pair of pajamas, and crawled beneath the covers. I'll admit, when I'd fantasized about getting into bed with Rick, this wasn't what I'd had in mind.

# Chapter Twenty-One

The B-52s yelling "Love Shack!" blasted me awake at six. It took a moment for my brain to clear and determine the day. *Tuesday.* Which meant work. I rolled over to find the bed empty of my overnight guest. I'd checked my calendar before going to bed last night and knew there were no breakfast meetings on the calendar for today, which meant it allowed me some extra time. I hit the snooze button and snuggled deeper beneath the comforter.

The scent of the nectar of the gods had me opening my eyes again. Light trickled through the crack beneath the door, and I realized my visitor might still be here. Throwing off the covers, I drew on my robe and padded into the main living area.

Rick wore the same jeans and Henley shirt as yesterday but had clearly showered and shaved. He was typing on his phone at the kitchen counter with a cup of coffee and empty plate at his elbow.

"What time did you wake up?" I yawned and shuffled to the coffee pot, drawn like a bee to her hive.

"Just after four thirty."

"You got a little over twelve hours of sleep. You must have needed it." The dark brew sloshed into my favorite yellow smiley face mug, leaving just enough room for cream and sugar.

"I don't know when the last time was, I slept so long and so deep."

I watched him over the lip of the cup. "Maybe it was the company."

"Honestly, I think it was the mattress," he replied sheepishly. "I woke without a single body ache. Can you tell me the brand?"

*Such a romantic.* I rolled my eyes but couldn't blame him. My own sleep improved greatly after it was installed. "I bought it last year. I'll get the specs for you."

"Thanks. I showered in your guest bathroom and found a razor in the medicine cabinet." He rubbed his clean-shaven jaw and delivered a smile. "I hope you don't mind."

A vision of Rick, naked, in my shower came to mind, and I got a rush.

"Oh, and the bathroom door wouldn't close properly, but I found your tools in the closet and fixed it."

*Fixed it?* My brain speed was too slow for the amount of data in front of me. It paused to buffer.

"I also made some eggs." He indicated the empty plate. "Would you like me to make you some?"

Buffering.

When I didn't answer, he snapped his fingers. "Karina? Are you in there? Eggs?"

My thoughts finally caught up to the live stream. I glanced away from the handsome specimen in my kitchen and sucked down a gulp of java. "No thanks. I tend to run on coffee in the morning. Sometimes I'll add a bagel or toast just to shake things up. Anything new on the Silverthorne front?" I tilted my chin toward his phone and leaned against the island. "Yesterday, you were dead on your feet. It seemed, you needed the sleep, and I didn't have the heart to wake you," I explained. "I told Jin to call me if there was an emergency and you were needed. I never heard anything. I figured no news was good news."

"Nothing earth-shattering. I've got some paperwork I need to catch up on." He put his phone down. "Hernandez will be released in a few days and start his trek home."

My brows went up. "Trek?"

"He can't fly. Too risky after surgery. We've acquired passage for him on a ship bound for Norfolk."

Wow. Rick really did have connections. "What about the Talley guy?"

"Things are looking good. We'll know more by the end of the week." He downed the last dregs of his coffee.

"Good to hear. I was wondering . . . how did they get captured to begin with? Overwhelming force? Was this a well-planned kidnapping?" I couldn't help the slight cringe that went with my question. *Is it callous of me to ask?*

Rick frowned. "More like dumb luck for the kidnappers. The pair of Talley men snuck off to find cigarettes without their security. Hernandez was doing a perimeter check when he saw them outside of the gates. He called for backup and ran out. The kidnappers must have been watching the refinery, waiting for the right moment to strike. They took advantage of an opening and were gone before the rest of the team started the Land Rovers."

I studied Rick. The tension around his eyes had dissipated and the weight of the world no longer lay quite so heavy on his broad shoulders. My own worries had also dissipated. Mike's situation was resolved, or in the process of it. The Silverthorne team would be returning safely to home base in the coming days. And Rick sat in my kitchen, freshly showered and clean shaven, with a cup of coffee in his hand, sharing much more about the op than I'd ever expected. As a matter of fact, I cocked my head, it was a little out of character.

"What? Why are you looking at me like that?"

"I'm surprised you told me all of this. Normally you play your cards close to the vest. I don't get much more than monosyllables out of you."

Sighing, he slid off the stool and refilled his coffee. "Joshua told me I needed to be more open with you."

"Josh is a smart man." I ran a finger around the lip of my

mug. "That still doesn't explain why you told me about the Talley exfil to begin with."

He sipped thoughtfully. "What if I told you my reasons were twofold?"

"Go on."

"I'm trying to be more open with you," he sighed and stared down at his Timberlands. "And . . . I didn't rule out the possibility that we might need your help."

My empty palm went up in a "you lost me" manner. "My help?"

"Your contacts on the Hill. And the FBI."

*So, he did listen to me.* "Are you saying I was your last line of defense?"

"I knew if things went sideways, you'd raise hell." He ran his thumb down my cheek and a delicate tingle coursed down my spine. "You wouldn't stop until we were found or dead."

I licked my lips. "Uh, I didn't know you had that kind of confidence in me."

"I'm so confident in your doggedness to help your friends, I believe that, given the opportunity, you'd have stowed away on a military C-130 bound for South America." Rick's intense silvery gaze speared me like a swordfish.

I think I stopped breathing.

"I feel lucky to count myself among those people in your life."

*Oh, he's good.* I waited, my tongue caught between my teeth, for him to move in for a kiss.

He didn't.

Discomfited, I glanced away and made an effort to diffuse the tensity. "Pshaw. Besides, I would've flown commercial."

His features relaxed. "You need to realize there are still things I can't reveal. Ever."

"I get it." Nodding, I gulped more coffee.

The silence stretched, and I finally broke it to ask, "So, where are you taking me on our date?"

He frowned in thought. "You like soul food?"

"Who doesn't like soul food?"

"Georgia Brown's?"

At the mention of a D.C. restaurant known for its low-country cuisine, my mouth watered for their buttermilk fried chicken and gumbo. "I can get on board that soul food train. Saturday?"

"Saturday it is. I'll make a reservation. What are your plans for today?" He stepped away to rinse his plate in the kitchen sink.

I drew in a breath and let it out with a sigh. "Work and more work. If I have time, I need to do some car shopping."

"What are you thinking of purchasing?" He dried his hands on a towel.

I set my empty mug down and debated pouring another. "Probably a boring four-door sedan. Got any recommendations?"

He shook his head. "Do your research. Don't make an impulse buy."

"Okay, *Dad.*" I smirked sarcastically.

His gaze bore into me and the smoldering tension returned. I couldn't break the plane. He moved in slowly, and his lips feathered across mine. My breath hitched, and I pressed closer, allowing him to deepen the kiss. If the coffee didn't start my engine, the kiss certainly did.

When we broke apart, he whispered into my ear, "Do you kiss your dad like that?"

"Eww! Gross!" I pulled away with a laugh and slapped him on the shoulder.

"C'mon." He grinned, put both our mugs in the sink, and held out a hand.

My toes curled and desire flowed thick through my veins.

Only, instead of walking me back to the bedroom, Rick

escorted me to the front door, picking up his leather coat on the way. "I've got to go home before I head to work." He swooped in for another smokin' hot kiss that sizzled my brain. Then with a smirk and cocky swagger, he caressed my bottom and waltzed out with a "see you Saturday" thrown over his shoulder.

*Bastard.* I slammed the door so hard the foyer table and its contents rattled. He knew exactly what he was doing. I'd be dining out on that kiss for the next twenty-four hours.

# Chapter Twenty-Two

It was a good thing Rick left me with the memory of a lovely kiss, because the rest of my Tuesday went downhill from there. I took an Uber to the office and spent the morning with my nose to the grindstone, catching up on what I'd missed the day before. By eleven, I received a call from my boss, informing me that our urban health care initiative bill was stalled in committee and wouldn't come to the floor for a vote in the House as originally expected. Which meant it was my job to inform the swath of folks who'd partnered with us to start making calls and see if we could get the bill moving again.

At noon, I took the metro into D.C. and met with an attorney from Jessica's firm, Bernard Theodore Evans III, Esquire, to give my statement to the FBI. Bernard (pronounced burr-nerd in the English manner) was as snooty as his name implies; however, he was one of Jessica's best associates and knew exactly how to handle the FBI. I was out of there in little more than an hour. Even so, I was running late for my meeting with the Urban Health League to discuss our options regarding the stalled bill and had to settle for a street vendor pretzel for lunch.

My day ran so late, I didn't have a chance to swing by to pick up my rental car. By the time I returned home, it was past nine. I'd survived the day on coffee and a pretzel and was so hungry I could've eaten my left arm. When I checked the fridge for food, I realized I'd been so busy dealing with the Mike/Matheson affair, I'd never had time to go to the grocery store over the weekend, and my dinner options were limited. I settled on eggs and toast.

While my bread toasted, I checked my voice mail and text messages and realized I'd heard not a peep from Mike, Rick, or any of the Silverthorne folks. Surprising. I texted Mike, letting him know I'd given my statement, and I needed to return his burn phone. During dinner, I gave some serious consideration to sending a suggestive text to Rick. A little payback for this morning's tease. Everything I wrote sounded too Hallmark channel smarmy, or porn film trashy. After typing, deleting, and retyping half a dozen texts, I simply gave up.

By Wednesday, my life returned to relatively normal chaos, as opposed to the mad-as-a-March- Hare chaos that had governed the past week. Mike returned my text and told me he'd call after work for an update and determine a time to get the phone. I planned to give the bat phone to Rick—who still hadn't called or texted—on Saturday. It was nice not having to worry about who might be listening in on my conversations and only having one cellphone to keep track of. Juggling multiple phones had become cumbersome. Best of all, during my lunch hour I took time to order groceries. They were waiting for me when I arrived home. I whipped up a salmon dinner with fresh asparagus.

Mike arrived, unannounced, at half past eight.

"Well, this is a surprise," I said, leading him into the living room. "Would you like something to drink? Beer? Wine? Water?"

He wore his normal FBI uniform—dark suit, white shirt, colored tie. "I'll have a beer, please." He took off his coat, draped it on the couch, and sat next to it, stretching out his long legs.

I came back with Mike's beer and a Chilean Chardonnay for myself. "Bring me up to date. What's happening with the case and Newcomb?"

"Quite a bit has happened since we last spoke." He took a long draw from the bottle. "They found a rash of damning evidence at Matheson's hideout."

"Did they get his computer?"

"Yes. They also found the glass he took from the Red Dragon, along with a silicone fingerprinting kit."

"That sounds like good news for you." I slid into the club chair. "What about Keller and Newcomb? What's going on with them?"

"Apparently, Newcomb wanted to find Matheson as much as I did. He was the one who tipped off Senator Tate all those years ago. Tate gave Matheson the tip, and then . . . well . . . we know what happened. When Matheson took off, he left with a million dollars of the Serbs' money. He didn't think they would miss such a paltry amount."

"But they did."

"And they were not happy. Petrovic knew Matheson also did work for Tate. He put pressure on the senator. However, the senator had no idea where Matheson went. Instead, he gave them Newcomb."

"Tate gave them Newcomb? Why?"

"Maybe because Petrovic threatened him, or he panicked." He lifted a shoulder. "We'll probably never know why."

"Did the Serbians cause Tate's accident?"

"Possibly. The investigation into his death is being reopened." He took another slug of his beer. "After Tate gave Petrovic the dirt on Newcomb, our agent was pressured into working for the Serbs. He's been tipping them off ever since."

I frowned. "How did that work for so many years? Why didn't Organized Crime get onto him?"

"Newcomb is smart. He knew what intel he could give them that wouldn't lead directly back to him, or that they could find through a different source. However, when Matheson returned to town to settle his debt with the Serbs, Newcomb started working his own angle. The Serbs wanted two things"—he held up two fingers—"their money, and Matheson dead. Newcomb wanted out from under Petrovic's thumb. He promised to deliver

Matheson and has been using any means necessary to do so. However, in an effort to save his hide, Matheson contacted Petrovic to make a deal. He offered twice the amount he took, but Petrovic wanted more. He told Matheson to get the baseball."

"Wait." I raised my hand. "Question. Was Newcomb aware of the side deal Petrovic made with Matheson?"

"We don't know. We're also unsure if Petrovic ever planned to allow Matheson to live even after he made his payments. Meanwhile, Newcomb has been scouring the city in search of both Matheson and me. Apparently, he's known all along Matheson was the person who framed me. He figured, when he located me, he could apply pressure, and I would help him find Matheson. Which, given the chance, I probably would have fallen in line and led him directly to Matheson. However, when Newcomb realized he'd been led on a wild goose chase Monday morning, he knew something was up. Newcomb reached out to a colleague in OC."

My hand went up again. "What's OC?"

"Organized Crime." Mike fidgeted with the label of his beer, peeling it off bit by bit as he spoke. "McGill was playing his cards close to his chest, but he insisted on looping in some folks in OC. One of the agents didn't realize Newcomb needed to be left out of the loop. He passed the information along. Newcomb informed the Serbs that the FBI was closing in on Matheson and gave them his location." He bunched his little pile of beer label scraps into a ball. "You know the rest."

"It would seem everyone was working their own angles." I took a sip and allowed the acidic pear-flavored wine to rest on my tongue before swallowing. "Where did all this intel come from?"

"We pieced it together from a few different sources. Keller, after realizing Newcomb wasn't on the up and up, figured he'd better switch teams or go down with Newcomb. He gave us everything that he knew about Newcomb's investigation.

Matheson copped a deal and gave us what he knew."

"What kind of deal did Matheson make?"

Mike's mouth twisted. "He's going to testify against the Serbs."

"WITSEC?"

He sighed. "Yeah. Matheson knows where a lot of the bodies are buried, so to speak."

"Even after all the B.S. he put you through?! He gets a new life courtesy of the government!" I cried.

He nodded ruefully and continued, "The rest of it came from OC. Apparently, two months ago they began turning Petrovic's mistress into a criminal informant. She's been dribbling morsels of intel, but not enough to build a case and take down the syndicate. However, once she found out Monday's hit went awry, she panicked and made her own deal. She's been spilling her guts ever since." He spun his empty bottle. "Including what she knew about Newcomb—whom she identified from photographs."

"What's happening to Newcomb and the Serbs?"

"One of the Serbs who shot at you, is dead, and the other is in critical condition. Organized Crime arrested Petrovic and half a dozen of his men this morning. Newcomb's trying to work a deal."

"Will he get it?"

Mike shook his head. "Not full immunity, but, if he cooperates, it's likely he'll see a reduced sentence."

"Well, at least someone's going to jail for this shitshow." I tapped his bottle with my glass.

"K.C."—he leaned forward, placing his elbows on his knees—"I couldn't have done it without you."

"More like you couldn't have done it without Silverthorne." I tried to keep the smirk out of my tone, knowing how many times he'd warned me about their questionable tactics.

He ducked his head. "True. True, they were helpful. You were the one to retrieve Matheson's package, *and* you came up with the fake baseball idea."

"Ha." I pointed at him. "You admit I occasionally have good ideas."

"I've often admitted you have good ideas," he replied tartly.

"No." I drank a deep gulp wine before continuing, "I believe you've often referred to them as 'harebrained schemes'."

"Okay, okay, maybe I said that once or twice. I apologize profusely for ever doubting you." He had the humility to acknowledge the truth.

I delivered a self-satisfied grin at my small victory. However, I felt Mike had groveled enough and changed the subject. "Did you get the scoop on the Silverthorne rescue?"

"Just the bare minimum. What do you know?"

I gave Mike the rundown on what Rick and Jin had told me about Hernandez and the Talley guy.

"I'm glad to hear they'll be okay." He gave me a funny look. "Did you hear about . . ."

"About what?"

He shook his head. "Nothing, just . . . something I heard on the news . . . about the DEA, they captured the head of Los Rojos Cartel . . . in Venezuela."

"Yeah, I saw that." I sipped my wine and kept my face neutral. I was fairly certain the Los Rojos head was the guy Rick captured for the DEA. However, I figured those who needed to know . . . knew it.

"Listen, K.C." He shoved the wad of paper fragments into the empty bottle and leaned toward me. "There's something else I wanted to talk to you about."

I remained relaxed against the cushions and put my feet up on the coffee table. "Okay. Shoot."

"Well . . . I was thinking . . . we should . . . consider getting back together."

The wine went down the wrong pipe, and I began hacking. I'll be honest, I did not see that coming. Rick had warned me. I should've believed him.

"You okay?" Mike asked.

I nodded, cleared my throat profusely, and wiped away tears. "Mike, nothing has changed since we broke up. You're still . . . well, you. Uptight FBI guy. I'm still the harebrained-scheme girl I was two months ago."

His head moved back and forth.

I realized I had to nip this in the bud. "No, listen to me, I care about you. I always will, but . . ."

"But you don't want to get back together," he said, completing my thought.

I licked my lips and stared moodily at the bottom of my glass. On so many levels, Mike and I worked when we were together. We had a similar sense of humor, enjoyed the same movies, were compatible in the sack, and our long-standing friendship made day-to-day interactions easy. But when it came to the nerve-wracking predicaments, I'd gotten sucked into, either he wasn't around, or he'd been dismissive, or he'd railed against me. Don't get me wrong, when the chips were down, Mike *always* came through, even if he did it begrudgingly. It was much easier to accept his criticism as a friend, but it felt hurtful as his girlfriend. Worse, his dismissiveness and censure made me prone to doing the exact opposite of what he wanted or told me to do, as demonstrated by my actions Monday. I needed someone willing to listen to my instincts and be a little more accepting when I jumped headlong into danger.

"Is there someone else?" he asked, breaking my reverie.

The Tuesday morning kiss flooded my memory, and I was afraid I blushed. "I—I don't know. There might be."

"I wondered," he said regretfully. "You know, he watches you when he thinks no one else is looking." His soft, chocolate gaze examined me. "You listen to him. He understands how to handle you."

"Nobody 'handles' me," I bristled.

He gave a rueful smile. "Donovan does." Rising, he scooped up his jacket. "I'd better be going. Thanks for the beer."

"Anytime. Oh, don't forget your burn phone." Reaching into my purse, my hand connected with a plastic bag. "Ah, you can return this to the FBI, with my compliments." I handed Mike the bag with the broken pieces of the bug.

He held it up to the light. "What happened to it?"

"There was an incident . . . with a hammer," I deadpanned.

Shaking his head, he pocketed the phone and the bug and kissed me on the forehead. "Goodbye, K.C."

I felt like utter crapola after he left. There was no reason I should . . . but I did.

# Chapter Twenty-Three

Friday afternoon, the front desk receptionist at my office phoned. "Karina, there's a man here from the FBI. He says he needs to see you."

"I'll come get him." I figured Mike had stopped by for some reason. Imagine my surprise when I rounded the corner to find a tall African American man, wearing a perfectly tailored gray suit and a congenial smile. "Director McGill." I swallowed. "I wasn't expecting you."

"Is there someplace we can talk?" he asked in his dulcet tone.

"Yes, right this way." I led the way to my office, passing many work cubes and garnering plenty of curious eyebrows. Rodrigo had the temerity to lean back in his chair and watch us all the way down the hall. Closing the door behind us, I indicated McGill should take a seat.

"Director McGill, it's nice to see you again. However, you must know that I've already provided my statement to the FBI regarding Terrance Matheson. I have nothing more for you without my attorney present."

"I'm not here for a statement." He laid his coat across his lap.

"Oh?" Using the armrests, I lowered myself into my desk chair. "Then what are you here for?"

He steepled his fingers. "It's been made clear by multiple parties that you have played a key role in the capture of Matheson."

"Uh . . ." I wasn't sure where he was going with this line.

"Did you not?"

I shifted. "What role exactly are you speaking of? I'm sure you've read my statement and spoken to other agents on the scene."

"Didn't you hit him with your car door, incapacitating him, which eventually led to his arrest?"

"I would argue it was the other way around. *He* ran into *my* car door. He was in a bit of a hurry, you see." I repeated the story I'd told with my lawyer present and the one I was sticking with.

"Be that as it may, Agent Finnegan has allowed that the baseball with the tracker was your idea," he drawled.

I wasn't sure why he was here, and my Spidey sense went on full alert. Was there something the FBI wanted to hang around my neck? Had Mike not been fully forthcoming last night? Was *I* a person of interest? "Director, where are you going with this? If I'm under interrogation, I insist on having an attorney present."

"As I said, it's not an interrogation. I'm trying to ascertain your role in the capture," he repeated quite calmly.

I replied hesitantly. "Ye-es. I was there when he ran into my car door. And the false baseball with the tracker *may* have been my idea. I would like to point out that Matheson directed Mike to break into an evidence warehouse. The fake baseball seemed like the best way to track Matheson to his lair."

He nodded in agreement. "It was a risky plan, but it paid off."

I nervously drummed my fingers on the desk "Is there something else I can help you with?"

"No. I have something for you." He reached into his inside pocket, drew out an envelope, and laid it on the desk in front of me.

The FBI logo and address emblazoned the upper left-hand corner, and dead center in bold, black, uppercase lettering was my name. My stomach flip-flopped. "What is it? A summons? Subpoena?"

"Neither. Open it. I promise it won't bite," he said rather

pleasantly and smiled.

I pulled out a piece of paper with FBI letterhead. Unfolding it, a check slipped onto the desk. "This is a check for twenty thousand dollars." I held it aloft. "I don't understand."

"If you read the letter, you'll find that there was a reward for information leading to the capture of Terrance Matheson."

"Well, this is . . . um . . . unexpected."

"I understand your car sustained heavy damage. Perhaps this will help you finance a new one?"

"Yes." I perked up and waved the check in the air with relief. "It'll certainly come in handy. Thank you." I replaced the check in the envelope and slipped it into the front pocket of my computer bag with a smile.

McGill made no move to leave.

"Now, Director"—I folded my hands, one on top of the other—"there must be something else I can do for you. You could've easily sent this over with an intern or put it in the mail."

Those bright white teeth flashed at me. "Actually, I gave a talk over at T.C. Williams High School, not far from here." He pointed in the general direction of the school. "My nephew is a sophomore there in the Governor's Health Science Academy program."

"Nice," I said, impressed. The specialty program was filled with highly motivated and intelligent students. "He wants to be a doctor?"

"Sports Medicine. I remembered your office was nearby and offered to bring the check." He finally rose.

Relieved, I stood, too. "Thank you. I appreciate your time."

"Ms. Cardinal—"

"Call me Karina."

"As nice as it is seeing you again . . ." We shook hands; his was slightly rough, and he didn't release me, rather added his other hand on top. "I hope it's the last time having to do with any sort of FBI business."

Uneasiness flooded back into my system. Was it a threat? A warning? I tilted my head and gritted out a smile. "Me too. I'm *sure* this will be the last time."

He released me. "Lovely."

"Let me walk you out."

We garnered fewer looks on our return trip to the reception area. Rodrigo, again, stuck his head out to watch. Rodrigo can smell gossip like a black bear can smell a cheeseburger in a locked car. It didn't surprise me to find him waiting in my office when I returned.

# Chapter Twenty-Four

"What are you doing?" Rick asked.

"I'm at a car lot, buying a new car." I mouthed, "Five minutes," to Kevin, the helpful associate setting up my financing, and stepped out of his office into the showroom. You could smell the scent of new leather and fresh rubber tires permeating the air. "What are you doing?"

"Paperwork." I heard the clicking of computer keys in the background. He continued, "Are we still on for tonight?"

I couldn't help the grin that spread across my face. "Absolutely. What time?"

"We have a seven thirty reservation at Georgia Brown's. Should I pick you up?"

"No. I'll meet you there. I want to drive my new car."

The typing paused. "What are you getting?"

"I'm not telling. It'll be a surprise," I said coyly.

"Wear a dress."

"What?" I asked, thrown by his abrupt comment.

"Wear. A. Dress. Tonight," he said in concise tones.

"Why?" The windchill was supposed to drop into the twenties tonight, and I'd been planning to wear a cute pants outfit to stay warm.

"We're going dancing."

*Hm, interesting.* "We are?"

"I told you, dinner and dancing. It's a date," he explained as if I should've remembered.

Which I did. "A dress it is. See you at seven thirty."

\*\*\*\*

I pulled to a halt in front of Georgia Brown's in my new red Jeep Wrangler and handed my keys to the valet. Rick arrived before me and waited near the hostess station. He wore black slacks, a white button-down, and a dark gray sport coat. He looked F-I-N-E. I'd only seen him dressed like this one other time—after a funeral. I could get used to it.

"Interesting choice. Not what I expected. I figured you for another uninspiring sedan. The red is sassy." He helped me remove my overcoat.

"It goes with my dress." I gave a little twirl. "Do you like it?" After the car lot, I'd gone shopping at the mall and purchased the frock specifically for our date, though I'd *never* admit it to him. The V-neck dress hugged my curves on top and flowed to a flared skirt at the bottom, perfect for spinning around the dance floor. I paired it with tights and black, knee-high boots to keep my legs warm.

A slow, sexy smile creased his features. "I like it."

*Oh, my.* That little bolt of electricity I was becoming used to shot through my body.

"Sir, your table is ready," the hostess said, interrupting our staring contest.

By the end of dinner, I'd pried open the safe and dragged out a fair amount of information about Rick's life. He went to high school in Texas and was the captain of his baseball team. He'd been a pitcher and won a scholarship to Texas A&M. Sophomore year, he obtained a shoulder injury, sat out half of the season, and lost his scholarship. He joined the Army through an ROTC scholarship to finish school and majored in International Relations with a minor in Russian Studies. His senior year, he was selected for a global leadership program and spent a semester in Ukraine.

"I was recruited into a three-lettered organization following my time in the Army," Rick said.

So, he was going to play it cagey, was he? "How long did you work for the CIA?" I asked, nonchalantly nibbling a piece of bread.

"I worked for the company for six years."

"Would it be fair to say the organization you worked for had an I and an A and a C in it, not necessarily in that order?" I rested my chin on my fist and gazed in wide-eyed innocence waiting for him to confirm the CIA. When no confirmation was forthcoming, I moved on. "How did Silverthorne come about?"

"A friend from the Army, Jack Silver, had been with a security firm. He wasn't happy with some of their tactics and questionable clients. He approached me about starting one ourselves. I was looking for something new. It seemed like a good idea at the time." He shrugged.

I fiddled with the stem of my wine glass. "Why haven't I met this elusive Jack Silver? Does he run the west coast division or something?"

Rick finished the last of his beer before answering, "Six months into our brand new endeavor, Jack was diagnosed with stage four pancreatic cancer. He died two months later."

I stopped fidgeting with my glass. "I'm sorry. It must have been difficult."

"When I think back to those days, I wonder how I was able to keep it all going."

"I'm glad you did. Or we might never have met."

He studied me for a moment. "Me too."

Deciding the topic had gotten a bit maudlin, I moved on to questions about his family. I gleaned that his older sister was a high school math teacher in Oklahoma, and his mother worked for a bank in Arkansas.

Foolishly, I probed a touchy subject in hopes I might glean a deeper understanding, "Tell me about your father."

"He's dead," Rick said without inflection, then proceeded to wave the waitress over and ask me, "Would you like coffee or dessert?"

In the snap of a finger, the flowing spigot of "Rick's Life" shut off. I hid my disappointment and left it alone. After all, Rick had revealed more to me in the past hour than he had in the past year.

We shared a piece of chocolate bourbon pecan pie, Rick paid the check, and I drove us to our next destination. Rick had taken a taxi to the restaurant, so he could catch a ride in my new car. He directed me to a salsa club in Northwest D.C.

Once we arrived, there wasn't much talking involved, but rather a lot of concentration, on my part, and breathless laughing on both our parts. Lessons started at nine. A dozen couples littered the floor, and, for an hour, we had a blast learning the samba and merengue. Dancing revealed a different side of Rick. His normal intense personality traits dissipated, and his drop-dead smile came more readily as we, or, I should say I, faltered and stumbled through the learning process. Rick was surprisingly adept and light on his feet. Having had dance lessons as a teenager, I wasn't completely hopeless, but I struggled to get some of the footwork right. Halfway through the class, I realized this wasn't Rick's first salsa lesson.

I said as much to him after tripping over his foot for the third time and called him a cheater.

He laughingly whispered in my ear, "Stop trying to lead. Trust me, I've got you."

Embarrassed, but slightly turned on by his Fred Astaire like dancing abilities, I took his advice, stopped trying to fight my way through the steps, and allowed my body to follow his lead. The lessons went much smoother when I submitted to his masterful skill.

For those who don't know, the samba has quick, little

movements with an open, stiffer dance frame. The merengue, on the other hand, has a closed position where the man holds the woman at waist level and the partners dance closer together. Both use a lot of hip action, but the, up close and personal, merengue definitely makes things a little spicy. The first dance the DJ played after the lesson was a merengue. We must have put on a decent showing, because a woman wearing a slinky blue dress and with a chest to rival Dolly Parton's slithered over to ask Rick for a dance.

"I'm sorry, ma'am, but I believe there's a country song about dancing with the one who brung you. And this lady brung me." Rick winked, slid a proprietary hand around my waist, and led me back onto the floor as the DJ spun a samba.

"You are full of surprises. Where did you learn to dance? Did your mom force you to attend junior cotillion or was it Arthur Murray's six lessons in six weeks?" I asked, rocking back on the ball of my foot with the beat of the music.

"College. I was dating a girl who talked me into taking a semester long class with her. It counted as a physical education credit. I figured, why not? The relationship came to an end, but the dance moves stuck around."

I wiggled my hips. "I bet you were popular with the ladies when they figured out you could dance."

He delivered a sly smile. "It certainly didn't hurt." His hand twisted in mine, and I spun away from him with laughter on my lips.

After a handful of dances, we took a break to catch our breath. Rick ordered beers for the both of us, and we watched other couples shimmy around the floor. Our dance instructors were particularly enjoyable to observe. Maceo was tall and lithe, with long elegant limbs accentuated by his black slacks and black button-down shirt. His partner, Gabriela, was average height with Latina curves that emphasized her rolling hip and shoulder movements. Her thick, black ponytail hung straight and crisp down the back of the yellow salsa dress she wore, while the fringe around her thighs flared out as she spun and dipped.

The accordion and guitar strains of an Argentinian tango came on over the loudspeakers, and the floor cleared of all but three couples. Maceo and Gabriela moved in synchronicity, with long strides across the floor punctuated by swift, agile, little kicks, while gazing intently into each other's eyes. A flip of the head, a quick turn of the body, and they glided away in the opposite direction to continue their mating dance. The pair had no equal on the floor. I couldn't take my eyes off them and only vaguely registered Rick's hand curling around mine. Finally, Gabriela slid down Maceo's body with one long leg splayed out behind her. Maceo cupped her cheek, and the song came to an abrupt end. It was one of the most sensual performances I'd ever witnessed. As I clapped in appreciation, along with the rest of the patrons, I realized I'd been holding my breath with my tongue caught between my teeth.

A moment later, a twangy guitar piped through the room. Rick slid of his stool, beckoned me with a curled finger, and, with the other hand, drew me onto the dance floor.

Grinning, I shook my head. "I don't know what this is."

"It's called a bachata. Follow my lead."

I wasn't sure if it was the sexy strains of the guitar rhythm, or if Maceo's and Gabriela's tango influenced Rick's next actions. He plastered me against his body and scarcely broke eye contact as my hips swiveled in conjunction with his. I waited for him to take my hand and spin me around or break away with some sort of fancy footwork. He never did. Our bodies rubbed against each other, and his hand slid down cupping my backside. It was like a scene from the movie *Dirty Dancing*. If you didn't think it was an utter and completely erotic turn-on, you'd be wrong.

The bongo drums wound down to their last beat, and Rick

suggested it was time to leave. "Before we're kicked out for indecency," he whispered in my ear.

I delivered a slow smile. "My place or yours?"

"Why don't we go to your place? I'll teach you the horizontal mambo," Rick breathed across my collarbone.

How could I refuse?

# Author's Note

I knew two things when I began writing *Swindler's Revenge*. First, Karina and Mike would be split up. Second, Mike was going to be in trouble and need her help. I also had vague ideas that a money launderer would play a role in framing Mike. With small bits of the plot line forming in my head, I reached out to an FBI contact who once worked White Collar crime. After laying out my ideas, my contact sent me in the direction of Operation Bullpen, a 1990s investigation into a group of individuals forging, fraudulently authenticating, and distributing sports memorabilia. The yearly sports memorabilia market is approximately a $1 billion industry, and it is estimated that the perpetrators of the fraud venture were raking in over $100 million every year. In 2000 twenty-six individuals were charged and convicted in the operation; 2001 saw even more convictions. A book by Kevin Nelson came out in 2013 called, *Operation Bullpen: The Inside Story of the Biggest Forgery Scam in American History,* and a movie is in the works. According to the FBI's website, the investigation resulted in:

- 63 charges and convictions.
- Seizures exceeding $4.9 million including 5 homes, cash, bank/investment accounts, jewelry, a Ferrari, a boat, and a Harley Davidson motorcycle.
- 18 forgery rings dismantled.
- Over $300,000.00 in restitution paid to over 1,000 victims and continuing.
- $15,253,000 in economic loss prevented in the seizure of tens of thousands of pieces of forged memorabilia through 75 search warrants and over 100 undercover evidence purchases.

In addition to this information, I also researched articles

about money laundering using sports memorabilia through eBay sales. If you Google José Uribe's 1990 Fleer card, you'll find theories that it is being used to launder money on eBay. An individual was selling it for $758,000 which raised eyebrows among legitimate collectors. It would certainly be one way to either pay off a debt to organized crime or clean your money.

The idea for Mike's money launderer to have an interest in baseball memorabilia came from the above research, as did Karina's idea to use a forged baseball to trap their bad guy. Having a dirty agent within the FBI came from my own imagination; a necessary plot device to keep Mike off balance and uncertain about who he could trust. I personally have no knowledge of any unlawful agents, and fully respect the investigations and hard work the FBI does on a daily basis.

# Acknowledgements

As usual, this latest Karina Cardinal mystery couldn't have happened without the help of certain people. Thanks to Matt Fine for his usual tidbits and insights on FBI life, which I used to develop Mike's storyline, along with Matheson's baseball collector plot. Thanks to Mark Bergin for his insights having done time as a Lieutenant for the Alexandria, Virginia, police department, and as a crime reporter in Philadelphia.

Finally, I'd like to thank my awesome team, Emily, *Lucky 13*, and Carolan, who help me make Karina's stories better. Also, to my friends and family who read Karina Cardinal and continue to support my writing.

# About the Author

Ellen Butler is a bestselling novelist writing critically acclaimed suspense thrillers, and award-winning romance. Ellen holds a master's degree in Public Administration and Policy, and her history includes a long list of writing for dry, but illuminating, professional newsletters and windy papers on public policy. Her time working in the D.C. area inspired the Karina Cardinal Mysteries. She lives in northern Virginia with her husband and two children.

You can find Ellen at:
Website ~ *www.EllenButler.net*
Facebook ~ *www.facebook.com/EllenButlerBooks*
Twitter ~ *@EButlerBooks*
Instagram ~ *@ebutlerbooks*
Goodreads ~ *www.goodreads.com/EllenButlerBooks*

## Novels by Ellen Butler
### Suspense/Thriller
*Isabella's Painting (Karina Cardinal Mystery Book 1)*
*Fatal Legislation (Karina Cardinal Mystery Book 2)*
*Diamonds & Deception (Karina Cardinal Mystery Book 3)*
*Pharoah's Forgery (Karina Cardinal Mystery Book 4)*
*Swindler's Revenge (Karina Cardinal Mystery Book 5)*
*The Brass Compass*
*Poplar Place*

Made in the USA
Middletown, DE
08 October 2022